The Prodigal Returns

Don Horne

Horne Publishing

Red Oak, Texas

The Prodigal Returns

ISBN-13: 978-0615553443

ISBN-10: 0615553443

To order, or for quantities:

Amazon.com

And other retailers

Horne Publishing

302 Cascade Drive

Red Oak, Texas 75154

Preface

Houston, Texas, in 1905 was a growing commercial town with the Southern Pacific Railroad bringing in passengers and freight. Ships arrived from all over the world. They offloaded goods and services at the dock off Market Square by coming up the ship channel. After Galveston to the south was blown away by a hurricane in 1900, Houston was the heir apparent for Texas' major port city.

From a small Holiness church just off the square, William Seymour went to Los Angeles, California, and taught on the baptism of the Holy Spirit in a small building that had been a livestock pen on Azusa Street. Pentecostal evangelists went out all over the world after the Azusa Street Revival from 1906 to 1911. One evangelist who went, saw, and believed was August Johnson from Paris, Arkansas. He was a white widower who had twin boys, Luke and Levi.

He owned a lumber mill, and his boys grew up working hard pulling a crosscut saw and swinging axes to cut the trees and trim them of branches. They used horses and chains to pull the timber out of the forest, and a steam engine ran the saw which made the logs into siding and timbers for construction.

August sent his sons to the University of Arkansas in the fall of 1907 to allow him to become an itinerant evangelist on the weekends. Luke and Levi played football, baseball, and Luke was on the boxing team. Luke studied to be a civil engineer, and Levi studied journalism.

The University of Arkansas went undefeated in football the season of 1909, and the coach said the team, "fought and clawed like Razorback hogs". To this day they are still called the Arkansas Razorbacks. The young men came home in June 1910 to a "Welcome Home" party. They were treated like heroes.

Chapter One

After a bath and dressing in a sport coat and tie, Levi was getting impatient waiting on Luke.

"Come on, Luke!" chided Levi. "You spend more time in front of the mirror than women do!"

"I just want to look nice for Maddie Howe. She is home from the University of Texas for the summer. She looks mighty fine, and she promised me a dance at the party!"

"Daddy said we could drive the Model T. I have already put the wheels and tires back on from the barn."

Luke made one last pass through his dark hair with his comb, put it in his back pocket, turned and smiled the smile that made all the girls swoon at the University of Arkansas. Levi rolled his eyes, held the door and playfully pushed him as they went out on the porch. They both jumped the three steps from the porch to the sidewalk, and jogged toward the car.

"You have to admit, Levi," said Luke, as they rolled up the oilcloth that protected the seats, "Daddy knows how to take care of mechanical equipment. We are the only people I know that take the wheels and tires off every time we drive anywhere."

"Yes, but we don't have a flat every time we want to go somewhere either," he agreed. "Now, let's go! You drive going and I will drive coming home. Just in case Maddie remembers you, and you don't want to come home when I do!"

They both laughed at the remark. Luke got in the door on the passenger's side for there was no door on the driver's side on the 1910 Model T Touring Car, slid across the seat, turned on the ignition, set the spark, and told Levi, "Give it a big crank!"

Levi turned the crank hard and the magneto fired the spark plugs to make the car pop once and then the engine settled into a tinny idle as Luke readjusted the spark. Pushing in on the clutch, he put the car in gear, and backed out of the barn.

They drove carefully down their lane to the dirt road leading into Paris. People waved and honked at the boys as they drove into town and went to the cotton gin warehouse where the party was being held. They parked the car away from the trees, but with the top down, they pulled an oil cloth over the seats anyway.

The band was tuning their fiddles and guitars to the upright piano some of the men had brought from the church. Girls and women were on one side and boys and men on the other, but a beautiful, brunette haired, brown-eyed girl managed to coyly lift her hand to shoulder level to smile and wave at Luke. He raised his eyebrows and shook his head up and down as if girls did that every day. Actually, they probably did at the University.

Levi watched, frowned and shook his head, because he realized he was invisible when Luke was around.

"Is that Maddie?" Levi asked in a whisper.

"Oh, yeah," smiled Luke. "That is Madeline Joyce Howe. Little Maddie is all grown up! I bet her daddy sleeps outside her door with a shotgun!"

They were still laughing when the music started. At first, mostly the young marrieds started dancing, but it was only a few minutes until Maddie was on the dance floor with a young man, and a line of anxious males was starting to form.

"You better go get in line," teased Levi.

"Don't worry. Watch this. Two can play the flirting game."

One of the most attractive girls in the place was a petite, blue-eyed blonde named Ellen Gray. She was a little shy, but her eyes sparkled when Luke asked her to dance. It only took a dance or two with him before the other guys noticed her and also started to ask her to dance. Maddie's line suddenly evaporated. So much so that she frowned at Luke when he first went over to ask her to dance.

"You did that on purpose, didn't you?" she crossed her arms and held her chin up.

"Did what?" Luke asked so innocently that she got even more angry.

"You started dancing with Ellen Gray knowing anyone you danced with would be noticed. The great Luke Johnson, University of Arkansas football player."

Luke laughed, which made her so petulant her lower lip started to quiver.

"So, are you going to dance with me or not?"

"Luke Johnson, you can make a girl crazy!"

"You love it! You know you do!"

With that, she gave him her hand, and soon she was laughing and smiling, realizing the charade was all for her benefit. Luke had confessed he had done it to have her all to himself. After two dances, they were over by one of the big, double sliding doors of the warehouse that was open to let in any night breezes. Luke waltzed her out the door, and, giggling like little kids on a prank, they ran hand in hand to the well house. In the doorway it was dark and she was in his arms without a word ever being said.

"Whew!" said Luke first, trying to catch his breath. "That is not the same kiss I used to get when we played hide-and-seek."

"I am not the same little girl I was back then."

Luke stepped back and held her at arms length and looked her up and down.

"You know, I think you're right!" he laughed.

She punched him in the stomach so quickly he almost lost his breath. She laughed and started running back toward the dance. He caught her in just a couple of strides, whirled her around in his strong arms as if she were still a little girl. She put her arms around his neck, and kissed him like a woman, while he held her in the air with the toes of her shoes barely touching the ground. They were a long distance from hide and seek.

Luke and Maddie were still laughing and holding hands as they walked back into the dance. Everyone noticed, especially the young men. No one but Levi dared ask her to dance for the rest of the night. Luke had cut her out of the herd, and at least for the night, she was his.

Maddie rode home with her folks of course, and even if her dad frowned at her about her "carrying on," he was secretly proud she had picked and won for herself the best looking, richest guy at the dance. In the back seat Maddie's mother did not say a word, but she squeezed her daughter's hand in the darkness and they both giggled.

"Knock it off, you two!" growled Maddie's dad, but the tone of his voice gave him away and they all just laughed. It had been a good night.

Chapter Two

The next day was Sunday, and Luke and Levi were up early to get ready for church. They rinsed off the Model T with a rag and a bucket of water. Using an old towel, they carefully wiped the black paint to get off the dust from the night before.

"You know, Levi," began Luke. "I think the next best looking girl at the dance, after Maddie Howe of course, was Ellen Gray. I saw you dance with her and the rest of the night she watched you while she danced with the other guys."

Levi looked down for a moment, as if the thought embarrassed him, and said, "I never know anything clever to say, but I noticed her too. Both girls will be at the church this morning, maybe she will let me sit by her. We get to hold hands when everyone prays. I am too shy to hold her hand any other way yet. I just met her last night."

Luke laughed at his twin brother and teased, "You realize you look just like me. Just try to imagine what I would say or do. Okay, just imagine what I would say, because you would never do what I would do."

"Why? What would you do?"

"Well, I would get her alone and just kiss her right on the mouth!"

"You're sick, Luke. You know that?" He threw a towel at him, which Luke caught in midair, and they both laughed.

People were just starting to arrive as they parked the car, and the boys went to find the girls. Both were sitting together as if they were expecting company. They smiled as if it had been a long time since they had seen one another, and Luke stepped through the aisle and sat beside Maddie.

Levi sat down on the end of the pew as Ellen moved over, after he politely asked if he could sit by her. Luke looked at Maddie, they smiled at one another, and both shook their heads. Maddie whispered to Luke that Ellen had told her how much she hoped Levi would sit by her. Both Ellen and Levi were smiling as the service began.

After about an hour or two of continuous preaching, the girls asked to be excused, and the boys stood up to allow the girls to go outside to the outhouse. After a few minutes, the boys got up and went out to see what was taking so long. Luke and Levi walked around behind the church toward the women's restroom.

"Rayburn Collins, leave me alone!" exclaimed Maddie, trying not to disturb the church service, which by now was singing an ending altar call song. Luke sized up the situation of the scruffy looking young man named Rayburn Collins holding Maddie's hands and bending down as if to steal a kiss. Luke eased up behind Rayburn, and his big roundhouse right punch caught him right on his ear, almost breaking his eardrum and causing him tremendous pain while it knocked him to the ground.

"Well, well, Rayburn Collins. You haven't changed since the 8th grade," smirked Luke. He stood over him for a moment, backed away a couple of steps with his fists raised. He smiled and beckoned the man on the ground to get up. Collins smiled a little crookedly and said, "You must need another whippin'. I whipped you in eighth grade and I can do it again!"

However, when he stood to his feet, he realized as Luke took off his suit coat, handed it to Levi, and rolled up his sleeves, that Luke was several inches taller and a lot more muscular than he had remembered from the eighth grade. His eyes widened, and he made the mistake of not running. Luke used a left jab straight from his shoulder that broke Rayburn's nose, causing blood to start flowing, and the last thing he remembered for a while was a big right handed fist that almost broke his jaw. When he came to, there was a big crowd of jeering people and he was wet from having a bucket of water thrown in his face.

He looked around for a sympathetic face and when he did not find one, he pushed himself off the ground and started jogging toward his car holding his nose with his handkerchief.

Luke was already back in his suit coat as he spoke loudly to Rayburn, "Come around anytime, Collins, I owe you a lot more whippings than one!" The crowd laughed and Maddie put her arm through Luke's so everyone would know "her man" had fought for her honor and won.

Rayburn Collins left town in a hurry and headed for Hot Springs, Arkansas, to soothe his face and feelings in the hot, mineral springs. He also wanted to put some distance between him and Luke Johnson. He was killed in a card game a month later when he was caught cheating.

Luke and Levi had been invited to the Howe's home for lunch after the church service. August, the boys' dad, was on the road evangelizing in Dardanelle a few miles away. Ellen Gray and her family joined the group, and Ellen sat by Levi during the meal. There was a lot of laughter and talk about Luke's taking care of Rayburn. Rayburn had been after Maddie since they were all in school together as kids. The first fight between Luke and him had been over him almost assaulting Maddie. However, even though it was broken up before a decision was reached, the first fight Luke had won, because Luke won Maddie's heart for coming to her aid at such peril to himself.

After a huge lunch of fried chicken, new potatoes, turnip greens, a salad of fresh garden vegetables, and Mrs. Howe's famous rolls, the kids went for a walk while the

Howes sat on the porch and visited with the Gray family.

As the kids disappeared around the barn on their way to the lane toward town, both couples were holding hands. Mr. Gray asked Mr. Howe, "What do you know about those boys?"

"I know you are new to town, George, but those are two of the finest young men in town. Their dad runs the sawmill during the week and is a Pentecostal Evangelist on Sunday. The boys go to the University of Arkansas and will be Seniors in the fall. Luke is in engineering and Levi is studying journalism and wants to write for the *Arkansas Gazette* after school. Both are star athletes, and, as Rayburn Collins found out, Luke Johnson is a conference champion in boxing!" When he laughed, Mr. Gray frowned.

"I don't know if I want my daughter around those ruffians if they are going to be doing that sort of thing!"

Mr. Howe was finding it hard to not let his anger show, but he said, "I am proud of my daughter's relationship with such a fine family, and those young men are going somewhere in life. Trust me, if they are good enough for my daughter as protective as I am, you can trust them too. You will not be disappointed in the behavior of Levi and Luke."

The relief showed on Mr. Gray's face as he smiled and thanked Mrs. Howe when she handed him a cup of tea.

"I am too protective I know, but Ellen is so pretty and the young men are calling and coming around all the time."

"That won't be a problem now, George. If Levi Johnson likes her, no one will dare to ask her out."

"You're right, of course, but good, young men are hard to find. She is 20 years old, and has already had two years of prep school. I am sending her to the University of Arkansas in the fall where she will be a Junior. I am glad she will know someone we can trust." Reassured, Mr. Gray visited laughing and talking. The two families found they had more in common than the two prettiest daughters in town. It was enough to make them friends.

The Howes lived in a two story brick house just a few blocks from the square. Norman Howe and his wife, Bonnie, owned and ran one of the two banks in Paris. The lumber mill, the railroad now stopping in Paris, and the increased rate of industrialization was making him a very rich man. George Gray was an accountant Norman had hired, and had been working for the bank only a few weeks. Norman thought George was a little strict and straight-laced, but he was an excellent accountant.

He knew what George was going through. He smiled to himself because he was learning more every day about raising a pretty, stubborn daughter. Why, she was even trying to start a movement in Paris to give women the right to vote! "The times are surely changing," he thought to himself.

Chapter Three

The two couples walked arm in arm to the Barnes'
Apothecary, the local drug store, which had small
tables and wireback chairs to sell ice cream and fountain
drinks. All four ordered Coca-Cola floats. They watched as
Tommy Barnes, the owner's son, squirted a little
concentrate into a glass, put in some carbonated water,
stirred and added 2 big scoops of homemade ice cream to
each one. Levi paid the 10 cents apiece for the 4 glasses
with a 50 cent piece and told Tommy to keep the change.
Luke and Levi carried two glasses apiece over to their
companions seated at one of the small tables, and received
warm smiles and "thank, you's" from the girls.

As they sat and talked, other young people came and
went. All made a special point of saying their welcomes to

the Johnson twins. The small crowd of laughing young people turned to listen as Levi tapped on his glass with a spoon. He held up his glass, studied it for a moment, and said to the group, "Did you know Coca-Cola used to actually have cocaine in it?"

"Oh, great," smiled Luke. "Here we go again. Is there anything you don't know? You are a walking library!"

Ignoring Luke, Levi continued, "It was first mixed and sold as a patent medicine by a doctor named John Pemberton in Georgia in 1886. It was made from coca leaves for the cocaine, cola nuts for the caffeine and did have medicinal qualities. It would soothe colic babies and people with upset stomachs."

"With cocaine in it, I am sure it did soothe people," snorted Luke. The girls, and the young people sitting on chairs around the foursome, all laughed.

"No, really. In 1903 the government made the Coca-Cola company take out the cocaine if they were selling it as a fountain drink. By then a man named Asa Candler had bought the rights to the formula and incorporated a company known as The Coca-Cola Company to differentiate from all the competitors that had sprung up."

"Levi, where do you come up with all this stuff?"

"I can read, my brother, and I have subscriptions to several out of town newspapers and magazines. You ought to read something other than the sports pages in the newspaper."

"Okay," said Luke. "Anything else?" And he just shook his head as if there were no way to stop him.

"It was Candler's idea to just sell the syrup and keep the formula secret. They sell the syrup to bottling companies all over the United States and Canada already. If you purchase it by the bottle, the name of the bottling company is on the bottom of the bottle. Using the local water is why there are sometimes a little variation in taste."

"You know," spoke up Ellen. "Levi is right! I got a bottle last week from Russellville. I am glad to hear the whole story!"

"Oh, you are just taking Levi's side," a giggling Maddie countered. At that everyone laughed and it made Ellen blush.

"Did I tell you my dad was going to start a tent revival at the fairgrounds after the Fourth of July?" said Levi.

"He has leased a tent and has two or three musicians already lined up. It ought to be great!"

Even a tent revival seemed like fun agreed most of the kids, when they thought about looking forward to another dull summer.

"I bet Maddie and Ellen get to sing," said Luke.

The girls shrugged their shoulders and nodded affirmatively. Singing publicly was a burden most pretty girls had to bear according to Maddie's dad.

"Well, at least all the young men in town will be there!" laughed Luke. "Oh!" He exclaimed, as Maddie kicked him in the shin under the table, bringing another round of laughter as Luke rubbed his injured leg.

"You don't have to come, Luke Johnson," teased Maddie.

"Oh yes I do. My dad insists on it. Why else would I come?"

Everyone laughed as Maddie stuck out her tongue at him.

"You could probably use it," smiled Levi.

"Probably," stated Luke. "But all this talk about speaking in tongues and the Holy Spirit that Daddy preaches about is all new to me. He started preaching like this after he came back from California."

Several of the kids agreed as to the mystery of it all, and stated they would be looking forward to hearing about it from someone that had actually been at a meeting on Azusa Street in Los Angeles.

Later, Luke and Levi walked the girls to Maddie's home, said their goodbyes, and drove to their house through the square. They passed by the high school they had attended, and where Luke had won the state boxing championship. They still had boxing matches in the gymnasium.

They drove slowly by the jail. It was a small, red brick building where the jailer and his family lived downstairs, and the prisoners were kept in cells above. The jailer's wife cooked for the prisoners and washed their sheets and clothing. Usually the worst inmates they had were locals for public drunkenness, and most times the sheriff knew them. Sometimes they would sit and play cards with the cells unlocked. There were a few criticisms that the same people seemed to get "locked up" on Saturday night just to get a meal and play cards with the sheriff!

On one corner of the square there was a new newspaper business going in. The printing presses were already installed, and when Luke pointed it out, Levi said, "Yes, and I am real excited! Mr. J. W. Wagner is starting a new paper called *The Progress*. I am interviewing tomorrow about working this summer for him. It is just going to be a bi-weekly to start, but he hopes to become a weekly soon!"

"I thought we had a newspaper already," said Luke.

"We do, and it is called the *Express*. Actually, it is the oldest business in Paris. It started in 1880, and is being published by Mr. Greenwood, former publisher of the Chismville *Star*. I asked him first because he has connections to the *Fort Smith Tribune*. However, they didn't need anyone right now because, according to Mr. Greenwood, nothing much ever happens in Paris."

"So why are you interested in working for a start up newspaper?"

"This is my Senior year, remember, and the experience would look good on my resume."

"Good point. I am going to work for Daddy until I can find something else. The thought of a crosscut saw and the summertime does not sound like fun!"

"Now, you are getting smarter! I don't want to work in timber either. And they call you the dumb one! HAHAHA!" laughed Levi.

"Smart alec. If I were not driving, I would kick your..!"

"Aah, aah, aah, don't say it!" Levi said, shaking his finger at him. Both wound up laughing.

As they turned into the lane to go up to their house they saw their father's pickup.

"Yea, daddy's home!" exclaimed Levi.

"I am glad. I am sick and tired of your fried ham and egg sandwiches," said Luke. "Maybe he will take us into town to Molly's Cafe."

When asked, the thought of Molly Smith's Cafe sounded good to August too. Molly only opened her restaurant for the evening meal on Sunday. It was originally for the people who were in the hotels in town to have a place to eat. The locals, however, went sometimes on Sunday evenings to eat and then sit and visit.

Levi got in the back seat as they drove back to town in the touring car. At the restaurant, the three men enjoyed some of Molly's meat loaf, mashed potatoes with gravy, and topped it all off with her homemade coconut meringue pie.

Molly Smith was an attractive 40 year old widow who purchased the restaurant after she received a goodly compensation for her husband's death in a mining accident. After a short lawsuit, it was deemed the fault of the company for not providing enough safety equipment.

She was always very well dressed and made up. She had a "scandalous" short length hair cut, and on Sunday wore beautiful silk brocade dresses which were ordered from as far away as New York. The married women, except for a few, were very cool at first toward her when she became a widow, thinking she might be after their husbands. But, Molly was very outspoken, and when she saw what was happening she put an end to it by telling them all at a book club meeting, "Ladies, no offense, any man who would be living with any of you, I sure as Hades don't want!"

A couple of the ladies walked out at the use of such language, but when Molly started closing the cafe on Wednesdays at noon and invited all the women in town to come for a free noon meal and book discussions, the place was full.

No men were allowed, and it was the high point of the week for most of them. It was a chance to talk about the men, current events, women's suffrage, prohibition, and sometimes they even discussed books!

After the meal, Molly came and filled up the men's water glasses, and, looking straight at August, said, "Will that be all?"

She smiled and walked away as August blushed a beet red. Both Luke and Levi kept their heads down as if they were studying something minute in their plates, and tried not to choke as they did their best to keep from laughing out loud.

After a moment, it settled enough for Luke to say to his dad, "You know, Pop, I want to know something."

"Sure, son. What?"

"We come here several times a week and whenever you are with us, your piece of pie is always bigger than ours. What is up with that?"

To August it was simple. "Because I am the one that pays!" he said.

All three men laughed, but it was no secret to anyone except August the only man in town who would ever have a chance with Molly was August Johnson. It seemed complicated to August with his two sons and all, but secretly the boys were hoping the two would get together. Molly, to the boys, would be welcome as their step mom, especially the way she could cook, and being the best looking single woman in town did not hurt.

"Actually, boys," began August, "I need to talk to you. As you know, the Fourth of July is on Monday this year and there will be a parade, probably some public speeches, a big dinner on the grounds, followed by a big fireworks show. I will be escorting Molly Smith to the festivities."

Luke and Levi looked at each other and Levi said, "Hey, way to go, Pop!"

"Well, I wanted you to be the first to know, but I am sure by the Fourth everyone in town will know. Molly is going to tell her book club this Wednesday. It is a little embarrassing."

"Not for us," smiled Luke. "We are proud for the both of you!"

"Anyway," continued August. "The day after the Fourth I will start setting up my revival tent and I hope to hold my first meeting on Friday the Eighth of July. I will need your help as well as many of your friends that can help also."

Both boys were excited to help, and looked forward to it, knowing all the men in town would also help. Of course, the boys knew with all the men, young and old, at the fairgrounds, the girls and women would be there too to provide lunch and encouragement. Luke winked at Levi and both boys smiled. August just shook his head, even though he smiled too.

By the time they finished their pie and tea at the end of the meal, the Johnsons were the only ones left in the restaurant. Molly went and locked the door and turned the sign around to say closed. She came over and smiled as the men stood for her to sit down in the chair which August held for her.

"How was the meal, guys?" she said, as she fished for a compliment. After being reassured avidly by all three men it was the best meat loaf they had ever had, she was beaming and looked radiant. She won the heart of all three.

Molly kidded the boys about their being seen with Maddie Howe and Ellen Gray. It was a pleasant conversation finally ending with August announcing to the boys, "Tomorrow is a work day. I know Levi has an 8 o'clock appointment with Mr. Wagner, and Luke and I are going to start early too."

Luke grimaced, but he liked working with his dad. They laughed and kidded a lot, and now that the relationship with Molly and August was going forward, he and his dad would have a lot to talk about.

They drove home and the boys put the car in the barn. After removing the wheels, they went and sat for a few minutes on the porch with their dad to watch the last of the sunset.

"Hey, Luke, I read where there is to be a prize fight between a black guy, Jack Johnson, and the former undefeated world champion, James Jeffries, a white guy, on the Fourth of July. What do you think about that?"

"I am probably the only man I know who thinks Jack Johnson is going to defeat James Jeffries, the white man. Jeffries is out of shape and has not fought in 6 years, while Johnson has already won 50 fights. He has not lost since December '08 when he beat Tommy Burns in Australia for the World Heavyweight title!"

"Well, Luke, don't say anything out loud about it. There are a lot of whites <u>and</u> blacks having loud and violent arguments already about the fight."

After a round of good nights, the boys went off to bed while August sat and thought about the boys, Molly, and after all these years, how nice it would be to have a woman around. He smiled at the thought, got up, and went to bed happy.

Chapter Four

L evi was up early Monday morning to get dressed in a suit and tie to go interview with Mr. Wagner at the newspaper office. Luke and August gave him a ride on their way to the sawmill, and though his appointment was not until 8:00, Mr. Wagner smiled to see Levi early. He unlocked the door and took him to a small, crowded little office and made a seat for Levi by putting the papers from his seat onto a filing cabinet.

"Good morning, Levi," began Mr. Wagner, a middle aged, prematurely bald, pleasant looking man in a tie and white shirt with the sleeves rolled up. "I have seen you around town, and I know your dad well. Now tell me why you want to be a newspaperman."

"It is about people, sir. I like people and being able to tell about what goes on in their lives, both good and bad, is like keeping a journal of people's lives. I actually have done quite a bit of writing and reporting at the University for the school newspaper. I have several articles with me if you would like to see them."

Levi handed him a folder with several news clippings, and after reading quickly through them, Mr. Wagner smiled and said, "This is a very impressive portfolio, young man. I want you, but be advised, you will not make a lot of money to start. In fact, you will be required to help me sell advertising, but I will augment your salary with a commission. I can pay ten dollars a week salary, and I hope you can make a couple times that in commissions, fair enough?"

They shook hands and Levi asked, "When do I start?"

Mr. Wagner said, "Right now! I am swamped!"

Levi hung up his suit coat, rolled up his sleeves, put on an apron and went to work. Working for his dad had made him know how to work with a sense of urgency, and by lunch the inside of the office did not look the same. He had filed everything which could be filed, threw away what was duplicated, and swept the wooden floors after spreading out oiled sawdust to keep the dust down.

"Good job, Levi," said Mr. Wagner, after looking at all he had done. "Let's go to Molly's for lunch. My treat!"

Obviously excited, Levi exclaimed, "Sounds good to me!"

The two men washed their hands, and though they left their coats off, they rolled their sleeves down, pulled off, and hung up their aprons. They wanted to look professional at Molly's.

Molly smiled at the two men as they entered, and then privately winked at Levi. The men feasted on smothered pork chops, corn, beans, and salad. As they lingered a few minutes to let their meal settle, Mr. Wagner asked Levi, "Is your dad doing well as an evangelist?"

"He is doing well, and he hopes the upcoming revival will help here in Paris."

"What do you think about the baptism in the Holy Spirit part?" asked Mr. Wagner.

"You know, Mr. Wagner, some new ideas are hard to gain acceptance, and sometimes even hard to understand. I can tell you this, my dad is a different person since he came back from the revival in California. He offers Luke and I encouragement all the time. He is a real inspiration to us both."

"That is a nice thing to say about your dad, Levi. In my own mind I have questions, but his sincerity goes a long way to offering me hope there is more than just salvation in God's plan for me. Say, I need some more news for the first issue. How about going to the fair grounds and see what sort of preparations they are making for next Monday's Fourth of July celebration."

"Sure," said Levi.

Mr. Wagner left a nice tip for Molly, paid for the meal, and the two walked back to the office where he gave Levi a notepad and a "PRESS" pocket sign for his hat. Levi sharpened several pencils and started for the fairgrounds a few blocks away. As he left the office he met Ellen Gray who had been on her way to see him.

"Why hello, Ellen. What a neat surprise! Walk with me to the fairgrounds."

"Sure. Are you on your first assignment? How exciting!"

"Well, it is really mostly work, but getting to see you will make it fun. Thanks for coming over."

Ellen took Levi's offered arm and they walked along talking and laughing. At the fairground Levi took notes about the preparations being made, including the podium for the speakers and the canvas and wood shelters for the food court and the games. Ellen was impressed with his thoroughness. Levi even interviewed a few of the workers. After several pages of notes, Levi and Ellen held hands as they walked back to the shop.

"I was wanting to get the right time, but next Monday would you let me escort you to the Fourth of July Celebration?"

Ellen stopped and looked at him for a moment. "I would have been disappointed if you took someone else, Levi. If we were not standing on a city street, I would kiss you!"

She put her arm through his and hugged his arm tightly as they walked. At the shop Ellen went in too and Levi introduced her to Mr. Wagner who was very impressed by her. He even offered her a small job on a part time basis for her to work mornings answering the phone and taking messages while Levi and him printed the paper.

After Ellen left with a promise to start the next day, Mr. Wagner told Levi to go ahead and write what he had and he would edit it. Levi finished the first page of copy and Mr. Wagner took it to start editing.

"Good job, Levi! I like the way you know to write in upside down pyramid form. You know, by telling the facts in the first paragraph, and then building and defining the facts through the rest of the article I can size and edit where I need to without destroying the information in the article. Good job! You are a real find! Did by any chance you learn to use a Linotype machine?"

"Yes, sir! I was the best typesetter on the paper at the University."

"You know, we could have our first issue out by Friday in time to put in the schedule for the Fourth of July Celebration. That would be a good way to start!" exclaimed Mr. Wagner. "Our professionalism in the first issue will go a long way in getting us off the ground."

With very little editing, the text was ready for the Linotype machine. Mr. Wagner watched Levi on the console and how quickly he worked. As Levi finished each line Mr. Wagner put the pages together and the first page was finished speedily.

"The other paper still uses movable type," began Mr. Wagner. "I tried to get them to buy a Linotype, but Mr. Greenwood told me it was the way they had always done it, and it is the way they will always do it. He claimed because he was a weekly newspaper it did not make any difference. To me that is nonsense. If a new device will save time and money it is all the more reason to use it. It is the same thinking which people are using about automobiles not ever replacing horses. Automobiles are changing America. Soon we will be able to live in <u>one</u> town and work in <u>another</u> town!"

"Easy, Mr. Wagner. There are less than 100 miles of paved roads in all of Arkansas," smiled Levi.

"You are right, Levi, but these are exciting times!"

"Oh, I feel the same way don't take me wrong, and that is why I want to report on those times."

A little after 6 p.m. Levi helped shut down the shop and waited outside for a few minutes, and then started for home. But soon he heard the unmistakable "oogah" horn of the Model T. It was Luke and August on their way home too.

"Hey, thanks! I don't mind walking, but I will take a ride anytime!"

They started off down the street, all three crammed into the single bench seat of the pickup. Luke all of a sudden started laughing out loud, "Levi, we had a new man start today at the mill. He was thinking he was tough and in good shape. So, I put him with Lightning."

"That is so old, but it is funny every time. What happened?"

"Well we unloaded a huge pile of gravel to put up on the roof, and we started using the conveyor belt with Lightning doing the shoveling from the big pile to the belt. You know how he does with perfect shovel loads every few inches all day long. After about 30 minutes, I asked Billy Bowden, the new guy, to go down and take over for Lightning and give him a break. Well, he jumps down off the roof and gets a shovel and goes to work. Up on the roof we get these huge piles of gravel in just a steady stream from him! After about 30 minutes, the piles get smaller and smaller, and further apart, until I looked down, and there was Billy leaning on his shovel with his chest heaving and sweating like he had been running for miles flat out. I said to him, 'what's up?' He looked up and sweat was just pouring. I said, 'Hey, Lightning, give old Billy a breather!' We all started laughing and pointing at Lightning as he started shoveling even, methodical, and piled just like always. Billy just looked at Lightning with his mouth open. He could not believe that old man could outdo him!"

"So then what happened. Did you tell Billy Bowden the joke?"

"Yes, and after we explained he was called Lightning as a nickname because he was <u>slow</u>, not because he was fast, we all had a laugh at his expense, and he was laughing too. He said he wanted to be the one to tell the next new guy to 'spell' Lightning!"

All of a sudden, the boys realized the truck had stopped in front of Molly's Cafe.

"You boys are probably hungry. Right?"

"Yeah, Dad, and that is the <u>only</u> reason we would stop here!"

All three laughed because they knew why they were stopping.

Molly was genuinely pleased to see them, and patted August's shoulder as she waited on them. A move which was not lost on the boys who looked at one another and smiled.

Molly asked about Levi's first day, and commented she would buy advertising if he wanted to come by the next day. He assured her he would.

After the meal, the boys told their dad they would walk on home and he could come later. They smiled when they saw Molly put the closed sign up as soon as they left.

The two brothers walked along kidding one another about girls, and who was better in football, Arkansas or Texas. Their mother had perished giving them birth, and in 20 years of togetherness, they were best friends. Luke could get them in trouble for his pranks sometimes, but everyone knew them and even the sheriff waved when he saw them.

At home they sat on the front porch and waited for their dad. It was a couple of hours before August came home, and Luke and Levi thought they detected just a trace of lipstick on one corner of his collar and a slight smell of Molly's perfume. They both smiled as August went on about Molly Smith and how well she could cook.

"We are glad you two are finally getting to go out together. You are a perfect match for one another," smiled Luke.

"Luke's right, dad. You like to eat and Molly likes to cook. It's a match made in heaven. Of course her being the prettiest woman in town doesn't hurt!"

They all laughed as August's face began to turn red. The boys and their dad got up to go up to bed and August grabbed both by the back of their necks and said, "No more kidding. I would not be interested in any woman who would come between us three!"

He put his arm around the shoulders of his sons and hugged them tight for a moment before he let them go.

"Now, get outta here!" he growled. Both boys took off for their rooms laughing and pointing back at their dad.

Chapter Five

The next day Levi came into work and without being asked or told, took the broom and started sweeping. Mr. Wagner smiled to himself and thought, "That young man is going somewhere. Too bad it won't be here! Paris, Arkansas, won't be able to hold him."

Levi had already swept and cleaned the inside of the shop, and was sweeping the sidewalk in his apron when he looked and saw Ellen coming. She smiled at Levi as he held the door for her, and she patted his shoulder as she passed. Levi smiled as her touch was warm where she touched him.

Mr. Wagner, Levi, and Ellen sat and visited about the job in front of them. He wanted to have an issue on the streets by Friday. He also needed some advertising sold. Levi and Ellen volunteered to go out and sell for a couple of hours. Mr. Wagner handed the two a hand written price sheet apiece and a receipt book. The team of Levi and Ellen Gray was formidable. They were back at the office by 1:30 with full page ads sold to the bank, the Johnson saw mill, and Molly's Cafe, where they had eaten lunch.

Everyone they spoke with bought advertising, even if it was a small ad, to try and help the new paper get started. Of course, the time spent walking together was great for them to get to know one another as they laughed and commented on people and places. Everyone knew Levi and he introduced Ellen as his friend, not just a fellow employee.

At Molly's, she was especially nice to Ellen and Levi. She liked Ellen immediately, and of course Levi was already special for being August's son. They had sandwiches and fried potatoes to eat, and Cokes to drink with apple pie for dessert. By the time the meal was over, the young couple was "in like" and caused smiles everywhere they went.

After they closed for the day, Levi walked Ellen home, and her mother, Lettie, seemed to really enjoy seeing Levi again. She was proud of her daughter's choice in a friend.

Even George, her husband, had to admit he liked Levi. He invited him into the library and they visited about Levi's goals in life and what he intended to do after college. Levi and George found they were both interested in a lot of the same things. Both were interested in current events, especially technology of all kinds. After a long conversation, George was glad Levi was dating his daughter. He could see Levi was interested in Ellen as a true person not just a pretty face.

When it came time for Levi to go, George started to get up to walk Ellen and Levi to the door, but his wife put her hand on his arm and nodded no. He shook hands warmly, invited him back, and then sat back down. The young couple walked out on the porch and sat in the swing for a few minutes holding hands as they swung back and forth.

"Ellen," Levi began. "I can write anything, but I never know anything great to say to you when we are alone. Don't think me too forward, but I really like you. Does that make you feel uncomfortable?"

"Why should it, silly. I feel the same way too!"

She turned her face to Levi, and kissed him sweetly.

"Luke would really be proud of me," Levi thought to

himself. When he smiled, Ellen said, "What is the smile about?"

"You really make me happy," Levi answered. With his answer she lay her head on his shoulder for a few minutes until Levi said, "I guess I really had better be going, but I will see you tomorrow. I am already looking forward to it."

"Me too!"

Levi walked down the walk onto the sidewalk, turned and waved, and started humming to himself as he walked home. Luke noticed the smile as he came into the house and said grinning, "Oh, man, you got it bad!"

"Yep!" said Levi. "Guilty as charged, but I love it! I am not like you, this has never happened to me before."

"Tell you a secret, Levi. The only girl who has ever made me feel that way is Maddie Howe. She can make me blush, laugh, and mad all at the same time!" They both laughed as Luke gripped his brother on the shoulder. "You ever tell her I will beat you to death!"

Chapter Six

B y Friday morning the first issue of 500 copies was printed and ready for sale. By late in the day, only a few copies were left. The population of Paris, Arkansas, in 1910 was less than 1000, but people from around the county came in from the farms and outlying homes to shop for groceries and supplies for the upcoming week. Also, there were extra people in town for the Fourth of July celebration. In the new paper the local merchants had advertised products, there was a schedule of events for the Fourth, news of the revival coming the next Friday, and almost hidden on an inner page, was the news of the upcoming prize fight between a black man and a white man.

Jack Johnson was born in 1878 in Galveston, Texas, and fought under the nickname "Galveston Giant." He was one of six children of former slaves and he was taught to read and write by his blue-collar parents. He had only 5 years of formal education.

Johnson won his first title on February 3, 1903, by beating "Denver" Ed Martin in 20 rounds for the World Colored Heavyweight Championship. Black and white boxers could meet in other venues, but the world heavyweight championship was off limits to them. However, Johnson did fight former champion Bob Fitzsimmons in July 1907, and knocked him out in two rounds. The reigning world white champion, Tommy Burns, was finally fought and beaten in Australia on what was called a TKO, (Technical Knock Out), December 26, 1908. It was clear he had beaten the champion. Every time Burns was about to go down, Johnson held him up, beating an already helpless man.

After Johnson's victory over Burns, and the taunting before, during, and after the match, coupled with such a merciless beating, racial animosity was so great among the whites that even a socialist like Jack London called out for a "Great White Hope" to defeat Johnson and take away the title.

As the title holder, Johnson had to fight in several matches against several "white hopes" including Stanley Ketchel, the Middleweight Champion. In the fight Ketchel knocked Johnson down in the twelfth round. Johnson got up very slowly, and as Ketchel bent over him, with one sucker punch to the mouth, Johnson knocked him out for several minutes including several of Ketchel's front teeth. He also fought the great middleweight, Jack O'Brien. Although Jack Johnson outweighed O'Brien 205 pounds to only 161 pounds, he wound up with a disappointing 6 round draw.

In early 1910, former undefeated heavyweight champion, James Jeffries, came out of retirement and announced, "I am going into this fight for the sole purpose of proving that a white man is better than a Negro!" He had refused a few years before to fight Johnson, and had even been a referee for one of Johnson's bouts, the only one to end in a draw, on his vote.

The fight took place on July 4, 1910, in front of 22,000 people in a specially built ring in Reno, Nevada. In the fifteenth round, after Johnson had knocked the champion down twice for the first time in his career, his people called it quits to prevent Johnson from knocking him out.

For the "Fight Of The Century" Johnson earned $225,000, a tremendous amount of money at the time. The outcome of the fight triggered riots between the blacks and the whites all across the United States. Although the whites felt humiliated, the blacks were jubilant, taking to the streets, but in some cities, like Chicago and North Little Rock, Arkansas, the police and whites tried to stop the parades. [3]

In Paris, Arkansas, there were just a few black families in the entire town, and even though they marched to celebrate, they were very conscious of where they were. Luke and Levi attended the parade. Levi was there to report, but Luke was there to celebrate. He secretly had won several hundred dollars from the dozens of white people betting on the black man. He had placed a bet also in Levi's name, but Levi would not accept the money from gambling. Luke split all the money in half anyway, and put Levi's money in a special savings account under Levi's name the next day. Luke kept out a little for "walking around money" and set aside the rest to put in his own bank account.

The parade was not really very noisy, and a number of the spectators even waved at the participants.

The Fourth of July had been "business as usual" as far as the celebration went. The mayor gave a speech, there was a cakewalk, a pie auction, and lots of fireworks afterward.

Paris was quiet as Levi and Ellen walked along in the late evening arm in arm.

"You know, Levi," began Ellen, "I was frightened hearing about the race riots in other places. I hope the blacks here in Paris realize we think of them as one of us."

"Yeah, I agree, Ellen, but the sad fact is, lots of whites are resistant to change and any act of the blacks to uplift themselves is considered a challenge to their superiority. In other places with a higher concentration of blacks, I am sure this is just the start. However, right now I am more worried about women wanting to vote in Arkansas than anything else."

"You are so rotten! You have been hanging around Luke too much!" She laughed, hugged him tight for a moment, and then quickly kissed him on the mouth and whispered, "Levi, don't ever change."

Chapter Seven

The revival tent went up without much ado. The men that owned the tent helped lay it out and showed August and the others just what to do. Levi wrote an article for the next week's paper about the tent, and fliers were made and handed out on Thursday and Friday. Others were nailed to posts around town or put on trees.

The upright piano was brought from the church and put on one end of the platform built by the men from August's company. In a town of only 1000 with half of them being young, August counted out only 300 wooden folding chairs, but then cement blocks and boards were readied in case they were needed for seats.

On Friday evening there was an aura of excitement as the tent filled with friends and family of August Johnson. Levi and Luke were sitting on the back row beside Maddie and Ellen. The two couples accepted all the smiles and knowing nods from people as they sat together. The girls went forward and sang a beautiful rendition of "Amazing Grace" which left very few dry-eyed.

August preached from the Bible without getting into the baptism of the Holy Spirit. The service was only a couple of hours long, and there was an altar call and a few came forth to be prayed for with a laying on of hands. Everyone went away feeling blessed and strengthened. It was a very typical church service. Although August was encouraged by the number and the participation, he wanted more.

August went upstairs to his "prayer room" on Saturday morning before the second night's service. He prayed intensely that God would move, no matter what it took.

As the people started to find their way into the tent for the evening service, a few went down to the altar and prayed quietly. The mood was somber as the people visited in whispers among themselves as if God were present. The song service was mostly worshipful four part harmony. August's sermon touched on the baptism in the Holy Spirit but he was mostly calling on people to come forward and be "saved" or "justified".

Luke and Levi slipped outside to catch a breath of cool air in the warm, summer evening. They noticed Jake McGraw standing by his beat up pickup truck. Jake was the town drunk, or at least one of them. He was a hero from the Spanish American War, and would sometimes call out to invisible comrades when he was drinking. He imagined he was in battle, or worse, he was reliving being in battle. The people knew and cared for him, and the sheriff would even take him home sometimes when he had too much to drink.

The service was building in crescendo and Luke got the idea of setting off a leftover firecracker behind Jake. He thought it would be funny. Levi did not think it was funny at all. However, after Levi went back inside, Luke waited until the service was especially loud, lit the firecracker, and threw it on the ground not far from Jake McGraw.

No one but Jake and Luke heard the cannon-like report it produced. Jake screamed and took off running toward the tent, with his arms flailing and screaming unintelligibly, he ran down the sawdust covered main aisle, tripped, and fell on his face right in front of the evangelist, August.

"Look!" someone cried. "Jake McGraw has come forward to give his heart to the Lord!"

It was bedlam as people started praying and shouting. Women pulled errant husbands and children to the altar to be prayed for, and the husbands and children broke down and were truly moved by seeing Jake's obvious transformation. They had revival!

Tongues broke out by several people. Some just stared at such an experience. Jake was so moved by all the tears and love he really did give his heart to the Lord. No matter how conservative people thought they were, they knew they were witnessing something life changing.

It was over two hours before things quieted. People just sat. No one wanted to go home, because the presence of the Lord was so strong! Luke and Levi were very quiet on the way home. As soon as they were alone, Levi grabbed Luke and told him, "Thank you for not setting off the firecracker!"

Luke just smiled and said, "The Lord really moves in mysterious ways!"

Several months went by before Luke confessed to Levi what he had done. Both agreed as unholy as it was, God used it to His benefit. They never told anyone about what had happened. Being a witness to the revival caused both of them to believe it was meant to be. Of course, they also did not want to face August and his wrath if he were to find out!

The revival was originally intended to be a week, but it ran for over three weeks. People came so early they had two meetings a day, and sometimes they ran together until the meetings were several hours long. Luckily, several of August's Pentecostal evangelist friends would preach sometimes to let him rest. It did not seem to matter who spoke, because as soon as the prayer line started, each service took on its own agenda. Some nights there were healings, some nights people prayed for salvation, and some nights tongues were spoken. Most of the people came in not knowing what it was, and had to have it explained. August was very careful to take his Bible and explain using chapter and verse to prevent any confusion.

The very nature around Paris changed. There were random acts of kindness every day. Paris was a friendly town before, but after the first Pentecostal revival it was like a huge extended family.

Chapter Eight

By mid July Mr. Wagner and Levi were printing the newspaper as a regular bi-weekly. Levi was given a Brownie camera by Mr. Wagner, and he was taught how to develop his own prints and etch metal plates to be able to print from them. Ellen had to start working full time with the paper to take all the news over the phone and schedule Levi to cover different events. Ellen and Levi enjoyed working together so much they forgot how demanding the work could be. Every evening after the shop closed, Levi would walk Ellen home and sometimes Ellen's mom would make him stay for supper, but she always had a snack for the two. Levi and Ellen would sit on the front porch and visit with Ellen's parents for a while before Levi would walk on home.

The afternoon of Wednesday, July 20, Molly fed the girls in the book club, and shooed them out by two o'clock.

From the kitchen of her restaurant, she fixed meatloaf sandwiches, a salad, covered half of a leftover coconut pie, put iced tea in a gallon jar, took plates, napkins, silverware, and put it all in a large picnic basket with a blanket and table cloth. A few minutes later Molly smiled as she heard August's Model T ease up to the back door. Everyone in town knew that Molly and August were taking an occasional Wednesday afternoon picnic together.

"Where we going?" Molly asked as she put her head on August's shoulder.

"Someplace cool. I thought we could drive out by the lake and sit under the pines. The needles will make a soft, smooth place to put a blanket." She squeezed his knee as he smiled.

The drive off the road to the lake was a smooth wagon trail from all the fishermen and visitors, but so early in the afternoon none were present. August carried the basket as Molly found a small rise to spread the blanket and the table cloth under a canopy of green pines. Having been together daily for so long, Molly and August were very comfortable with one another as they spread out the meal, sat, and laughed as they talked.

"You know," began August, "everyone knows about our afternoon picnics."

Molly looked at him and said, "I don't care, do you?"

"Well, I do have my reputation to protect, and people see me cavorting around with a young, beautiful widow there is bound to be talk."

"So? Whatcha gonna do?" Molly asked and smiled. She was thinking she did not care what the townspeople thought. She knew most were jealous.

"You know things could be different, even though I really don't care what they think or say either."

Molly furrowed her brow as she looked at him intently, "Different, how?"

August reached into his vest pocket and pulled out a small black box wrapped in a handkerchief.

"Oh, August," Molly whispered as she started to tear up. She was guessing what it contained. After dreaming of this moment for so long, it was overwhelming.

August took her hand, handed her the box, and as she opened it he said, "Molly Smith, I love you with all my heart. I never thought it would happen to me again, but will you marry me?"

Molly opened the box, gasped at the size of the ring, and as she put on the ring and held it up in the sunlight there were rainbows everywhere on the leaves and trees as the ring flashed in the sunlight.

"Yes, August. Of course I will marry you! I never let myself even dream it might happen again until you came along. I have loved you for a long time."

"My boys love you nearly as much as I do. This is going to make them very happy."

They picked up everything they had brought and not ate. Holding hands to the car, Molly rode back to town with her head on August's shoulder. However, this time when they entered downtown, she did not sit up straight or move over. She waved happily to everyone they saw, looking at them and smiling.

On Thursday evening, Levi arrived home and noticed Luke, Maddie, Molly, and August were sitting on the big front porch smiling at him.

"What?" Levi asked.

"Come on up and sit down, son. Here's a glass of lemonade. Did you have a good day? Oh, by the way, Molly and I are getting married. How is the paper going?" August deadpanned the whole thing.

It took a moment for it to sink in what his dad had said. Levi shook his head as if to clear his ears and asked, "What did you say?"

"I asked did you have a good day."

"No, no, no. After that."

"I asked about the paper."

By now it was obvious something was afoot. Everyone was looking like they were about to burst! Finally, the air exploded with laughter, and August stood and held up Molly's left hand to show the ring finger and said proudly, "Molly and I are getting married!"

Levi grabbed and hugged his dad. Molly stood and he hugged both of them at the same time while tears flowed from everyone.

"I can't believe it!" Levi exclaimed. "Luke and I were hoping this would happen! You are so welcome, Molly, into this crazy family!"

Everyone hugged everyone, and Levi went inside to call and tell Ellen and Mr. Wagner the news. Mr. Wagner said, "We will put it on the front page for next week's paper!" After things had settled down, Levi started taking notes on when, where, and what about the wedding. It was to be on Saturday, August 6, at the church. Because both had been married before, they wanted to keep it small and among just friends. However, after the paper came out, nearly everyone in town was making plans to come although there were no invitations sent out.

Molly and August had decided that August would move into her new, big brick home. It was built and only lived in by Molly, using some of the large money settlement of her dead husband. There would not be any "ghosts" to deal with of either her or August's dead spouses. The boys inherited the house in which they were born.

Molly asked Maddie and Ellen to help her plan, and she showed them the Edwardian style dress she had purchased a few months before when she was in Little Rock. It was a light yellow in color and had a very fashionable high waist, and did not have a bustle that fashions had from previous years. The trend, she claimed, was for a more natural, slim look. The girls were both impressed because she was going to be an absolutely stunning bride. It had a large hat with a veil. She looked like something out of *New Yorker Magazine*.

August had several suits, but he wanted a new one in which to be married. So, August and the boys all drove to Fort Smith up the old Military Trail which by now was so well-traveled it was becoming considered a highway. August purchased a new, vested suit in a dark, charcoal gray with a top hat for a semi-formal afternoon wedding. Luke and Levi purchased matching suits with new "patent leather" shoes to match.

"I imagine Maddie Howe will be asking me to marry her after seeing this outfit!" laughed Luke.

"I guess you don't look bad," smiled Levi, "but I am so much better looking than you."

All three men laughed, because it was like looking into a mirror to see Luke and Levi together.

They looked at new automobiles at the Ford house, and other places. August almost purchased a new Ford Town Car, but he was afraid he would look too pretentious driving it around Paris. Luke also pointed out the Town Car was meant to be driven by a chauffeur, and as much as he loved his dad he was not cut out to be a chauffeur. There was lots of kidding and laughter on the way back.

Both boys could not quit smiling as they traveled. They had never seen their dad so happy.

Everyone agreed it was the most beautiful wedding ever in Paris. The high fashion wedding dress and suits for the men were talked about for years. Having two of the most attractive couples in town as part of the attendants just added to the wedding. Maddie and Luke, Ellen and Levi, and the decorations were on a scale never before seen.

Afterward, there was a huge reception in the back yard of Molly's home with a string band and dancing. Each of the boys took turns dancing with their beautiful step mother. There was a long line to dance with the new bride, and she was very generous to the point it made some of the women pout at being left alone. However, August, Luke, and Levi took turns dancing with all the left alone girls and women. Of course, it just took a dance or two until Maddie and Ellen reminded Luke and Levi they had come with them. The party was very classy, and though some men sneaked a drink from vest pocket containers, no one got drunk or started a fight. They knew full well

August and the two Johnson boys could finish anything they started.

Both newspapers carried accounts of the wedding, but the *Progress* came out first and Levi's articles and pictures completely out did the *Express*. Mr. Greenwood came by and shook Levi's hand and told him, "Great job, Levi. Maybe I should have hired you. For a young man, you are very gifted. If you should ever want a job, come and see me."

Although Levi would never think of leaving the *Progress*, it made him feel better about being snubbed by the other newspaper when he had interviewed at the beginning of the summer. Without saying anything, Mr. Wagner quietly raised Levi's salary to a very substantial, for the time, twenty dollars per week.

The happy couple left on a two week honeymoon in Hot Springs. They watched the horses run at the new race track and went for walks along Bathhouse Row, but August was shy and did not want to partake of the bathhouse scene. Molly and August stayed at the historic Arlington hotel, and went out to eat at the finest restaurants. They were admired by everyone as they made such a beautiful couple. August rowed Molly around on the small lake that would later become Lake Ouachita with Molly holding an embroidered parasol.

Hot Springs, Arkansas, in 1910 had a population of 14,400 according to the census. The town was originally part of the Louisiana Purchase of 1803 from France. Then president, Thomas Jefferson, sent a 2 man team to find the Hot Springs, and in December 1804, Dr. George Hunter and William Dunbar found the springs with only a few rudimentary "outhouses" to allow bathers access to the 143 degree waters known for their healing properties. The first permanent settler was in 1808, but others followed soon with some wanting to "cash in" on selling baths to people.

On August 24, 1818, the Quapaw Indians ceded the land around the hot springs to the United States in a treaty. After Arkansas became its own territory in 1819, the Arkansas Territorial Legislature requested in 1820 that the springs and adjoining mountains be set aside as a federal reservation. Twelve years later, in 1832, the Hot Springs Reservation was created by the US Congress, granting federal protection of the thermal waters. Thus making Hot Springs National Park as the first in the nation.

After the Civil War, an extensive rebuilding of bathhouses and hotels took place in Hot Springs. The year-round population soared to 1,200 inhabitants by 1870. By 1873 six bathhouses and 24 hotels and boardinghouses stood near the springs. In 1874, Joseph Reynolds announced his decision to construct a narrow gauge railroad from Malvern to Hot Springs. Completion in 1875 resulted in the growth of visitation to the springs.

Samuel W. Fordyce and two other entrepreneurs financed the construction of the first luxury hotel in the area, the first Arlington Hotel which opened in 1875.

There were places a Pentecostal evangelist such as August would normally not have gone, but on his honeymoon Molly and August listened and even danced to a couple of bands and watched several floor shows. They visited the Ohio Club which was originally built and owned by Otis McGraw to be a private club and gambling saloon. The New Ohio Club still had the original Italian mahogany back bar. Each place of business was, a different style of architecture to stand out from the others.

The honeymoon was a treasure to be remembered and relived the rest of their lives. When the weather forced a fire and inside activities, they would be able to reminisce fondly about their honeymoon.

Both agreed, after only ten days, it was time to go back to Paris and get the boys ready to go back to the University. There were some things Molly and August wanted to do to Molly's house to make it "theirs" while the boys were home to give their input.

Chapter Nine

L uke and Levi were making plans to go back to school by the end of August. Maddie and Luke were spending every moment they could together. They were at the boys' home one afternoon in the porch swing with Luke's arm around her and her head on his shoulder.

Maddie asked Luke, "Are you going to date others while we are apart?"

"Are you? Is that where this is going?"

"I asked you first."

"Maddie, you have to know I love you. I may see other girls but my heart belongs to you. Is that a fair enough answer?"

She looked straight ahead for a moment then answered, "Well, fair enough, I guess. Are you going to be mad if I do the same and see other boys?"

"No, not in the least. Truth is, it is not really fair to the University of Arkansas for a University of Texas girl to deprive all the girls of Luke Johnson."

"You are the most cocky, arrogant person I have ever met!"

"Oh, really. Try looking in the mirror. You and me are in love with the same person...YOU!"

At that she grabbed him in his side and pinched as hard as she could. In obvious pain, Luke exclaimed, "That's not fair! You know I am not going to pinch you back. Norman Howe would come after me with a shotgun if you went home with bruises all over you."

Laughing out loud at his discomfort, Maddie kissed him. "I did pinch you a little hard. I'm sorry."

Luke held her close for a moment and whispered into her hair, "Don't ever find anyone else, Maddie. I love you."

She pushed him back to arms length, looked at him for a moment, and said, "You are the only boy I will ever love, Luke Johnson."

They laughed and teased one another for a little while longer and Luke walked her home. On the porch, Luke and Maddie looked around to see if anyone were watching, and then kissed one more time. Maddie had to leave the next morning, while the others did not have to leave until the next weekend which was just before Labor Day.

With everyone gathered to see Maddie off at the train station, Luke and she gave each other a small kiss on the lips. She put her head out of the window and blew kisses until the train went around the curve going south toward Hot Springs and Texas.

Luke, Levi, and Ellen all began preparations to go to school. Clothes were purchased or cleaned and pressed. The suitcases were packed and ready to go.

The University of Arkansas at Fayetteville was founded in 1871 on the site of a hilltop farm that overlooked the Ozark Mountains, giving it the nickname "The Hill". The University was established under the Morrill Land-Grant Colleges Act of 1862. The Morrill Act specifically directed that the endowed institutions were "to teach such branches of learning as are related to agriculture and the mechanic arts." The underlying idea was that educational institutions should support occupations in industry and the professions. The University's founding also satisfied the provision in the Arkansas Constitution of 1868 that the General Assembly was to "establish and maintain a State University."

Initially, to fund the University, $130,000 was raised by the citizens of Washington County. This was in response to the competition created by the Arkansas General Assembly's Organic Act of 1871, providing for the "location, organization and maintenance of the Arkansas Industrial University with a normal department, i.e., teacher education, therein." Classes started in February 1872.

Completed in 1875 at the University of Arkansas, Old Main, a two-towered brick building designed in the Second Empire style, was the primary instructional and administrative building. Its design was based on the plans for the main academic building at the University of Illinois, which has since burned down. However, the clock and bell towers were switched at Arkansas.

The northern, taller tower is the bell tower, and the southern shorter tower is the clock tower. One legend for the tower switch is that the taller tower was put to the north as a reminder of the Union invasion during the Civil War.

The lawn at Old Main serves as an arboretum, with many of the trees native to the state of Arkansas found on the lawn. Sitting at the edge of the lawn is Spoofer's Stone, a place for couples to meet and pass notes. Students play soccer, cricket and touch football on the lawn's open green.

Beginning with the class of 1876, the names of students at The University of Arkansas are inscribed in "Senior Walk" and wind across campus for more than five miles (2.5 miles of sidewalk). The sidewalk is one of a kind nationally. More recently, the names of all the recipients of honorary degrees were also added.

One of the more unusual structures at The University of Arkansas is the Chi Omega Greek Theatre, a gift to the school by the national headquarters of the sorority. It marked the first time in the history of Greek letter social organizations that a national sorority had presented a memorial of its foundation to the institution where it was founded. Chi Omega was organized on April 5, 1895, at the University of Arkansas and is the mother (Psi) chapter of the national organization. The theater has been used for commencements, convocations, concerts, dramas and pep rallies.

Luke, Levi, and Ellen loaded everything they could carry into as few suitcases as they could. It still looked as if they were moving, August said. George and Lettie Gray, the Howes, August and Molly, and dozens of friends and extended family were at the station to see them off.

The trio rode the train to Fayetteville. Ellen was very appreciative when she arrived on campus for the first time, for she had help offloading and finding her way around.

The dorms, as they were the first of every school year, were madhouses of yelling and laughing young people renewing friendships and moving into their respective rooms.

The boys had a top floor room being Seniors, and Ellen found she had a pretty, talkative, brown-haired girl from Missouri named Lela Mae Thompson for her roommate. When she introduced Lela Mae to Levi she was very careful to hold his arm to reinforce the fact Levi belonged to her. Lela Mae had no problem though getting asked out from the start, and the boys came and went from the "Spoofer's Stone" for her.

Lela Mae and Ellen would go to the practice field and watch the football team practice. The first time the girls waved at Luke and Levi the coach had to blow his whistle to regain focus from the team. All of them were staring at the girls instead of practicing like they should.

Arkansas played Missouri State for the first game of the season in 1910. The Razorbacks won 100 - 0. The new name for the team, the Razorbacks, gave the team a new identity and a pride they had never had before. The team only lost one game that season, and it was to a huge Kansas State team.

With the football season going on, and spending so much time studying his Senior courses, if Luke went out at all it was usually with a bunch of guys or with Lela Mae, Ellen and Levi.

He received several letters at first from Maddie, and he answered every one. As the semester lengthened, the letters came more infrequent till they stopped all together about two weeks before Christmas break.

Luke was wondering if Maddie had a new friend or something, and the few times he had been out with Lela Mae, it was just not the same. By the end of the semester he was ready to go home.

Chapter Ten

L uke, Levi, and Ellen came home to Paris from Fayetteville for the Christmas break. Maddie rode the train up from Austin, Texas, and Luke and the Howes were at the station waiting for her. However, there was a young man with Maddie whom she introduced as her friend, Richard Allen. Luke did not shake hands, but took one look at Maddie and Richard, smiled at Maddie, turned around and walked away. It was an awkward moment for all.

Richard spoke first in a nasal tone, "I am not sure that country boy likes me."

Norman Howe, obviously offended for Maddie surprising everyone, said, "I don't know you, boy, but while you are here you don't want to see him again. That country boy will break you in half, and leave you on the ground jerking, if you get into a fight."

"Richard, go get the bags!" ordered Maddie, trying to change the subject. Richard put his nose up, sniffed, and did as he was told.

Norman laughed under his breath, and thought to himself, "All the money in Texas would never buy peace in that relationship."

Maddie's mother pulled her aside and asked, "What are you thinking? You could have at least told Luke before you got here."

"There wasn't time for a letter to get here. We decided to come together at the last minute. Richard and his family are very, very rich and they are part of the elite in Austin. He has taken me to the biggest homes and the grandest parties I have ever seen."

"What about Luke?"

"Luke was last summer's romance. This is more serious than playing children's games like before."

"Maddie, your dad is rich now, but he did not have much when we got married. The journey of working together to build something has been the best part of my life. You go ahead, but you will regret it if you lose someone like Luke. He will be rich in his own right, not rich in his daddy's name like your friend."

Maddie frowned, turned back to Richard, and took his arm as they loaded everything into the Howe's car. She was very quite for the trip home. Seeing Luke was different than what she had thought it would be. She had imagined a scene where Luke would fight for her, or at least try to beg her into coming back to him, and she would separate the two men and make her choice in dramatic style. She had not considered the possibility Luke would just walk away.

Day after day went by and still Maddie had not heard from Luke. She did see him once drive by in the touring car with Levi and Ellen in the back, and someone she did not know in the front with him. For some reason, that hurt her more than she would have thought. If she wanted him, Richard would do anything for her she knew, but she wanted to at least talk to Luke.

The snow started to fall two days before Christmas Eve which was on a Saturday. In Arkansas, with many evergreen trees, the snow fell silently and created an almost surreal landscape. The snow bent the limbs on the cedars and pines with its weight. Everyone shut the barn doors to protect the automobiles, and hitched up the horses either to a sleigh or to ride. The common joke was, "The snow put the cars in their place...in the barn! Nothing will ever replace a good horse!"

There were two Christmas parties on Christmas Eve, one at the Howes, and one at Molly and August's. Several older people, mostly bank employees, came to the Howe's, but there were no young people. Maddie knew why. Hurt and angry at the town for siding with Luke, Maddie made Richard take her to Molly and August's house over her parents' objections.

Norman had to hook up the sleigh because Richard did not know how. He had always had a servant do it before. Maddie did not like it, but she had to drive because the servants had also done the driving before, while Richard and his family sat under big comforters in the back.

Norman stood on the porch with his arm around his wife, and they and the little group of guests watched smiling as Maddie had trouble getting the horses under control. They were not used to her voice. Finally, they settled enough to pull the sleigh down the middle of the road.

As if everyone had thought of the idea at the same time, Norman said loudly to everyone, "Get what food you can carry while the men get the sleighs! I am not going to miss this!"

They were all in agreement, and in less than two minutes, the whole party was on their way to go the mile and a half to Molly and August's home. There was much laughter as they slapped the reins to make the horses trot faster. They were all there ready to disembark as Maddie and Richard walked up on the porch.

Maddie knocked loudly, but no one opened the door. However, she heard Luke say, "Who is it?"

Maddie stomped her foot, and said angrily through clenched teeth, "Luke Johnson, you open that door this instant!"

Luke was on the other side of the door with his hand over his mouth to keep from laughing while he answered, "Why? You are having your own party aren't you? Besides, this party is just for my friends!"

The shocked Maddie could not believe <u>anyone</u> would not jump when she said jump! She stood in silence with her mouth open staring at the door. It was so quiet that Luke opened the door just enough to look out with one eye.

When Maddie saw Luke she pushed the door so hard Luke almost lost his balance. He let it open and was ready to cover up like a boxer under a fusillade of blows, or whatever was going to come, from Maddie. He was completely surprised when she put her arms around him and hugged him with all her might. She started sobbing and crying out loud.

"Luke, I am so sorry. I was just trying to be silly and obviously I succeeded." She looked up at him with tears and makeup streaming and said, "Will you forgive me? Please?"

"I don't know," drawled Luke in his best ham hillbilly accent. "I am just a country boy, and I ain't used to these hi-falutin', high-toned city women!"

The crowd of over 50 people roared. Luke turned to them and said, "What do <u>yall</u> think?"

In unison as if they had practiced, the crowd answered loudly in their best fake hillbilly accent, "We don't know. We're just country people!"

Everyone laughed as Maddie turned red and put her face into Luke's chest. She realized she had been put in her place by the people who loved her. She looked up at Luke, and put both hands behind his head and pulled his face down to hers and kissed him for a quick moment while everyone cheered or cried or both!

"Where's Richard?" Luke asked.

"Oh, my goodness!" exclaimed Maddie. "We shut the door on him!"

Maddie went to the door and opened it to reveal a somewhat nervous Richard standing holding his hat as he warily looked at this crowd of people where he didn't belong. Maddie pulled him on into the room by the arm, and said to everyone, "This is Richard Allen, my friend from college. He traveled with me so I would not have to make the long trip from Texas by myself."

"Thanks, Richard," spoke up Maddie's dad, Norman Howe. "But I would feel sorry for anyone who messed with

Maddie! Come on in. You are welcome here. We are just country people."

Afterward, all the young people and everyone gathered around introducing themselves and offered him punch and food. Molly whisked him off by the arm and started introducing him to all the pretty girls she could find. She pulled him under the mistletoe, kissed him on the cheek, and in just a few minutes he had lipstick all over his mouth and face as the girls got in line to kiss him!

Luke and Maddie sneaked away from the crowd and into the library and shut the door. Maddie leaned against the door while Luke tried to put his arms around her to kiss her. She pushed him back to arms length, and he saw tears on her cheek and said, "What now?"

She looked him directly in the eyes and said, "I really am sorry."

"I know <u>that</u>, but I love you anyway."

She hit him softly on his chest with her fist.

"Do you really, Luke? Tonight showed me I will always love you, but it is complicated now with my having met Richard. He has even asked to marry me. I have not said yes or no. I wanted to see and talk to you first."

"Then marry me, Maddie! I cannot even imagine my life without you!"

She hugged him again as she started crying, "Luke, I am so confused. Things were simple when I was at home, but being away makes me look at things a little different."

"Like how? You either love me or you don't. Does having a lot of money mean that much to you? You are already wealthy in Paris."

"That is just the point...in Paris. You have no idea of seeing the life Richard and the Allens live. They have numerous servants, cooks, gardeners, chauffeurs, a huge house, several cars, and the newspapers even report whenever they are seen in public. It is a different world than Paris, Arkansas."

There was a knock on the door and Levi said, "Hey, you two! We are getting ready to pass out gifts and we need you two out here!"

They opened the door a little sheepishly and everyone smiled at first, but from the tears on Maddie's face, and the look on Luke's face, everyone knew something sad was going on.

Maddie walked out, took Richard by the hand, ignored the gasp from the crowd, and, facing them, said, "You have known me all my life. I love every one in this room dearly, and I am asking from a sincere heart you accept Richard as my friend."

Everyone looked at Luke as he raised his eyes to Maddie, smiled a little, and walked over to Richard and held out his hand. There was a collective sigh as Richard shook his hand.

Since it was their home, Molly and August started handing out gifts from the huge pile around the Christmas tree. Maddie and Ellen got several gifts from their parents, and one or two clothing gifts from Levi and Luke. There were brown paper bags with oranges, apples, and hard candy for everyone. Finally all the gifts were gone. Levi stood up, set his punch on a table, and said, "There are only two gifts left. Molly has been hiding them from everybody until now. Okay, Molly, bring mine out."

Molly had on an apron and she reached into one front pocket and brought out a small black box. There was a murmur from the crowd as they guessed what it might hold. Levi got down on one knee and took the left hand of a blushing Ellen Gray.

"I know we have talked about it, but now I am asking. I love you, Ellen, will you marry me?"

Everyone held their breath until Ellen said, "Of course, Levi. I love you too!"

Levi put the ring on her finger as everyone cheered and clapped. Finally, the noise died down and everyone turned and looked at Luke standing next to Maddie.

"What do you want me to say?" said Luke. "She didn't even come to the party with me!" There was laughter, and then Luke looked at Molly who was grinning from ear to ear. "Do you have any more gifts?"

The crowd looked at Molly. She fished around in her other pocket as if she were really having a hard time finding something. "Well," she started. "I do have one here for Maddie Howe."

"Let me see it," said Luke.

A pin would have sounded like an anvil if it had dropped in the silence as Luke took the box, opened it, looked at the shining diamond ring for a long moment, and then closed the box and put it in his pocket before an absolutely flabbergasted Maddie who put her hands up to her cheeks and started crying all over again. He turned away from her, and said, "Merry Christmas, everyone! Let's party!"

Although the atmosphere was somewhat subdued, Luke acted like Maddie and Richard were just good friends home for the holidays. He hugged Ellen and Levi and even kissed Ellen on the cheek. It did not take long for the party to become festive again.

Luke went off sleighing for a couple of hours while the party was going with a girl on each arm. He did not have to drive as a third girl did the driving. They wound around the countryside and the girls took turns driving and sitting in the back seat making out with him. He was trying to forget about Maddie for a little while.

After the guests left, the Johnsons, the Howes, Richard and Maddie, and the Gray families sat at Molly's long dinner table and discussed not only what had just happened, but what next.

Luke and Levi, when asked, explained they had purchased the rings from a jeweler in Fayetteville who had ordered them from a catalog. Luke said, "I know Levi was confident, but I was having my doubts about Maddie when I saw she had brought home a friend, and it turns out I was right. It is just one of those things. We all were afraid Paris did not offer enough for Maddie. So, for my sake, no one is going to treat her any differently than before."

Maddie smiled a little smile at Luke and in a small voice said, "Thank you, Luke." She squeezed his hand for a moment, but Luke pulled his hand away slowly.

The only one not a Senior and due to graduate in May was Ellen, but Levi was willing to get a job in Fayetteville and study for his Masters until she graduated the next year. Money was not really an issue, and graduating from the University of Arkansas was a dream of George and Lettie Gray for their daughter since Ellen was a little girl. Her degree was going to be in Journalism too. She and Levi would be able to work together.

Luke would be remaining in Fayetteville also for him to get his Master's degree in engineering with a minor in architecture. He had designed buildings and highways as a hobby while he was at the University, and he was gifted enough several professors had encouraged him to go on. After the wedding, Levi and Ellen would stay together in a nice house leased by August and Molly from friends who had purchased the house for their children while they attended the University.

Luke would spend the last semester of his senior year in the dorm until he could send out applications for employment. He would rent a small off campus apartment when he came back until after his master's graduation. Levi watched him and was proud of the way he was handling everything. He knew him better than anyone and he could tell from the very polite, controlled speech and resolute expression inside he was seething. It might be better if Maddie and Richard went on home. As if sensing the same, Maddie pulled Richard up by the hand, kissed her mother, glanced at Luke, and then took the sleigh as she drove around town to show it to Richard in the snow.

Richard confessed he had never seen that much snow. He was looking at the snow as it continued to fall in large soft flakes and melt on his face. His face was wet as he closed his eyes and looked up. Maddie's face was wet too and she was grateful for the snow. It hid her tears.

Chapter Eleven

The last few days of Christmas break saw the threesome of Levi, Ellen, and Luke together everywhere. Richard Allen and Maddie went with them occasionally. He was kidded about being a snob, but he became friends with everyone, especially the local girls who all tried hard to win his favor before he left. However, he only had eyes for Maddie. She seemed to take him for granted by only occasionally holding his hand.

One day Luke and Richard went to town to get ice for the house icebox, and Luke was interested in hearing more about Richard's family. Even though Richard had a couple of personality "quirks" that were mostly just irritating, Luke thought underneath the affected accent and dress, he seemed to be a "good ol' boy." When Luke questioned him about it, Richard opened up.

"We are actually from Corsicana, which is in the central part of Texas. My father made some money in cattle, sold out, and went into the oil business. He had noticed when the drilling companies were looking for water, they kept complaining about having to drill through pockets of oil to get to the water. Some friends of his, H. G. Damon and Ralph Benton, talked him into investing some money, and they formed the Corsicana Oil Development Company. They brought in a Pennsylvania driller, John Galey, and they drilled several barely successful wells that averaged 25 barrels a day or less by 1896. So, Galey and his partner sold their interests in the wells and went back to Pennsylvania thinking there was no oil in Texas, if you can believe it!

However, my dad and more locals drilled on their own and by 1900 they had produced more than 2 million barrels from the Corsicana field alone. While that is not a tremendous amount by Pennsylvania standards, it did prove there was oil in Texas.

My dad believed in the future of oil, and he happened to meet a one-armed mechanic who was also a self-taught geologist by the name of Patillo Higgins. Higgins believed the oil lay beneath salt domes like the Spindle Top salt dome close to Beaumont, a small town in the southeastern part of Texas.

He reasoned the oil dome was more porous than just the soil, and held tremendous amounts of oil. So, Higgins organized the Gladys City Oil, Gas, and Manufacturing Company in 1892. Higgins drilled several wells and none amounted to much, but he still believed in the salt dome wells. He advertised for investors, and my dad and an Austrian Navy Captain by the name of Anthony Lucas were the only ones interested. No one but them believed in the theory of salt domes holding oil in large amounts.

Another problem with drilling on the Texas coastal plain was there was so little rock in the soil and so much sand the holes kept collapsing. One of Lucas's drillers, Curt Hamill, came up with a revolutionary new idea of pumping mud instead of water into the drilling hole to flush out the cuttings produced by the drill.

This helped in not only retrieving the cuttings, but the mud stuck to the sides of the hole and kept it from collapsing. Mud is used in nearly every oil drilling operation in the world since.

They had started on October 27, 1900, and after 2 exhausting months of drilling they shut down for a week over the Christmas holiday. They came back fresh and pushed the original 880 feet to a depth of 1,020 feet in just a week. They pulled the drill out to change the bit and other equipment on January 10, 1901. When they reinstalled the drill and got to only a depth of 700 feet, mud started bubbling back up the hole! In just a few seconds the drill pipe shot out of the hole, but then....nothing!

The frustrated drillers started to clean up the mess and salvage anything they could. Suddenly, a noise like a cannon shot came from the hole, and mud came shooting out of the hole! Within a few seconds, natural gas, then oil came shooting out of the hole in the first "gusher" that was taller than the derrick in size! Captain Lucas and the company had hoped to produce at least 5 to 10 barrels a day, but, get this, Luke, that oil well named 'Lucas 1' flowed initially at 100,000 barrels a day! That is more than all the oil wells in the United States combined!"

"Wow! No wonder your dad got rich! My hat is off to your dad and you!"

From then on, they were good friends. Each respected the other.

The day they left for Texas, Luke shook Richard's hand and Richard told him, "If you ever get to Austin, look me up. My family and I know everybody!"

Luke and Maddie embraced for a moment and Maddie kissed him on the cheek. She reached up and softly patted his cheek as she looked into his eyes. She turned, put her arm through Richard's and walked away. She put her head out the window and waved until the curve carried her out of sight.

Luke stood for a moment watching the spot where the train had been. Molly came up on one side and put her hand in his, and August stood on the other side with his arm around him.

"That was rough, Luke, but I have to say you handled it very well." said Molly and squeezed his hand.

"Thanks, and I am not too sad. Truthfully, I have known for a long time it was coming. Better now than after we were married."

As the train bounced along on the way back to Fayetteville, Luke was quiet as he thought about Maddie and how his life was going to change. He decided he could handle what had happened, if Maddie was really going to be happy.

He laughed out loud when he thought about Maddie demanding that he open the door. When he told what he was laughing about, Levi and Ellen joined in also, and all three agreed they just wanted to get the semester over and get back home.

Once back at school, the busy routine helped Luke deal with missing Maddie. They no longer wrote to one another, but there was so much to plan for with the upcoming graduation and Levi getting married in the summer, the days and weeks passed quickly.

One warm Spring day, Luke was escorting Ellen and Lela Mae back to their dorm from class. A Ford Sportabout with two local hoodlums in it slowed to keep pace. Luke changed position to be near the street as they walked along, and the one in the passenger seat called out, "Wouldn't you two fine little ladies like to go for a ride?"

All three ignored them and the car sped up and stopped. The passenger got out and told Luke, "You look real cute in your letterman's sweater."

He saw the stripes and icons for football and baseball, but overlooked the boxing gloves and the insignia that said "Conference Champion."

The man was older than Luke and the girls, in his late twenties, and Luke immediately looked at the man's hands. They were scarred as if he had fought a lot. One of his ears was flat and his nose had been broken at least once. He had a beer belly, and Luke sized him up as a puncher, not a boxer. Luke put his arm out and stopped the girls. He and the man were at eye level and the man was close to Luke's face. Luke smiled a little smile, and said quietly, "I can smell you have been drinking, why don't you go on home? We don't want any trouble. You are not supposed to be on campus anyway unless you are a student."

"My, aren't we a prissy one," and he put his arm out to push Luke.

Luke grabbed his arm by the wrist, twisted the man around, and kicked him in the pants, making him fall to his knees.

"You girls get out of here!" Luke raised his voice.

"No! We are not leaving you here alone with this jerk!" said Lela Mae, and put up her own little fists making Luke smile. Ellen moved away a few feet to prepare for what was going to happen. She had never seen Levi fight except sparring with Luke, but she was wishing that he was there.

"You are in trouble, college boy. I love beating on you pretty boys."

"You won't after today, my friend," said Luke. "I can cover the ground I stand on. Come on. Let's see what you got."

The man stood, and, instead of going into a sparring stance, he tried to use a surprise roundhouse right punch for a knockout blow. Luke easily slipped away, and using a jab, hit the man in the left eye, effectively closing it. He moved his feet making the man turn around and around and swing at the air.

"Stand still, and let me hit you!" the man yelled.

Seeing the man could only hit and not box, Luke went to work using short jabs to the man's face while he darted one way and then the other, and kept away from him. The man was already tiring from the hard punches he was taking and the foot movement. He was used to finishing off people, who were usually drunk, in one or two solid punches, but he had yet to land one on Luke. He was getting confused and he could not see Luke's fists as they came at him in a blur. He swung aimlessly with his left, and then his right. Luke stepped in close and hit him so hard in the stomach his fist almost went out of sight. It took all the fight out of him as he backed up trying to get his breath back. Luke kept coming. He wanted him to get a lesson he was never going to forget.

The man put his hands up to try to protect his face but Luke would hit him in the stomach. He would put a hand down to protect his stomach, and Luke would hit him in the face. He tried blindly to reach out and grab Luke, but Luke kept moving and hitting him over and over until with both eyes beaten closed, and his sore nose broken again, he backed up and put his hands down and said, "I quit! Don't hit me again. Please!"

"Are you going to come back? Because next time I won't be nice."

"This was nice?" He asked, or mumbled, from a fat lip. "We won't be back. You made a believer out of us. Who are you?"

"My name is Luke Johnson, and I have a twin brother who is a <u>lot</u> tougher than me."

Levi came running up at that time and the man's eyes went as wide as he could get them in the circumstances when he saw Levi. He went limping off to the car as fast as he could move, jumped over the door into the seat, and yelled at the driver. "GO! GO! Lord help, there's TWO of them!"

The crowd which had gathered by that time laughed hard at what was happening. The guys in the Sportabout had beaten up several students, and were wanted by the Sheriff for putting a few of them in the hospital. The police stopped the car a block away for speeding on campus, and one of them had seen Luke whip the man but did not try to stop it, and he asked, "Who did this?"

The driver, who was unmarked, exclaimed, "It was a whole gang of college kids! They just jumped on Jackie for no reason and beat him up!"

The officer who had seen it start, and finished, laughed and said, "Wait until I tell all over town a little college boy kicked your bottom bad. You will be the laughing stock of the town. If I were you I would move to another state.

From now on, no one will be afraid of you. They know all they have to do is call the Johnson twins. So, GO!"

They knew they had been whipped, and they went to a flophouse hotel where they had rented a room, packed hurriedly, and left town within the hour. After being informed by the two officers what had happened, the Sheriff just waved and smiled as the boys came through town. They would not look at him, and they could hear people on both sides of the street laughing and jeering. They had built their "bad boy" reputation on intimidation, and now that it was gone they were looking for some place far away.

The rest of the semester of Luke and Levi's senior year was spent studying hard for finals and making plans for the wedding in the summer. After making sure it was okay with Luke for Maddie to help Ellen with the wedding, Maddie was in constant communication with Ellen, who in turn would pass the plans on to the boys. Although the boys already had their suits, there was a number of things to plan such as the reception, location, and more.

The wedding was to be at August's church with him doing the service. Norman and Bonnie planned the reception for the cotton gin warehouse. No one's home seemed to have enough room for all the people the couple was expecting. There would be a band, and numerous college friends had already RSVP'd. Both small hotels were already fully booked, and people the couple knew well were sent to the homes of family and friends. Finally, the planning was mostly done, and it was just anticipation and the waiting for the big day.

Chapter Twelve

L uke and Levi graduated at the top of the class in their respective colleges in May, class of 1911. Both now had degrees and both had some extra experience from part time and summer work in their respective fields. Luke was going to spend the summer after the wedding designing houses and buildings for several local builders in Paris and also in Little Rock. Levi was ready to help with the *Progress* again for Mr. Wagner.

The wedding between Levi and Ellen took place in June and the only wedding deemed comparable to it was the wedding of August and Molly. Norman Howe gave Ellen and Levi a trip to Europe for the honeymoon. The three women, which included Ellen's mother and Molly, took the train to Little Rock and stayed for 2 days buying a wedding dress and bridesmaids dresses. Plus, they also purchased traveling clothes for Ellen.

It was a pretty wedding. Richard Allen came up from Texas with Maddie and presented the couple with expensive luggage for their trip to Europe and back to school. Ellen had invited her roommate, Lela Mae Thompson, and afterward they saw very little of her and Luke around town. He not only spent every possible moment with her, but she stayed over for two days and stayed with Ellen at the Gray's home till after the couple departed for their honeymoon.

Luke had a chance to say hello to Maddie, but he just smiled, nodded and did not speak. He did shake Richard's hand. He would not look at Maddie even though he knew she was watching him. They left the day after the wedding and only Mr. and Mrs. Howe saw them off at the train station. Maddie was a little disappointed, and on the long ride back to Texas it was beginning to sink in about the sacrifices she was having to make to get what she wanted.

The wedding was on June 10th, and two days later the couple took the two day train ride to New York City, boarded a ship, and went to England and France. The trip took four weeks, and their time was spent looking at the countryside, old castles, and museums.

Every night was a party of sorts with numerous people trying to buy drinks and meals for them. They visited village after village with neat sounding names only Ellen could pronounce because she had taken French in school. Levi and Ellen were captivated by the people themselves. They were just working people like the ones back home in Paris, Arkansas. No one was prepared for what was going to happen a few years later.

Maddie did not stay in Paris for the summer. No one questioned it because of Richard and the engagement. Luke was busy again going back and forth between Little Rock and Paris designing houses and businesses. He dated a few times with some of the women he met, but nothing serious.

In the fall of 1911, when they returned to the University of Arkansas, Levi and Ellen moved into the little house owned by Norman's friend. Luke and Levi studied for their Master's degrees while Ellen finished her undergraduate.

All the families came to see the boys receive their Master's degrees, and Ellen her undergraduate, in May 1912. August, Norman Howe, and George Gray, along with their wives, were reduced to tears to see the proceedings. As each walked across the stage, the men stood and clapped loudly enough to draw attention and their wives had to gently pull them down to their seats.

After a huge reception for all the graduates at the Chi Omega Theatre at the University, the group loaded all the automobiles they could find, packaged the rest to be shipped by train, and drove back to Paris for another "Congratulations" party. This time Ellen and Levi danced the first dance together. There was still a line to dance with Ellen, but Maddie was not there this time. Luke and Levi got one more chance to dance with all the girls.

The threesome had agreed after graduation they would like to move to Little Rock for more opportunity. Luke got a job as an architect with a very prestigious firm in Little Rock, and Levi interviewed in Little Rock also with *The Arkansas Gazette*, his dream job. They were so impressed with Levi he was given a job as an assistant editor over several departments based on his experience with the

Paris Progress and the University of Arkansas *University Weekly*. Mr. Wagner had given him such a glowing letter of recommendation, one of the owners remarked privately, "He might should run for Governor!"

The biggest stipulation from Ellen was it was time to have separate houses. Of course, that was fine with the men. They built new homes, designed by Luke, right next door to one another on the Rebsamen Golf course, and joined the Country Club. Ellen and Levi's home was very formal and beautifully landscaped like all the other homes.

Luke's home, however, was a work of art. With extra time on his hands, he built a glass and stone masterpiece. It made the newspapers and even several trade magazines.

In Austin, although she was not surprised for she knew Luke was gifted, Maddie bought a copy of every newspaper and magazine that had an article about him. Although she looked for pictures of him and other women, even after a year the title of "Most Eligible Bachelor of Little Rock" still belonged to Luke Johnson. Several comments were made about the "reclusive genius" of architecture.

Levi and Ellen gave beautiful parties for the women in the Country Club, and were in turn invited to all the best parties in Little Rock. Ellen was young and beautiful, her husband and brother-in-law were good looking and well-to-do, and she was active in the politics of the time including prohibition and women's rights.

As the months went by, from 1913 into 1914, Levi, Luke, and Ellen were liked and admired by everyone. With Europe talking about war, the young couple had many long conversations with other couples and friends about the possibility of the United States entering the war. The Germans had many friends and relatives of German natives around Paris and in Arkansas, and the question of which side America would take was not a moot point.

One of the main reasons for WWI was nationalism. When the war was declared on Germany, people burst out on the street celebrating in France and Britain. If the population had not been primed to support the war, the government might not have started it.

WWI was the result of a long string of events dating back to the 1890's. Conflict in the Balkans and complex European alliances were the main causes. Germany had a huge role in this. They fought for the independence of Morocco in an attempt to break the alliance between France and Britain. Germany also participated in an arms race. Kaiser Wilhelm II started building up a navy, trying to surpass Britain's fleet. Since Britain was an island nation, and had many overseas colonies, it had a gigantic navy, so what the Kaiser was attempting to do was no easy feat. Germany wanted to increase its own colonial empire, and most of the good colonies were already taken. These actions and policies helped fuel the fire. Long-term feuds and disputes, caused by imperialism and nationalism, resulted in the "Triple Entente". England, France and Russia created a common alliance opposed to the "Triple Alliance" of Germany, Austria-Hungary, and Italy. When war finally broke out, it was between the Entente and its supporters and the Central Powers (Germany, Austria-Hungary, Bulgaria, and the Ottoman Empire).[1]

The people who came and went at the Johnsons' homes were hoping the USA could remain neutral. Although a noble thought, very few really believed it was possible. Luke and Levi had private conversations about what they would do if war came. Unless Germany attacked

America directly, neither one wanted the war. However, Luke and Levi both agreed they would volunteer before they were drafted. The draft would happen two years later.

Chapter Thirteen

In March of 1914, Levi and Ellen traveled to Paris, Arkansas, for Levi to report on the arrest of Arthur Tillman, who had been arrested for the murder of his 19 year old girlfriend, Amanda Stevens. Her body had been found in a well on the property of Ambrose Johnson. Ambrose was a cousin of August Johnson. The *Gazette* was only one of several newspapers that covered the brutal slaying.

Levi and Ellen stayed in the old home place and it was a daily event to telegraph or telephone from Paris back to Little Rock the day's events. Mr. Wagner was given several "scoops" not offered to the *Express,* and his newspaper outsold the *Express* 3 to 1. Mr. Greenwood was even offering overtures to Mr. Wagner about selling or combining the two papers.

The newspaper reported that Amanda Stevens had disappeared from her home, and was found about eight days later in a well on the farm of Ambrose Johnson, partly submerged in water with a large stone attached to her neck by a telephone wire, a bullet through her head and approximately a wagon load of rock covering it as an additional precaution of the body's rising. It is believed the girl was not dead when she was put into the well because her hands were filled with dirt that was probably acquired either trying to get out or as she was put in.

A letter found at the home of the Stevens girl's parents was from a young man named Arthur Tillman requesting that she meet him at their usual place on the night of her disappearance.

According to her parents, the girl left home on the evening of March 10th telling her parents that she was going to a dance with Tillman. When she did not return, it was thought she was persuaded to leave the county because of her approaching motherhood.

A damaging statement was made by Tillman's mother. She said she thought the girl had driven from the country and she was positive that Arthur had nothing to do with it. To back her statements she said with the exception of a few hours, Arthur was at home the entire night. The time he was away from home was when he left about six o'clock carrying a 22 caliber rifle. He returned, she said, between eight and nine o'clock. The girl was shot with a rifle of that caliber. So suspicion was already pointing to Tillman.

In the meantime a report was current that a warrant charging him with seduction had been issued for Tillman, and he went to Knoxville to consult his uncle who was an attorney. On advice from his uncle, he returned home and his action led to his arrest on a more serious charge.

The well in which the girl's body was found was located on the farm of Ambrose Johnson. Mr. and Mrs. Johnson returned home Sunday, March 6. Noticing that the wooden curbing had been entirely removed from the well and a greater part of the stone curb was missing, they knew something was wrong. While discussing the strangeness of it, they noticed Arthur Tillman approach the well and peer intently into the depths. When questioned regarding this, Tillman said he too had noticed the changed condition of the well and looked inside it for this reason.

Johnson, knowing of the intimacy of Tillman and the girl and noticing the strangeness of the boy's acts, immediately collected several neighbors and the following day they began removing the rock from the well. It took several hours to remove the rocks, and it was late afternoon when the girl's body was removed and taken to the Johnson home for an inquest.

Arthur was later arrested at his uncle's home in Knoxville and escaped. A man was arrested in Fort Smith a few days later and thought to be him. The Sheriff of Johnson County went there and failed to identify him. While going to his hotel however, he met the real Tillman and placed him under arrest. He was delivered to Sheriff Cook and placed in jail in Paris. While en route to the penitentiary for safe keeping, Tillman again escaped by jumping from the train as it sped through Perry County at the speed of thirty miles per hour. Tillman had two trials and was granted an appeal. An appeal to the governor like wise failed to save him. Prominent Little Rock people took a hand in behalf of the boy and it is said that Governor Hayes received a thousand letters asking for commutation.

"I didn't want to get away, I wanted to kill myself." Thus, Arthur Tillman addressed three stalwart deputy sheriffs who stood gripping him, one of them holding his coat as the train sped away. A few minutes before, Tillman tried to leap from the open door of the baggage car in which he was being brought to Paris.

Tillman was tried by Judge Evans and was sentenced to be hanged, at Paris (Arkansas). Since he learned that Governor Hayes offered no hope of respite, Tillman suffered much mentally. When early morning he set out from Little Rock for Paris, his attitude was of deep dejection.

Once on the train, with chains and handcuffs holding his arms tightly and with fetters about his ankles, the prisoner was an object of curiosity. Owing to the wide publicity given his case, Tillman was seen and being recognized by the passengers. He was taken to the baggage car. His escort sought to save him from embarrassing gazes and occasional remarks of the morbidly curious.

About five miles from Paris the railroad climbed a steep grade. Suddenly, with a terrific kick, Tillman broke the chain about his ankles before the officers could stop him, he rushed to the car door. There he turned momentarily for a last look at his escort. The glance cost him his escape from the gallows. One of the deputies quickly reached almost his full length and caught the youth's coat. Tillman was dragged back from the door and after his words of explanation, was re chained to continue the trip. None but the officer and one baggage man knew of the incident until Paris was reached at 6:30 o'clock. This was Tillman's third and last escape attempt.

On July 10, Tillman addressed a letter to Governor Hayes to which he made affidavit, implicating another man whose name was given, with many attendant circumstances, and asserting his own innocence. The affidavit concluded:

"I would make this statement again, and swear to it, if I had only one more minute to live, and all on God's earth I ask of you, your excellency, is that you give me a fair impartial investigation of my case, something I know I did not have, nor could have gotten at my trial, on account of strong prejudice against me in Logan County."

In Paris, Arkansas, July 14, 1914, Arthur Tillman calmly awaited death in his cell being fully resigned to his fate. This followed a visit from the minister of the Methodist Church.

Everywhere there was a spirit of unrest for repeated rumors of attempts to rescue reached there.

It was reported that Tillman's father purchased a high powered rifle and a supply of ammunition and this gave credence to the report that a sharp-shooter would attempt to pick the lad off the scaffold.

On July 13, 1914, holding him at arm's length the better to see his face, Mrs. J.F. Tillman bade farewell that afternoon to her son Arthur, condemned to die. Neither mother nor son expected to see each other alive again.

"My son," the mother sobbed as she looked through tear dimmed eyes, "my little boy. You were never sweeter or dearer to your mother than you are today. I'll always know you are innocent," and unable to restrain herself, the mother flung her arms about Arthur's neck.

Reverend Ray, the Methodist circuit rider, was with Tillman during his last hours. The only statement that Tillman made was in a conversation with his spiritual adviser when he protested his innocence.

"Arthur, for God's sake," said the minister, "tell the whole truth right now. Are you innocent or guilty? I want to know if you are guilty so I may pray and have you join me in sincere prayer for forgiveness. If you are innocent, I want to hear the whole truth."

"I am innocent," was the young man's reply, uttered in a firm tone of voice.

"But," the minister said, "suppose you are not telling the truth. Are you going to die with that thing on your head?"

"Brother Ray,", said Tillman, "I am not guilty. If I should confess to that crime when I did not do it, I would die with a lie on my lips. You don't want me to die that way, do you?"

"The courts condemned you," continued the minister, "and everything is against you. Can you produce proof of you innocence? Is there not something you can say at the last minute? If you are innocent, who is the man?"

Then Tillman mentioned the name of a relative of the murdered girl. He tried to shift the blame on him at the trial, but failed to furnish convincing proof.

"How do you know that man is guilty?" said Ray.

"He was the first man to meet the girl," answered Tillman. "Why once he proposed to me that I swap Amanda Stevens to him for his wife. I would not do it, and then he told me one day that he was going to kill her."

"Arthur," said the circuit minister, "that is a mighty serious thing for you to say if you have no proof."

"I can't help it, I can tell you nothing else. I am innocent," answered Tillman wringing his hands.

"I want to impress on you that you embrace religion and then make a false statement, you are in danger of going to hell."

"I can't help it, I tried to tell all at the court and they would not let me," wailed Tillman.

Several pathetic scenes took place when relatives of the boy called to bid him goodbye, but throughout it all it seemed the lad's thoughts were of his mother and two little sisters. His last night on earth was sleepless and he failed to eat the chicken supper Sheriff Cook had ordered especially provided. At one o'clock he asked members of the death watch for watermelon. This was secured and he ate ravenously. He afterward requested that he be allowed to sleep until four o'clock and laid down, but rest was broken and he was awake before the appointed time.

When Sheriff Cook called at the jail, the boy's condition seemed to be weaker and one of the physicians told the sheriff that the boy would have to be given morphine. This was done and Sheriff Cook told Ray that the services would have to be held in the death cell. At the request of Tillman the minister sang "Shall we Gather at the River" and "God be with You Till we Meet Again". In both these songs Tillman joined. Afterward he told the minister he wanted to pray.

After the prayer Tillman said to Sheriff Cook, "I'm ready, but you will have to carry me." It is not known whether this was intended as a threat of defiance or a reference to his physical condition. Without regard to the intent of the remark, Sheriff Cook motioned to his deputies. Wayne Cook and Sam Kin cannon took Tillman by the arms and the march began.

Once on the scaffold, Sheriff Cook in a trembling voice

read the death warrant and the ropes and straps were adjusted. He (Tillman) then asked someone to wipe the perspiration from his face and his uncle stepped forward. "Thanks, Uncle Jim," said the youth. "Tell Mama I'm certainly going to Heaven this morning."

At the site of the black cap, Tillman said, "Goodbye, people." The cap was adjusted, Sheriff Cook stepped back, pulled the trigger, and the boy shot down. This ended hanging in the State of Arkansas. A law was passed stating that the death penalty would thereafter be paid in the electric chair at the penitentiary. This law came into effect before Tillman was hanged, but he was alleged to have killed the girl before this law was passed. On the same day of the hanging, an electric chair sat at Little Rock.[1]

Whether good or bad, Paris has the distinction of being the site of the last public hanging in the State of Arkansas.

Levi's coverage of the Amanda Stevens murder trial firmly planted him as the top investigative reporter for the *Arkansas Gazette,* as well as an editor. He was given a little raise and he was well to do for the time. He traveled in the inner circles of society with friends all over Little Rock and Arkansas.

Chapter Fourteen

In April of 1914, the same year as the hanging, during a break from coverage of the trial, Levi and Ellen, Luke, August and Molly, and approximately 300 Pentecostal evangelists convened in Hot Springs to establish the denomination, first called a fellowship, named The Assemblies of God.

In the decade of 1904 to 1914, the number of independent, itinerant Pentecostal preachers and evangelists had grown to such numbers they began to recognize a need for an organization "to promote unity and doctrinal stability, establish legal standing, coordinate the mission enterprise, and establish a ministerial training school."

The approximately 300 delegates to the first General Council represented a variety of independent churches and networks of churches, including the "Association of Christian Assemblies" from Indiana and the "Church of God in Christ and in Unity with the Apostolic Faith Movement" from Alabama, Arkansas, Mississippi, and Texas.

After The Assemblies of God were formed, August was one of the first evangelists to receive "papers" or certification to preach as a minister. His first act after the meeting in Hot Springs was to return home and start the First Assembly of God Church in Paris, Arkansas, even though the process for his certification was not complete. The first revival back in the summer of 1910, and subsequent revivals, guaranteed him a firm base of Spirit filled people to fill the pews. Molly still ran her restaurant and August ran the sawmill and preached on the weekends.

However, not everyone believed in what August was preaching, even though he had experienced the Baptism of the Holy Spirit himself. James Tagger, a former friend and a resident of Paris, was a staunch Baptist, and these teachings were against anything he had been taught. The Baptists believed one received all the Holy Spirit one was to receive at the moment of conversion. The tongues were "not for us, but the group of people gathered in the Bible at that time." To August, the fact the Bible stated they spoke in tongues other than their own native tongues just made it more believable than ever. But, what seemed so evident to August was lost on James Taggert. He was a very stubborn, opinionated man that was very strict with his family to the point his oldest son had already run away to the Army. It became such an issue with Taggert he had tried to pick a fist fight with August several times over his beliefs.

James Taggert was one of two Taggert brothers who were both small time farmers. His brother, Olen Taggert, was a bootlegger and a bully. He especially bullied Willie Thompson, a slender young man who had only been living in Paris for a year or two, and who lived on the same lane across the road from him. Willie was quiet and worked hard on his farm while he kept to himself. Olen would let his cows eat in Willie's garden by tearing down a piece of Willie's fence. At times there were chickens missing on

Willie's farm, and Willie could smell chicken frying and knew that Olen had his chicken for dinner. Olen had no chickens of his own.

Willie complained once to the sheriff that Olen had made a pass at his wife, but she pulled a knife on him to defend herself. The sheriff talked to Olen, but he said she was just making that up to try to get him in trouble because Willie was such a "coward" himself and would not face him. He had spent several nights in the jail for fighting and drunkenness.

He was not one that got to play cards with the Sheriff. The Sheriff's wife gave him sandwiches to eat when he was in jail, and not a full meal like most others. Olen lived on a few acres of weeds a few miles from town with a still and a pig pen. At the time making moonshine was not illegal, and he made a small amount of money selling moonshine whiskey to out of towners and a few locals from his still. Most of the time he looked and smelled of pig manure and alcohol swill. He had been known to feed his pigs distilled swill and laugh as they squealed and lay on their side, or staggered around from the effects. The people in town kept their distance for several reasons; from the smell to the fact they considered him dangerous.

One cool Sunday morning the church doors were closed to protect against the wind. Suddenly they burst open and James Taggert, the brother of Olen Taggert, stood in the doorway red-faced and puffing.

"Preacher, I came to tear your play house down!"

August looked at him and asked, "James, have you been drinking? Go home!"

"No, I won't go home, and I ain't takin' orders from you anyway! So what if a man has a sip of homemade whiskey in his own home!"

"The whiskey is making a fool out of you, that's what," returned August calmly.

"James, get out of my church before you get hurt or hurt someone. I have heard how you slap your wife around and beat on your kids, but I won't let you do that to me. I will slap you back!"

"I thought you were tough, preacher. You gonna hide behind the pulpit or do you want to take this outside like a man?"

August closed his Bible, sighed deeply, and, almost sadly, spoke to the congregation, "Folks, excuse me for a moment. I will be right back."

James Taggert was a farmer on a small 40 acre homestead that never really did well because he didn't like to work, but tried to force his family to do it all. The day at church he was in wrinkled overalls, white shirt, and a suit coat. He smelled like he had had a lot more than just a "sip."

He backed out on the church porch as August approached him. August grabbed the man by the front of his overalls and shoved him backward off the porch that was five steps tall. Taggert fell flat on his back, and the alcohol and the suddenness of August's actions dazed him for a few seconds. August jumped down from the porch, grabbed Taggert's overalls by the bib, lifted him partially off the ground, but would not hit him with his fist. He held him with one hand and slapped him several times hard with the other.

He shoved him back down on the ground, stood over him, and told him very quietly, "James, don't ever come back to this church unless you want to worship. I will hurt you whether you are drunk or sober. Now, leave us alone. We are trying to have church."

August returned to the pulpit after closing and locking the doors. He had tears in his eyes as he spoke to the congregation, "If we were not making Satan mad, he would not be causing things like this to happen. I love brother Taggert. We once were friends, but he blames me for encouraging his son, Larry Joe, to stand up to him. When his son did, he held him down in the bed of a wagon and beat him with his fists. My son, Luke, was the one that pulled James off Larry Joe. Luke and Levi brought the battered boy to our home and we dressed his wounds and let him rest for several days, and I gave him money to go to family in Little Rock where he joined the Army. I have a feeling if Larry Joe ever comes back to Paris, James will leave him alone. He has grown a lot bigger and tougher than when he left here. The Army made him a man. That was three years ago."

The congregation looked at one another and shook their heads. They knew something had happened, but did not know the full story until now. They were very quiet for a moment as August prayed for God to intervene in this situation. In the stillness, there was a soft knock on the door.

"Pastor, August, let me in. I need to ask forgiveness from you and the congregation!" cried James.

Though a couple of people from the congregation were trying to warn August, he went and opened the door. Taggert fell at August's feet on his knees and grabbed August around the legs and starting crying and sobbing.

"I am so sorry, August. Please forgive me and pray to God He will forgive me too! My wife was gone with the kids when I woke up this morning! She left a small note which said she could not take it anymore." He put his head down and cried.

August patted him on the back of the head and said quietly, "Brother, James, this is where it all starts. Jesus died to bring forgiveness of sins to people just like you, and us too. No one here is without sin."

He put his arms under the man's arms and stood him up to his feet. By then several men from the congregation were there to help James to the altar where he threw himself face down and started praying for forgiveness from God. After several agonizing minutes of praying and sobbing, he sat up on the altar, looked at the people through tears and said, "Will you folks ever forgive me?"

All the men came around and cried and put their arms around James. He finally took a deep, ragged breath and said, "I wish Sarah had been here. The only way, she said, that she would come back is if I gave my heart to the Lord."

From the doorway there was a quiet voice, "She was, James!" It was Sarah! "I followed you to make sure you did not hurt yourself and I have seen everything. I love you, James, God help me, but this is the only way we can make our marriage and life together work. Let's go home."

They met between the altar and the doorway, hugged each other as if they were trying to squeeze the breath from one another, and cried loudly. The entire congregation gathered around praying and crying for the Taggerts. Finally after hugs and well wishes all around, James got up in the wagon beside Sarah and waved to everyone as they drove away.

Molly came up and put her arm around her husband and said, "I love you, August Johnson. I am so glad I am married to you!"

As the people came out of the church, they all shook hands with August and Molly. In a small community like Paris, where everyone already felt like family, it was strengthening to see love in action.

James Taggert was a changed man. The love of friends and a good family had made him the man everyone once knew.

August was afraid if people heard he let his temper flare they would be offended or upset. Molly held his hand and told him, "If they do, <u>they</u> have a problem, but I would be surprised if anyone ever blamed you for what happened."

Molly was right. His attendance went up by several families. More than one or two were confident in August's ability to protect his congregation, and told him so.

Chapter Fifteen

Only two weeks later, August dropped off Molly at the front door of the house after church, and drove around to the side where there was an overhang to protect the car. He had just gotten out when he heard Molly calling him.

"I'm coming!" August hurried to the porch where Molly met him.

"The sheriff is on the phone and needs a couple of men to help him. There has been a shooting!"

August went and grabbed his rifle and pistol, and hurried off for the jailhouse. Sheriff Cook and Norman Howe were already there and armed. They got into the sheriff's touring car and sped off.

"Willie Thompson has shot Olen Taggert!" exclaimed the sheriff.

"What happened?" said August.

"Willie and his wife came home from church early, and Olen was coming out of Willie's barn with his horse on a halter. When Willie confronted him, he took a whip to him. His wife got Willie into the house, but Willie went straight to his gun cabinet and pulled out a holster and a six-gun. Olen was just trying to tear the fence down around Willie's garden when Willie went back outside. He laughed when he saw Willie wearing a holster and gun. Olen had on his own gun. When he went to pull the pistol, Willie beat him to the draw and shot him dead with two shots to the man's chest. Willie's wife said that Willie is holed up in the pasture on thier property in a big thicket around a spring. She is afraid he is going to hurt himself, and she called me. I don't know what we are getting into, men."

August and Norman were both veterans and the sheriff called on them at times to form a posse if he needed. Both were already deputized for that purpose, and up until now they had only been used to break up a couple of big brawls at dances and the one saloon just outside of Paris.

As they drove into the yard of Willie's house, they could see Olen Taggert's body still lying by the garden fence with a gun in his hand. Mary Thompson, Willie's pretty, young wife came running down the steps to the yard and into Sheriff Cook's arms. The sheriff let her cry until she could talk.

"Help me, Sheriff! Willie is a good man and he has just had too much from Olen. When we got here and Olen had his horse, that was the last straw. Willie got down off the wagon and Olen tried to hit him with his whip. He nicked Willie, but when he drew back to hit him again, Willie took off for the house! I could hear Olen laughing for he thought Willie was running away. I chased after him because I knew where he was headed.

You know we moved here a year or so ago from Texas, but what you don't know is that Willie Thompson is a former Texas Ranger. He is deadly with a gun and he just did not want any trouble with anyone. What Olen and some folks mistook for cowardice was a reluctance on Willie's part to hurt people. Willie and I were living just outside of Fort Worth, and on my way home from church one evening five drunk cowboys tried to rape me. I should not have been walking at night by myself, but they tried to shoot Willie when he rode up and dismounted. He drew and shot two dead. When they kept coming he took a knife away from one and killed him with it. The other two ran for their lives!"

"What do you want us to do?" asked August.

"He left here talking about killing himself because he could not get away from his past. Up until now no one knew about Willie being a Texas Ranger, and he is afraid people will start talking and treating him different. He is in the big thicket by the spring. Would you men go talk to him?"

The men looked at one another, and Sheriff Cook said, "Now is the time if you want out. I will go and see if he will talk to me. It ain't against the law to protect your property and there stands Willie's horse with the halter still on it. Olen Taggert's hand is still on the fence! Willie hasn't done anything wrong, you agree?"

August and Norman agreed. The Sheriff took a fence stave which was about five feet long and tied a piece of white dish cloth from the clothes line to it. All three started walking with their hands raised the hundred yards to the thicket. They were only about thirty yards away when the sheriff yelled, "Willie! Willie Thompson! It's me Sheriff Cook! I have August and Norman with me. We laid down our guns and we are unarmed! Don't shoot, please!"

After a tense few seconds with everyone starting to sweat, Willie stood up nowhere near they thought he would be. He had his rifle in his hand but it was not pointed at them. It occurred to the three men Willie would have killed all three of them if there had been a fire fight.

Willie gave a short laugh and smiled as he said, "Put your hands down, boys. There has already been a shooting here today. I am holed up by the spring because I have water, and I didn't know if Olen had people or enough friends to come after me. They would have had to cross about a hundred yards of open ground and I could have defended myself."

The men sat down on a couple of felled trees that protected the spring from the cattle and horses. Willie seemed to want to talk.

"I guess Mary told you about Texas. I am not wanted or anything for protecting her from those guys from Billy Bonney's old gang. I just told the Rangers I was ready to settle down with Mary and resigned. No one questioned it, and here we are. I suppose we will have to move on when word gets around what happened."

No one spoke for a few moments, and the sheriff spoke.

"Willie, good people like you and Mary are what we need around here. The whole town knows what you put up with, and most of them are going to be glad you shot Olen Taggert before he hurt someone else. Mary and us three men are the only people in Paris, Arkansas, who know you are a former Texas Ranger. What if we showed people the evidence and say you got in a couple of shots before he shot you? We all will swear on the Bible in front of the judge that is what happened."

"You think it will work?" said Norman who had been quiet til then.

"A man has a right to bear arms and to protect his property and his life. Guaranteed by the Constitution," said the sheriff. "I will swear in court you are innocent, but it ain't going to court. I am ruling it right now as a justifiable homicide. I need to call for a coroner's wagon. You reckon Mary would make us a cup of coffee?"

Chapter Sixteen

Both Luke and Levi, and Ellen as his wife, were accepted by the upper class in Little Rock as well as the Progressives, a mostly middle class, church-going group interested in reform. The Progressives tended to be educated, modern, and technology savvy. Henry Ford, as well as President Theodore Roosevelt and President Woodrow Wilson were sympathetic to the Progressives.

This movement touched every aspect of American life. It transformed government into an active, interventionist entity at the national level, but also at the state and local levels. For the first time Americans were prepared to use government, including the federal government, as an instrument of reform.

Progressive reformers secured a federal income tax based on the ability to pay; formulated inheritance taxes;

devised a modern national banking system; and developed government regulatory commissions to oversee banking, insurance, railroads, gas, electricity, telephones, transportation, and manufacturing.

Education also became a self-conscious instrument of social change. The ideas of the educator and philosopher John Dewey influenced the reformers.

Progressive educational reformers broadened school curricula to include teaching about health and community life; called for active learning that would engage students' minds and draw out their talents; applied new scientific discoveries about learning; and tailored teaching techniques to students' needs. Progressive educators promoted compulsory education laws, kindergartens, and high schools. They raised the literacy rate of blacks from 43 percent to 77 percent.

During the Progressive Era, public health officers launched successful campaigns against hookworm, malaria, and pellagra. They reduced the incidence of tuberculosis, typhoid, and diphtheria. Pure milk campaigns also slashed rates of infant and child mortality.

Urban Progressives created public parks, libraries, hospitals, and museums. They also constructed new water and sewer systems and eliminated "red light" districts such as New Orleans' Storyville, in most major cities.

To bridge the gap between capital and labor, Progressives called for arbitration and mediation of labor disputes. Meanwhile, many Progressive businessmen called for a new-style "welfare capitalism" which provided workers with higher wages and pensions.

The Progressive Era was one of the most creative in the realm of culture and the arts. In the hands of Alfred Stieglitz, photography became an art form for the first time. Architects like Frank Lloyd Wright helped create modern architecture. The first exhibition of modern art, the Armory Show in New York in 1913, was held in the United States.

A new vocabulary characterized this era. Americans would speak about a "public interest" that was opposed by "special interests." They would also speak about "efficiency" and "expertise" in government and "morality" in foreign affairs. For the first time, Americans spoke of "social workers," "muckrakers," "trust busters," "feminists," "social scientists", and "conservation."

To increase popular control over government, Progressive reformers lobbied successfully for direct primaries; the elimination of boss rule; the direct election of Senators; woman's suffrage; and in many state legislatures, adoption of the referendum, the initiative, and the recall. Reformers also saw adoption of the first restrictions on political lobbyists and the first regulations on campaign finances.

To regulate corporate behavior, Progressives enforced new anti-trust laws and established the country's first effective regulatory commissions. They also established licenses for such professionals as pharmacists, veterinarians, and undertakers. To improve social welfare, they lobbied for workmen's compensation laws, minimum wage laws for women workers, and old-age and widow's pensions. To improve public health, Progressive reformers successfully lobbied for water standards, state and local departments of health, sanitary codes for schools, and laws prohibiting the sale of adulterated foods and drugs.

The Progressive Era also had a much more negative side. It saw the spread of disfranchisement and segregation of African Americans in the South and even in the federal government. This era also saw the enactment of reforms, such as at-large voting, that lessened the political influence of immigrant groups at a time when city budgets were increasing. Some critics frequently condemned Progressives as moralistic, undemocratic, and elitist.

Progressives did not agree on a single agenda. They disagreed vehemently in their attitudes toward such subjects as immigration restriction and prohibition of alcohol. They were a diverse lot that included Republicans and Democrats, Protestants, Catholics, and Jews, and urban and rural reformers. Women's organizations stood at the forefront of the social reforms and policy innovations during the Progressive era. Women activists were especially active in efforts to end child labor and to protest companies that had unsafe working conditions or produced unsafe products.

For the most part, Progressives were urban and college-educated, including journalists, academics, teachers, doctors, and nurses, as well as many business people.

For all its flaws and limitations, the Progressive Era was instrumental in formulating the rationale for much of the welfare state, including Social Security, unemployment insurance, and aid to single parent families.[1]

By using the "initiative and referendum" set forth by a constitutional amendment to the Arkansas Constitution approved in 1910, voters succeeded in 1912 in getting a prohibition measure on a ballot, but it failed to pass. The Progressives then turned to the legislature and were successful in pressuring them to pass the "Bone Dry" Law which was to be voted on in 1915.[1]

In Little Rock some time later, Luke, Levi and Ellen had several heated conversations about women's rights. Luke was conservative, but sympathetic. Ellen was liberal, and wanted prohibition and the right for women to vote.

"Now let me see if I understand this," Levi said.

The couple and Luke were sitting in the family room of Luke's home on a cool Fall evening with a fire going. They had just eaten, and they were all relaxed except Ellen. She could not understand why there was such a difference in opinion between she and Levi. "First, here it is 1915, there's a war going on in Europe, and you want to take away men's liquor with the new 'Bone Dry' law, which is probably going to pass, and now you want us to give women the right to vote. On top of that, you want me to embrace this encroachment on males with no reservations? Ellen, why don't you women just put on pants like men? What is so great about being a man that you women are jealous?"

Ellen sighed, "Levi, we want you men to accept us as equals! We can make intelligent decisions about candidates. We could not do any worse than you men! Besides, you have told me before that democracy only works if everybody votes. The true will of the people is served only with everyone voting."

Luke whispered to himself, "Uh oh. This is going to be bad!"

"Well, I didn't mean women!"

"You chauvinistic, self aggrandizing, pig!" huffed Ellen, and crossed her arms to herself.

In an attempt to defuse the situation, Levi said, "Let's don't make this personal, Ellen. As a reporter and journalist, the facts are we cannot legislate equality or morality. Right here in Little Rock we have the Pulaski

Heights neighborhood which is segregated and just for the wealthy. Prohibition is coming, but it is just going to drive the drinking underground, and create crime and other elements you women do not really want. Men and women are going to have their drinking even if it is illegal. Ellen, sitting in this room are the people that love you most in the world besides your mother and dad. We would never wish you harm, or do anything to you to belittle you."

Levi put his arm around a non-responding Ellen and said, "Besides being equal to a man for you women would mean a step down off the pedestal we put you on, why would you want that? I love you and I don't even put on my clothes in the morning without consulting you."

"It's just because you can't tell the difference between what goes with what and you <u>need</u> me!" she finally smiled at him. She put her head on his arm and Levi hugged her tightly for a moment.

"See, there you go."

"We women are tired of being defined by our husbands, like, Dr. Smith's wife, instead of JoAnn Smith, or Levi Johnson's wife, instead of Ellen Johnson."

"Okay, I can fix this," said Luke. "Next time we are introducing you two, I will say this is Ellen Johnson and her husband, Levi. Fair enough?" Everyone laughed and Levi kissed Ellen on the cheek. She responded by patting him on the chest.

The "Bone Dry" law was passed by the legislature of 1915 and became effective on January 1, 1916. Arkansas was officially dry. So, now it was time to address the right for women to vote. Several women from the Country Club invited Ellen to a parade down Main Street in Little Rock with over 300 more women all dressed in white and carrying signs. Luke and Levi had several conversations with other men and husbands at the Country Club and all agreed it was just a matter of time before women could vote. Why there were already women driving cars and flying planes!

Luke and Levi came home to a house full of women "suffragettes" nearly every day. Mostly the men tried to keep a very low profile, and even Ellen agreed that might be best. She knew how tender the subject of women voting was to Levi. However, finally, when pressed, he endeared himself to all the other wives and girlfriends by stating,

"You know, I have thought a lot about this. In fact, I have even changed my mind. In my relationship and marriage with Ellen I have a partnership in which her opinion matters to me. So, in a way she already has a vote in everything that goes on in our lives. I am no longer against women receiving the right to vote, because the truth is they deserve it."

He probably could have run for mayor of Little Rock if women had had the right to vote after that speech. He got a big hug and kiss from Ellen. She was proud of him for having the ability to think for himself.

The suffrage movement also gained an important ally with the election of Governor Charles Brough in 1916. His wife, Anne, was a good friend of Luke, Levi and Ellen. She, with the help of her husband, helped convince the legislature in 1917 to allow women to vote in primary elections. In the election of 1918, the right to vote for women became a law that required an amendment to the Constitution as the nineteenth amendment.

Chapter Seventeen

The Selective Service Act, or Selective Draft Act, was passed by the Congress of the United States on May 18, 1917. It was envisioned in December 1916 and brought to the President's attention shortly after the break in relations with Germany in February 1917.

The Army of the United States was dwarfed by the huge armies of Europe. Numbering only around 100,000, the Congress decided to enlarge the army to a national army numbering in the hundreds of thousands with which to fight a modern war. Every male between the ages of 21 to 30 were initially required to register. However, there were so many volunteers, the Draft age was extended in August 1918 from 18 to 45. There were over 23 million men that registered, and the army drafted 2.8 million by the end of the war. Out of the 4 million men that served in World War I, 2.3 million were volunteers.

Luke and Levi went to the Courthouse in Little Rock and registered for the draft. When told they might not get to serve there were so many men registered, Luke and Levi sat down with Ellen and explained they wanted to volunteer. She decided it was the men's decision and she would deal with whatever they decided. Luke and Levi decided to volunteer.

Luke and Levi called their dad and Molly to ask for an opinion more than to ask permission. Molly was quiet as she listened, and when she asked why they wanted to go, Luke answered, "If we enter now we can get better assignments than later. We might not even have to leave Arkansas!"

August took the news solemnly. "I hate war! We fight these 'glorious' battles with our brightest and best. We don't ever seem to learn. Our sons and daughters go marching off to war, and some don't come back. But, they all are forever changed. I am not trying, boys, make that men, to keep you as teenagers forever, but know this. You go with my blessing and my prayer that you both return in one piece. We will all be praying for your safe return."

"Dad, thanks," Luke spoke for both of them. "You have supported us in everything we have ever done. They are having a draft anyway, and we might have to go whether we want to or not. I know you will worry, but you keep the Faith you instilled in us that God will protect us. Love you, Dad!"

As he hung up the phone the two brothers and Ellen had a group hug with everyone in tears. The next day Luke and Levi joined the Army. On the basis of their education, Luke and Levi were given the rank of Second Lieutenant in the Army. Ellen decided they looked good in uniform, and she loved to show off her dashing husband and brother-in-law at their parties and at church.

The government had set aside 6000 acres to build Camp Pike on the north side of the Arkansas River from Little Rock, and Luke was instrumental in using his civil engineering experience to help lay out the camp to government specifications. The camp was to be used for training the 87th Division of the Army. Luke and Levi helped put the camp together and make it operational. It took several months.

Levi was part of the camp communications admin. He sent and received communiques between Washington and the Army. Plus, Levi continued to report local news to the *Arkansas Gazette*. Levi saw where the Army was looking for people to train to fly, and when he told Luke, they decided to volunteer for flight training. Already in the Army, they were immediately to be transferred to an Air Training facility in San Antonio, Texas, by the name of Kelly Field.

Ellen took the news very quietly, but did not try to discourage them. Luke and Levi left by train the day after New Year's in 1918. Both were excellent athletes and excelled in flying. They went to France after training and joined other American volunteers in the Lafayette Escadrille, a special squadron made up of a multi-national group of fliers.

By the end of February, both men were already aces with over 5 kills apiece. Both had had bullets flying close, but neither were hit. It was sobering to know they actually could have been killed. They realized August and Molly were praying as well as Ellen.

Ellen had taken a job as an assistant to the governor's wife, and was still a part time editor with *The Arkansas Gazette* with Levi and most of the men gone to war. Ellen kept everyone up to date on all the news from the front with all the wire services to the newspaper.

It was February 18, 1918, before any U.S. squadron entered combat in WW I, (the 103rd Aero Squadron, a pursuit unit flying with French forces and composed largely of former members of the Lafayette Escadrille which included Luke and Levi).

Luke and Levi were sometimes used for flying observation planes because of such a high rate of losses of planes and pilots. Observation planes often operated individually, as did pursuit pilots to attack a balloon or to meet the enemy in a dogfight. However the tendency was toward formation flying, for pursuit as well as for bombardment operations, as a defensive tactic. The dispersal of squadrons among the army ground units (each corps and division had an observation squadron attached) made coordination of air activities difficult, so that squadrons were organized by functions into groups, the first of these being the 1st Corps Observation Group, organized in April 1918.

On May 5, 1918, the 1st Pursuit Group was formed, and Luke and Levi both were transferred to fly fighters. They were part of the 94th Squadron with Lieutenant Eddie Rickenbacker as squadron commander.

The Johnson twins flew their first missions in the new squadron as air support for a bombing mission the second day at the airdrome. Levi marveled at how pretty and green, and even peaceful, the countryside looked as he and Luke flew along in formation with 13 others, all flying Nieuport biplanes. He remembered the long walks and the laughter shared with Ellen on their honeymoon in this same countryside. It was sad to both Levi and Luke to see it all destroyed. Wars, Levi mused, are fought by common people not the generals.

Just as the vegetation far below suddenly changed from green to black, grey and brown, Luke and Levi looked up toward the sun, for they knew from experience the Germans liked to attack with the sun behind them. They pointed toward the sun to the other pilots for some were on their first mission. They were right. The silhouette of the first German Fokker was coming in fast as Luke went left and Levi went hard right. The plane seemed surprised by the move and hesitated. By then, Luke first, and Levi next, came quickly back around and poured bullets into the plane. The plane started a slow, smoking spiral toward the ground.

It was only a matter of seconds before the 3 winged German planes were circling for position on all sides. By breaking formation and getting more altitude, Luke and Levi had an advantage, and in a matter of minutes, two more Fokkers were smoking and diving trying to get away. Luke followed one down until it hit the ground and exploded. Levi's target tried to get away but, after one long burst from Levi's Vickers machine guns, the plane exploded in mid air. The other German fighters had had enough. They pulled up and fled for the German lines.

On the ground, they were greeted by all the other men with cheering and pats on the back. They took their first drinks of fine champagne to celebrate, and were quickly accepted by the other men. Their company commander, Lieutenant Rickenbacker came by the table and as the men stood at attention he offered congratulations. They got to bed about midnight, but it was still wartime at 5:00 a.m.

Luke and Levi got up quickly after a lifetime on the farm, and the sun was just showing color as they took off again. This time to fly support missions for the troops.

The Germans were losing the war, but were determined to push against the Americans one more time. Both Luke and Levi strafed the German lines and dropped a couple of small bombs to help push back the German offensive. When they arrived back at the airdrome, both were quiet as they helped to patch the bullet holes in their planes. Neither joined in the usual laughter and pranks after a successful mission. Looking at the holes in their planes up close, the men decided this was serious business.

"What would you do, Levi, if I got shot down?" asked Luke solemnly.

"I would miss you, Luke. You have been a part of my life all of my life. You are such a part of me sometimes I have to stop and think about where my life and thoughts begin and yours start. Truth is, brother, I really would miss you." Levi clasped his brother's arm tightly for a moment and both knew without saying anything else what there was between them was special.

The Air Service, First Army, was activated August 26, 1918, marking the commencement of large scale coordinated U.S. air operations. Col. Benjamin Foulois was named chief of the First Army Air Service over Col. Billy Mitchell, who had been directing air operations as chief of the I Corps Air Service since March, but Foulois voluntarily relinquished his post to Mitchell and became one of the two assistant chiefs of Air Service AEF, at Tours in charge of personnel and training. Mitchell went on to become a brigadier general and chief of the Army Group Air Service in mid-October 1918, succeeded at First Army by Col. Thomas Milling.

Occasions to smile were hard to come by during the war, but one of the most famous was an exploit of the famous 17th Squadron. On the offensive patrol of the 12th of August when the squadron had escorted 211 Squadron over Ostend to their perpetual target, submarine shelters, marine works and docks at Bruges. In the melee on the way home Lieutenants Armstrong, Snoke and Alderman were wounded, Lieutenant Armstrong's wounds being serious, and he had barely sufficient strength to get back to the field where on landing he set down on the back of a

DH-9 waiting to take-off. The bullet which had wounded Alderman had gone through the petrol tank, wounded him where he "sat" convincing him he was mortally wounded. He succeeded in gliding west of the lines making the beach a mile beyond Nieuport and was not heard from for some time. The Belgians had captured him as a, "suspicious character."

Later, Alderman recalled the visit of his Majesty, King George V, to the hospital known as "Queen Alexandria Hospital" which stood not far from their airdrome near the little French fort from which antiaircraft batteries fired as many as 600 rounds per night at the relays of Gothas that went overhead on the way to Dunkirk and Calais.

Lieutenants Armstrong and Alderman were in this hospital during the visit. As the King was casual, he came down the ward, very simply, with a word for every wounded man, an expression of interest, a touch of sympathy. When he reached Lieutenant Snoke, he said, "Ah, some Americans. I hope you are quite alright. I see you were wounded in the head." Then to Armstrong, "How are you and where were you wounded?" Lieutenant

Armstrong answered, "In the back and arm, your Majesty." Finally he reached Alderman with another, "And where were you wounded?" Alderman had a moment of self-consciousness but his quick-witted reply was "Over Ostend, your Majesty." The King understood and a smile of delighted amusement spread over his face and the faces of the officers of his staff. Alderman's wound from that moment became a public possession and it's exact location was always thereafter referred to as "Over Ostend," for had not a King understood? [2]

The weather was foggy and cold as Luke and Levi took off mid-morning on 29 October. They were to fly support missions for the troop advancement all along the front. The war was drawing to a close and the fliers met with very little resistance from German planes, but ground fire was still dangerous.

The formation of 15 planes began strafing missions and on his second pass at a German machine gun emplacement Levi's plane was shot up by another machine gun. Luke, flying close behind could only watch as Levi's plane began smoking. With the engine stopped, Levi succeeded in setting the plane down close to the American front lines, but still in "no man's land". The plane came in faster than normal, flipped, and immediately a small flame began. Levi was knocked unconscious from the landing and was hanging upside down.

Luke landed his plane within a few yards from Levi's plane, jumped out and ran to the plane. He could see his brother unconscious and he pushed up on him shoulder to shoulder until he could unbuckle his harness and pull him out of the plane to lay him on the ground. All of a sudden he heard Levi exclaim, "What, Ellen! What?"

Levi came awake and started trying to sit up on the ground where Luke had laid him. Luke pushed him back and was trying to keep him quiet, believing he was delirious. After a few moments, Levi calmed and looked up into his brother's anxious face. "I heard Ellen calling out to me, Luke! I promise you I did!"

Luke patted his brother on the chest and said, "Okay, I believe you. Lay still. Are you shot?"

"No, or at least I don't think so."

At that moment the plane exploded, and Luke threw himself over Levi in case there was any flying debris.

"Are you okay, Levi?" said an anxious Luke.

"Yes! Now get off me!"

Both men laughed and Luke spoke, "What could be any more strange? Two rednecks from Arkansas laying in the middle of a muddy field in Germany. I am just glad you are okay. Ellen would beat me to death if you don't come back from this war!" They laughed again.

Luke stood and pulled his brother to his feet, and both men put their arms around each other and let the tears flow down their faces. The soldiers that came running up were moved at such an obvious display of affection. One of the men was an officer and assured Luke they would get Levi back through the lines and to his squadron on a motorcycle.

Luke enlisted the aid of a soldier to turn the prop and help get his plane started. The engine coughed once, but roared to life. The men helped turn the plane around into the wind which suddenly came up strong, blowing dust and smoke into the enemy lines a few hundred yards away. It completely obscured what was happening. The plane bumped along and all the men cheered as the plane left the ground. Luke gained altitude and saluted the soldiers by dipping his wings and doing a barrel roll over the troops as he headed for the airdrome. They shouted and waved, for they were all lifted in spirit by the events.

Ellen kept up to date on the news from the front and both she and the families back home were cheered and positive on news the war could not last much longer. On the evening of the 28th of October, Ellen cooked for August and Molly who were visiting from Paris. It was a welcome visit from family. Of course, Molly helped and the taste of her meat loaf brought back many memories of more happy times from all of them.

Ellen told of all the latest news she had heard of where the guys were and what she knew of what was going on. They all held hands and stood in a circle as August prayed for the men's safe return. Afterward, August sat and talked quietly.

"You know, I have believed from the time they went off to the war they would make it back. I still believe it, but for some reason my soul is a little troubled. I just feel like they are in mortal danger today more than usual."

Ellen spoke first, "That is the way I feel too, August. Today is different. I know we have prayed, but I want to pray some more. We have talked about this all afternoon. I did not want to speak about it, but something is different and ominous."

They stood again and this time the intensity of their prayers caused the group to speak in tongues. Afterward, everyone felt the burden lift, and they all went off to bed. August and Molly were in one bedroom and Ellen was alone in hers. Suddenly, in the middle of the early morning on the 29th, Ellen sat up and screamed, "Levi! Levi, wake up!"

An anxious August and Molly ran into the bedroom and when told the men were in trouble, they prayed again. This time August prophesied there was a mighty wind sent from the Lord that was helping the men.

After the men returned and Luke and Levi related the events of October 29th to the group, everyone was astounded it happened while they were praying and they were delivered by a mighty wind just like August had prophesied!

As the war began to wind down, the squadron would only fly when Group would issue orders to support the troops who where advancing all along the front. It was very common to have football and baseball games between squadrons, and sometimes even boxing matches. The 94th Squadron, mostly Americans, was challenged by the 17th , mostly made up of British, to a boxing match. Someone from the 17th had heard Luke was a Conference Champion from the University of Arkansas. The 17th had a British Champion from Oxford by the name of Thomas Cook who had won a couple of pro fights besides being a college champion.

A meeting was arranged, a boxing ring was set up, and a former pro referee located who volunteered to referee the fight to keep it honest. Of course, wagering began, and the odds were heavy against Luke as much as 3 to 1. The British champion was more experienced than Luke, ten pounds heavier, and an inch taller. Although Luke looked a lot more muscled when they took off their shirts, it was assumed the somewhat older Thomas Cook would make quick work of the American. The fight would be 15 three minute rounds but no one expected the American to survive that long.

Several of the American brass were planning to come to the fight, and the squadron commander asked Levi to tell him the truth about his brother. After telling him that

Luke had been a state champion in high school and a conference champion in college, the officer watched Luke work out and decided this might be a chance to get back at the snobbish British officers who had laughed at the thought of an American beating their hero. He convinced the American officers to "sandbag" or to "play down" the facts of how good Luke was to get the best odds for betting. By fight time the odds stood at 4 to 1 against Luke, and on the squadron commanders word, there were some very heavy bets made. So much so that Levi told Luke he would have to win or they would be hung if they lost.

The two fighters came toe to toe in the ring, and the British fighter was very pompous and arrogant as he exclaimed, "Is this hillbilly kid the best the Americans can come up with?" The bi-partisan crowd was in an uproar as both sides yelled back and forth. Even some of the Americans were a little unsure, but Levi smiled to himself for he had seen lots of men defeated that had underestimated Luke.

The referee explained no hitting below the belt; also if one boxer goes down the other goes to a neutral corner before the count begins, and both fighters agreed. When they got to their corner, Levi told Luke, "I watched him fight a little and he likes to jab over and over with his left. When he wants to hit with his right, he drops his left. Come in over that dropped left hand with a right cross on the point of his jaw. Otherwise, stay away from him because he can hit hard."

Someone had a cowbell to use as a ringer. At the sound both fighters came out quickly from their corners. There was an "ooh" from the crowd as Luke landed the first punch and danced away before the Brit could retaliate. Cook was used to standing "toe to toe" and using his size to punch. Luke knew that and kept moving and jabbing and not allowing the larger man to get him into a corner. One or two stinging blows from the other fighter confirmed to Luke this was not going to be a quick fight. By the end of the first round it was apparent Luke was faster, but could he punch hard enough to knock Cook out?

The second and third rounds saw lots of sparring, and the crowd began to quieten as they saw the American knew what he was doing. Even the British crowd started to look at one another as they saw their fighter begin to tire somewhat and swing clumsily. Luke hit him constantly as the other man moved back and forth trying to keep up with his footwork. Finally late in the 5th round, after a jab or two in succession, the British fighter lowered his left hand to put all his weight in a right cross, Luke beat him to the punch with his own right hand to the man's jaw and knocked the British champ down. Luke went to a neutral corner and waited while the count went to 8. The man started to raise up and fell back down. He was through. It was bedlam as Levi rushed to Luke and picked him up while all the Americans cheered. The British champ got up slowly but extended his hand to congratulate Luke on a good fight. Even the British soldiers clapped for Luke, but they were not happy to have to pay their bets. Although a rematch was a possibility, both sides agreed Luke beat the British champ fair and square.

That evening the squadron commander came by the guys' room. They immediately stood at attention. "As you were, gentlemen!" exclaimed the officer.

"I just came by to give you a little something off the record. The odds were 4 to 1 and several thousand was bet.

Everyone agreed to give you a share of the earnings. So, here is 4 thousand dollars for your trouble! You just cannot tell anyone."

This time Levi was thankful for his share of the winnings. They hid their money until time to go back to the States. Both were very watchful of anyone that seemed to get close to them and they only hoped they <u>both</u> did not get killed in battle.

Luke Johnson was mildly famous after beating the British Boxing Champion. It even made the wire service and Ellen saw it. She immediately called her parents, and they called August, and all of them were overjoyed. It was the news that he and Levi were alive and well that made it so great for they had not heard from them in several weeks.Luke and Levi were returning from a troop support mission after 6 months of almost daily air to air combat, and wondered at all the shouting and waving from the ground. The day was a cold, bright, sunny day. It was November 11, 1918. The War To End All Wars was over.

Ellen was the first to hear of Germany's surrender, and immediately called August. All over Little Rock bells were ringing and horns were sounding as people took to the streets in impromptu parades and shouted to one another. The war was finally over!

The days seemed to drag one into another from November into the middle of December. Ellen did not know if and when the men were coming home. She was with August and Molly, who had come to help her wait at her house, three weeks later when the phone rang.

"Hey, what's for supper?" asked Levi with a lot of emotion in his voice on the other end of the line.

"Anything you want! Just get your self home! Where are you calling from? Is Luke with you?"

"We are together. He went to find us something to eat and actually I am calling from Kelly Field in San Antonio, Texas. We got off the boat in New York, and they put us on a train immediately. This is the first chance we have had to call. It takes a couple of weeks to a couple of months to process out, and we may even have to stay here and train aviators. I love you, Ellen Johnson!

Ellen sniffed as she said, "I love you too."

"I promise to never leave you again, Ellen!" She heard Levi sniff too, and then she sobbed some more.

"Ellen, listen, do you remember the guy Maddie brought home from the University of Texas that Christmas named Richard Allen? He wound up not marrying her, and he spent the war here in San Antonio. He is one of the officers on the base here in charge of processing us out. He is actually married to your old roommate, Lela Mae. They happened to run into one another a couple years ago and fell in love and got married. He really is a nice guy, and he gave me Maddie's phone number. She works in Austin for the University of Texas now, and she was so happy and surprised to hear from me. When I told her Luke never married either, she actually cried and begged me to help her see Luke.

Ellen, Maddie will meet you at the train station in Austin as you come through. I have not told Luke. I wanted it to be a surprise. Catch the train down here, pick up Maddie as you come through, and we can stay at a nice house Richard's family owns on the river. Luke and I will have already moved in by the time you get here. We may have to stay here for several months to make sure the war doesn't start up again. We will have to train other aviators in the meantime."

Ellen had her ear to the phone and started nodding excitedly as if Levi could see her. "I can get one in the morning and be there about mid morning the next day!"

"Great!" Levi exclaimed. "We will meet you at the station!"

They were both at the station by 10:00 a.m. on the day the girls were to arrive. They were part of a large group of people who were waiting for their men to come home, but also there were several men meeting their wives too. There was a large amount of anticipation among the people, but finally the train arrived and hissed to a stop in the station. The men searched through the offloading crowd until Levi heard Ellen's voice, "Levi! Levi Johnson!"

He looked and he could see Ellen with her head out of a window waving frantically. He got to touch her, but had to wait for a few moments for her to get off the train before he got his first teary eyed kisses.

"I guess I will go get the car while you two do kissy face," exclaimed Luke.

"No, brother, we need to wait on Ellen's traveling companion. She is getting their luggage." Levi was looking over Luke's shoulder and exclaimed, "See? There she comes now!"

Maddie was looking down trying to carry an overnight bag and a suitcase in one hand and a large suitcase that seemed heavy in the other. Her dark hair had become disheveled somewhat and one long curl was over one eye. She was trying to blow the hair away by blowing out of the corner of her mouth when she looked up.

Her and Luke were only about ten yards apart. Neither barely breathed for a long moment as they stared into one another's eyes. It took a few seconds, but the tears started to come into her eyes. Luke went to just an arm's length away, and said with very little emotion, "What are you doing here? Your chauffeur couldn't come?"

With a rueful smile, Maddie tried blowing the hair out of her face one more time, gave up, and said, "I don't have a chauffeur. I never married Richard. I was already in Austin when I graduated, so, I just stayed.

I have a good job in the administration department of The University of Texas. I have a little apartment near school, and I have been there for the last 6 years."

"What am I supposed to do or say, Maddie, after all this time? I don't know!"

She walked into his arms and said, "I don't care what else you do, but kiss me!"

"And that is supposed to make up for everything?"

"Would it help if I told you I love you, Luke Johnson?"

Luke put his arms around her and held her off the ground and swung her around so that her toes barely touched the ground. As he kissed her it was like the well house again in Paris. He held her a long time as Levi and Ellen clapped.

Luke picked up her heavy suitcases, and she carried the overnight bag and put her free arm around him and held him tight.

No one seemed to notice as Luke and Levi kissed the girls on the station platform. After a few minutes, the men went and loaded the luggage into the new touring car that Luke had bought. There were so many bags and suitcases, Levi and Ellen sat on top of the luggage amid laughter and pointing by many bystanders. They did not care. They were together again.

The "little cottage" Richard had told them about was not far from downtown on the river, and was larger than the Johnson home in Paris. It was on a large fenced lot and very private with trees and the river. It had been used as a weekend location by Richard's parents when they needed to get away for a little while from all the bustle in Austin. It had a large family room, kitchen, and three bedrooms. Luke and Levi had only their personal clothes and belongings to move in and they were appreciative the cottage even had linens and a fully stocked kitchen including dishes and silverware.

The little group let themselves in and Levi and Ellen's bedroom was on one side of the house with the other two bedrooms across the living room on the other side of the house. As soon as the girls' luggage was put away. Levi grinned and winked at Luke and said, "I am sure Ellen is a little tired from the trip and all. So we are going to rest for a bit."

"You know it is still the middle of the afternoon. Maddie and I thought you might want to sit outside and talk awhile. This place has a nice covered patio with an outside cooking stove and table and chairs, right, Maddie?"

Maddie picked right up on the tease, "Luke's right. We have not seen each other in several years. Let's visit and catch up!"

Levi put his arm around the smiling Ellen and said grinning, "You visit, and we will catch up!"

As they turned and walked away with their arms around one another, Ellen turned her head to them, smiled, and stuck out her tongue at Luke and Maddie causing everyone to laugh out loud.

"Maddie, would you care to make coffee while I build a fire? We have a few things to talk about, don't we?" Luke smiled at her as she kissed him on her way to the kitchen.

Within a few minutes Luke had a fire going and Maddie brought the coffeepot from the kitchen on a silver tray, and served the coffee in beautiful china cups with painted roses on the side.

Luke took the offered cup, sipped it, and set it aside as too hot for the moment. Maddie sat down beside him on the large red leather couch, and spread a blanket over her legs.

"I don't even want to know if you were ever here with Richard."

"Yes, you do, Luke. Let me talk first. I <u>have</u> been here but only when Richard's family was too. I slept in my own room. Luke, I am still a virgin. Richard adored me, I know, but after a short time even he knew it was not going to happen for us. I was another trinket on his arm for him to show off as we went to parties and out to eat and college happenings. He was in a rich fraternity and it was fun for a while to be known as Richard's girlfriend. But, you know me well enough to know I am not good at living in someone else's shadow."

"Yes, I know," smiled Luke. "But go on."

"Well, just before we graduated I had a long talk with Richard and I gave him back his ring. We <u>both</u> cried. That was one fancy ring!" They both laughed as she moved closer to Luke on the couch. He put his arm around her, and she put her head on his shoulder as she continued to talk.

"We agreed to travel together to Ellen and Levi's wedding. I wanted to talk to you then, but you would not even look at me. After you took off with Lela Mae, I figured it was all over as far as you were concerned."

"Would you believe she was trying to get me to talk to you? She liked me as a friend, but she knew I would never love her the way I do you. I mean <u>did</u>."

Maddie raised her head up and looked into Luke's face. "<u>Did</u>? Luke Johnson, you are so transparent! The moment I saw you on that train station platform I knew you still loved me. I love you too, Luke. I don't know if I would ever have found anyone else."

As the tears started, Luke said, "Let me get a handkerchief. I will be right back." He got up quickly and went into the bedroom and came back with a handkerchief in his hand.

"Well, looka here! I found this little black box in this old handkerchief. Wonder what it is, hmm."

Luke sat beside Maddie as they both watched him open the box. Nestled inside on black velvet was the diamond ring Luke had bought for Maddie so long ago. It glistened in the firelight.

"Maybe not as fancy as the ring Richard gave you, but it will have to do. Maddie Johnson, I gave you my heart a long time ago, and now I am giving you this ring. Will you marry me?" Luke's own tears were flowing copiously as he took the handkerchief and wiped his eyes.

Maddie was crying so hard her hands were shaking as she held out her hand for Luke to put the ring on her finger. Luke gave her the handkerchief and as she wiped the tears, Luke said, "Just don't blow your nose in it!"

They both were crying and laughing as she said, "You are such a jerk!"

He held her tight as they kissed, and from the doorway to their bedroom they heard Ellen sob. They looked, and Levi and Ellen were standing there still fully dressed, both in tears, as Levi said softly, "Man I am glad that is finally over! Now, don't bother us for a while! We have been plastered against the door listening."

Both couples laughed as Levi playfully slammed the bedroom door. Maddie smiled, rolled her eyes and shook her head as she heard Levi lock the door as if her and Luke would barge into the room.

"Now, where were we?" she said as she put her arms around Luke and held her face up to kiss him.

Chapter Eighteen

They all traveled to Paris for Luke and Maddie's wedding two months later. Maddie's mother brought out a tightly wrapped package smiling, "I hope you can still get in this, but this is the wedding dress I bought when I thought you might marry Richard."

Maddie squealed with delight and ripped off the paper.

"Don't worry, I have <u>lost</u> weight, not gained, through the years. I don't eat as much as I did when someone else was buying!"

Just a small announcement in the paper and the church was full. Molly got everyone fed and even had time to bake a beautiful cake. Dressed in his officer's uniform, and Maddie in her expensive dress, it was a story book wedding.

Luke asked Maddie to see if she would care if he invited Richard to the wedding.

"Of course not. He is still our friend, and he even helped us get back together!"

Although surprised to hear of the wedding so soon, Richard and Lela Mae were there. Everyone had the same opinion this is the way it should have been.

Back home in Little Rock in 1919 there were numerous job offers for the twins. Levi went back to the Arkansas Gazette, but as a Senior Editor. Ellen worked for him as an assistant editor. Luke returned to work as an architect with the same firm where he had worked before, but technology had changed and he was having a little bit of trouble catching up. Though during the day he was too busy to think, Maddie came home one evening after Luke had been working only a few weeks on the job and found him sitting by the pool with a drink in his hand.

"Talk to me, Luke. You never used to drink."

"You're right, Maddie, but that was a war ago. I am having a little trouble assimilating back into the work routine. The men that never went to war seem very condescending to those of us that did. I am slowly starting to realize I don't have a part with them any more. They talk about movies and celebrities and events I never knew. I am good at what I do, but after being in the skies for so long, it is hard to adjust. I sit in a room full of architects and my co-worker is within arms reach. I need some space."

"How can I help, Luke? Do you want to get away for awhile? The old home place is being cared for by August and Molly, and we could go home for a while. My job is not fun now anyway with the changes in administration. We have plenty of money for a long time. Besides, I would like to see the folks too."

They packed clothes enough for a week or two, and left at daylight the next morning. Levi and Ellen stood quietly as they said goodbye. The foursome had been together so long they were sad to see Luke and Maddie leave, even though they were thinking it would not be for long.

The trip from Little Rock by car took 4 hours. For Luke and Maddie it was a chance to relax and both had memories to reminisce of their quick honeymoon in Hot Springs. The summer foliage was very uplifting to both of them. By the time they got to Paris, both were in a good mood.

"Let's go to Molly's for a meal," said Maddie. "She will just die. She doesn't know we are coming!"

The restaurant was very busy, and Luke and Maddie left on their driving hats and sunglasses as they watched and waited until Molly's back was turned, slipped in, and sat at a table in the corner. Molly walked right up on them before she actually looked them in the face and recognized them.

"Luke and Maddie! I don't believe it! You are a sight for sore eyes!"

Luke and Maddie stood and hugged Molly. She had tears in her eyes as she told everyone in the place her children were home from Little Rock, and Luke was a war hero home from the war. Everyone joined in the applause. It was like seeing family for all of them for they had known the couple from their childhood. For a few minutes everyone gathered around and shook hands and patted the couple on the back. It finally settled enough for Molly to take their order.

"I have a new item on the menu. It is called a hamburger, and most people order fried potatoes and a Coca Cola with it."

"Sure. Sounds good to me!" smiled Luke. He was hungry after traveling so long. Maddie had made sandwiches, but they were gone long before they got to Paris.

Maddie bent down to quietly tell them she was expecting August and Norman any second. They were coming for the noon meal and visit a little.

Maddie stood between them and the door as it opened. She had seen the men coming and the whole restaurant heard August's booming voice as he said, "Hey, good lookin' what time you get off?"

Everyone laughed, and Molly moved toward the door and away from in front of the couple. August and Norman's face brightened as they saw Luke and Maddie. Both rushed over and August grabbed Luke and Norman hugged Maddie. It took a minute or two before the emotions slowed enough to speak.

"We were in the neighborhood and thought we would stop by!" smiled Luke.

"Actually, Luke wanted some <u>good</u> cooking for a change!" laughed Maddie and put her arm around Molly and her dad.

The meal almost got cold from the conversation being so heated with everyone trying to catch up on almost two years of being apart. They had not had time to visit during the wedding a few months before. Luke was answering questions about the war, and Maddie was being asked about the women's right to vote passing. Norman called Bonnie, Maddie's mother, and told her to come and join him and August for lunch. It was only a three block walk, and she came quickly.

The men stood as Bonnie came through the door. No one said anything. They all sat down at the table. Bonnie looked around the room and smiled at some of the people she knew. When her eyes saw Maddie and Luke on the other side of the room, she blinked, thinking it could not be them! She looked at Norman and August and both had tears in their eyes as they just smiled and nodded. She stood, and that was as long as it took for Maddie to run across the room and into her mother's arms. Both sobbed for a moment, and as she held Maddie she reached for

Luke to draw him close too. Everyone in the place was teary eyed.

The adults all ordered meat loaf and sides of mashed potatoes and green beans, which was Molly's trademark dish. Luke and Maddie took Molly's advice and ordered hamburgers, fries and a Coke. The hamburger was a round, ground beef pattie served on a round bun. The potatoes were deep fried the way the French were doing, thus the name became French fries.

"Okay, kids, what do you think?" asked Molly.

Luke spoke first, "I think you are on to something. The hamburgers are a portable meal. One could take a sackful, or one, have a picnic or ride in an automobile, and not have to deal with plates and cleanup like a sit down meal. The youth of America are starting to mobilize. We have more and faster cars. We don't waltz any more, we jitterbug or Charleston. Hamburgers and fries, of course with a Coke, is the future. We can cater the hamburger to any way we like it. I like sweet pickles, mustard and onions. Maddie likes dill pickles, mayonnaise and lettuce. This is already big in Little Rock, and we love them! Thanks!"

After the meal, Luke, Maddie, and Maddie's mother, Bonnie, went to the home place. The house was a little stuffy from it being a warm summer day and being shut up. They raised all the windows, removed all the furniture covers, and Bonnie and Maddie washed dishes and cleaned windows until by evening the house was sparkling. Luke went outside and turned on the water and primed the lines until fresh water was coming into the kitchen and bath.

Bonnie hugged the couple goodbye and went home to fix an evening meal for Norman, August and Molly, and Maddie and Luke. She also called and invited George and Lettie Gray. Bonnie loved the thought of having her daughter and all the family at home for a meal.

Luke and Maddie made the bed with fresh sheets in the master bedroom downstairs, and sat down in the big swing on the back porch in the shade.

"This is home, isn't it?" mused Luke quietly. He looked out over the pasture where he used to play and run with Levi. For a few moments he was a 10-year old and then a teenager. His mind was full of pleasant memories.

"Yes," said Maddie. "It will always be home."

Luke agreed. They walked with their arms around one another as they went into the house to change clothes to go to the Howes for dinner. They still were dressed in their traveling clothes.

After the evening meal, Norman and Bonnie, the Grays, August and Molly piled them up with boxes and pans of food. They were given coffee, and Molly was smiling as she came out to the car with a cake. It was Luke's favorite; white cake with chocolate icing. She was given a kiss on the cheek for her trouble, and she seemed to think that was enough as she smiled proudly. All the way back to their home the couple were laughing and kidding each other about who would get up early and make coffee.

"Yes, Princess, I will make coffee. I will have to make two pots so I can drink one and you can have some by the time you get up!"

Maddie put her head on his shoulder, and, still smiling, said, "It is really comforting to be home, isn't it? Funny, I didn't miss it while I was away, but being here I realize just how much I love this place."

The next morning as the room began to lighten from

the pending sunrise, Luke eased out of bed and smiled as Maddie never even knew he got up. He went, fixed coffee on the gas stove, and was sitting barefoot in one of the rocking chairs on the front porch as the first rays of sunlight reached the tops of the trees.

He heard the sound of Norman's new Buick H-45 Touring Car turn in from the road and watched as he came down the lane. The car was a highly waxed burgundy color with a tan touring top.

"What a pretty car!" thought Luke.

Luke met Norman in the driveway as he stopped, and he held the door for him as he got out. He was dressed in a suit and tie which were his "work" clothes. He always looked professional and wealthy.

"Hey, Norman. You are up early. I thought you bankers only went to work about 4 hours a day!" kidded Luke.

"If people only knew. It is a lot of hard work carrying money bags into the vault," Norman laughed.

Luke laughed too and said, "I don't want to know how much truth was in that statement. I have heard about Banker's Hours all my life."

They walked up onto the porch, and Norman sat down in one of the rocking chairs instead of going into the house.

"You surely know Maddie is not up yet."

"Actually, Luke, my boy, I came to see you. Are you up for a drive around town this morning? I have something I want to show you."

"Sure, let me leave Maddie a note and put on shoes and I will be right back."

Norman and Luke made the driveway circle in front of the house and went back to the road. As they drove into town only a few people were up but they waved at Norman and Luke. They all knew the car and the passengers. Only when they did not stop in town did Luke ask, "Where are we going?"

"Okay, think about this. Remember all the Curtiss 2 seater aircraft you used to train pilots in at the end of the war in Texas?"

"Sure, they were model number JN-4 and were affectionately called the Jenny. It is a little known fact the Army does not brag about, but there were nearly as many fliers killed in accidents as in combat. The planes were so crude and pilots were untrained, but the JN-4s were easy to fly for training. Why do you ask?"

"Well, I read where the army was selling all those planes for cents on the dollar. I bought 5 planes for only 200 dollars apiece!" Norman was talking faster and more animated.

"Also, the government is looking for people and private contractors to set up airmail routes. We could make a small fortune in flying air mail!"

"Great! I am listening! I am at the perfect point in my life to make a change. I still love flying, and if I could do it and make money, how much fun would that be?" Luke's voice was excited too.

Norman continued, "The first air mail route began last year on May 15, 1918. It is between New York and Washington, D.C., with a stop in Philadelphia for the exchange of mails or plane. The distance is only about 218 miles and it runs one round trip daily, except Sunday. This service was inaugurated with the cooperation of the War Department, which furnished planes and pilots. They also handled flying and maintenance, while the Post Office Department handles the mail and related matters.

In August 1918 the Post Office Department took over the entire operation of this route and is furnishing its own equipment and personnel. The operation of this experimental route was so successful that the Post Office Department began to lay plans for the establishment of a transcontinental route from New York City to San Francisco. That is why they are needing private contractors to make it happen.

There are two latter routes being used in conjunctions with trains by flying Chicago and Cleveland mail to Cleveland, where it is placed on trains that left New York the evening before. There is a savings of about 16 hours of delivery of mail from New York City and the New England States.

On the three routes in operation this year, there are only eight daily planes, flying a total of 1,906 miles per day. The record of performance is 96.54 per cent, and this was made with more than 30 per cent of the flights flown in rain, fog, mist, and other conditions of poor visibility.

To be honest, Luke, I don't know yet what kind of acceptance we will have because we will be in competition at first with others and even the Postal Department.

195

However, if we could get our little business going we might be assimilated into the air mail service for a tidy sum of money. You and I could go do something else, like start a passenger service. Who knows, first the mail, and then passengers. There may be a market someday for people to fly across the United States. It would be just a matter of a 16 or 18 hour trip instead of several days to cross America."

"You know, Norman. I have had the dream of flying passengers for a couple of years. It took us weeks and weeks of marching and mud to get anywhere during the war. A few planes could have ferried men and equipment to the front a lot quicker. It may have saved a lot of lives. Plus, here in the States, right now Chalk's Airlines has already begun air service between Miami and Bimini in the Bahamas in February of this year using flying boats. Now based in Ft. Lauderdale, Chalk's claims to be the oldest continuously operating airline in the United States."

"Well, I knew you would be interested, and as my son-in-law, I have the money and I will see that we get the chance, to do something in the emerging aviation industry."

At the small grassy pasture and hangar/garage that claimed to be the Paris, Arkansas, Municipal Airport, the two men got out and Norman smiled at Luke as he ran excitedly between the airplanes. He went from one to the next, grinning ear to ear as if he had met a group of old friends.

All five planes were some of the last built and used very little. These Jenny airplanes were equipped with Hispano-Suiza motors and very reliable for short distances. They could carry up to 200 pounds of mail plus the pilot, or about the weight of a man. A compartment was made where the second pilot would have sat when they were used for training.

Luke picked the best looking of all the planes, and started a preflight check. One of the mechanics spun the prop for him, and much to Luke and Norman's delight, the plane started on the first try. Norman stepped back and looked like a proud poppa watching his son on his first solo bike ride as Luke turned the plane into the wind and opened the throttle all the way. In just a few hundred feet the plane seemed to bound into the air as if it were more at home in the air than on the ground.

Luke flew around and over Paris, and marveled at how flat the country looked. He felt like he had just been let out of a cage to be back in the sky again. He buzzed a few cows in a pasture and laughed as they ran every which way, even running into each other, trying to get away from such a fearsome noise. He could see downtown and flew close over the saw mill until August and the men came out and started waving as they recognized Luke as the pilot.

He flew over his own property, and on a wild spur of the moment, he landed in the pasture and taxied up close to the house. Maddie came running out wondering what was happening. She was dressed in pants to take a ride with Luke on the horses later. Luke left the plane idling as he jumped out and grabbed Maddie in a bear hug.

"Go with me, Maddie. Even for just a few minutes! I will fly you back to the airport and we can ride back with your dad!"

Luke ran into the house and grabbed goggles and leather helmets for both of them, and helped a protesting Maddie into the passenger's cockpit and strapped her harness down snug.

"You know I trust you, Luke, but you take it easy. This is not the way I want to die!"

Luke just laughed and said, "At least we will die together!"

"Oh, sure, like that is supposed to make me feel better!" Luke laughed out loud while Maddie frowned.

Luke returned to the pilot's seat after strapping in Maddie, gunned the engine, and turned the plane into the breeze. He smiled to himself as he heard Maddie squeal as the plane lifted off the ground. When she saw the view of Mount Magazine and the creeks and farms from the sky, she was so overcome with curiosity and wonder she overcame her fear. She understood what Luke and Levi saw in flying, and she was wanting to fly more, but they had to go back to the airport.

Norman was not even surprised at seeing Maddie. He had thought Luke would probably stop and get her to fly with him. She was flushed with excitement as she hugged her dad.

"That was the greatest time I have ever had, Daddy! You ought to charge admission to take people up for a ride," exclaimed Maddie.

Luke and Norman looked at one another and both shook their heads affirmatively. Both had the same thought, but Norman spoke first, "Could be...could be."

Luke wanted to check out the rest of the planes, and he took Norman up on his first plane ride. Norman had believed that flying would only explode in size and usefulness, and now he understood why. Luke brought Norman back down so he could go to work, and Maddie forced Luke to take her with him on all the test flights. She even wanted to learn to fly!

One of the planes still had double controls for training, and in just two days of testing and maintenance on the planes, Maddie took off and flew with Luke sitting in the plane smiling as Maddie acted like a child with a new toy. She came back from the flight and Luke was bombarded by Maddie to let her solo.

"Okay, but you take it easy. You can do some basic things, but you are not ready for stunts of any kind. Do I make myself clear?"

"Yes, Daddy. I will, Daddy. I will be a good girl, Daddy." She stuck out her tongue as she climbed the steps into the cockpit.

Luke slapped her on the behind, and as she whirled around to look at him, Luke said in a tender tone, "Those planes are hard to replace!"

Maddie crossed her eyes and made a face at him. It made him smile and shake his head. She wound a yellow silk scarf around her neck to protect her throat from the coolness of the altitude. She looked beautiful. He could not believe he was letting her do this. He just knew he was asking for trouble!

However, Maddie proved to be one of the best students he ever had. She was quick to learn, and seemed to have an intuitive feel for the controls. Plus, she loved it! He was concerned she would overfly her abilities. He need not have worried.

Luke told her her how proud he was of her, and he started taking her up and training her to be able to control the plane. He wanted her to be able to fly her way out of any emergency.

After a couple of weeks, she even took her mother up! The whole family at one time or another got to fly. The "Howe-Johnson Flying Service Company" was born! Norman filed the papers for the new corporation and came out to the airport and oversaw the beginning of the building of comfortable offices for the company, which Luke had designed. The small complex included facilities for sleeping for the guest pilots and men. It also had a small area for people to wait.

Luke had plenty of war buddies to choose from to hire pilots and mechanics. With a few phone calls, Luke put together a very experienced organization of men he knew he could depend on and trust. He immediately hired two of the best pilots he knew that were available, Jimmy Anderson and Scottie Perlmutter. They in turn recommended a couple of more pilots, plus several mechanics.

After making final arrangements with the Postal Department to begin the short route for air mail between Fort Smith and Little Rock, an office and bunkhouse were to be built at both destinations. Although corporate offices were in Paris, permanent locations were made in both Fort Smith and Little Rock. The facilities were going to be finished within a month.

Chapter Nineteen

Luke and Maddie had been in Paris for 6 weeks when they called Levi and Ellen and told them to expect them the next day. They also asked would they open the windows in their house, and get the place ready. They wanted to come home for a few days. Levi and Ellen were excited. They had all sorts of questions to ask about the new business.

Early the next morning, Luke and Maddie packed just a few clothes to take because most were still in their house in Little Rock. They stowed the clothes in one of the planes that was freshly lettered with the name of the company, "The Howe-Johnson Flying Service Company Paris, Arkansas" painted in bright red letters on the side, and took off for Little Rock.

They followed the Arkansas River and flew over towns like Morrilton, Conway, and others. Once they got over

Little Rock, they circled the golf course to make sure no one was close. Luke landed the plane on the fairway and taxied almost up to the back patio of their house. As soon as they landed there were people running up to see what was going on. Luke opened the choke on the engine, which made it sputter and miss like he was having engine trouble. Everyone agreed just how fortunate it was it happened over a golf course. No one picked up on the fact the plane was sitting behind their house!

Levi and Ellen had taken the day off and were at home when they heard all the commotion. Levi knew the sound of the airplane and came out to see what was happening. He helped the couple down from the plane and even took pictures to put in the newspaper. Afterward, Levi and Ellen took them into their house and he interviewed Luke about the start up of daily air mail between Fort Smith and Little Rock and their new enterprise that already had an office in Little Rock.

Later that evening Norman called from Paris. He was very excited and when Maddie answered the phone he was almost rude to her as he demanded to talk to Luke. Maddie went and got Luke and then pouted as she stood with her arms folded to hear what her father had to say.

"Luke, this can't wait until you get back! I have just received confirmation that I won by bid an airmail route from Houston, Texas, to California with stops in San Antonio, Austin, Dallas, Albuquerque, Phoenix, Flagstaff, Los Angeles, and San Francisco! By having one contract already we got the rest! I contacted an investment firm run by you and Maddie's old friend, Richard Allen. I am leaving in the morning early. I am bringing two planes with Bonnie in one and me in the other. Jimmy and Scottie will stay over for a day or two for us all to have a way home."

"Okay, but what is up with all that?" asked Luke.

"I want to fly us all to Austin to meet with Richard tomorrow. His dad died recently and left him with a lot of oil money. I am a multi-millionaire myself, but he puts me in the shade! I thought we could fly down tomorrow, spend the night and fly back the next day!"

"Are you sure he knows what we want? It is going to take a bunch of new airplanes, and this time we need the new DeHavilland DH4s with the 400 horsepower Liberty engines and double the load carrying capacity that we have now. Men, mechanics, facilities in all those cities, and so on are going to take a lot of money, Norman."

"Luke, I agree, but when I said it was just us, he said he's in. We need to fly down and hammer out a contract."

"Tell you what, Norman. Fly down to Little Rock, and we will let Levi and Ellen take the extra plane and we can all be present. It sounds good to me. He was a snob at first, but Richard Allen can be trusted I believe."

"Okay, I should be there by 0900. Meet us at the airport."

"We'll be there, Norman!"

When Luke hung up the phone, Maddie jumped up and down and squealed, "We girls can all go shopping while you men do your thing!"

Luke rolled his eyes at Maddie because she did not understand what this could mean. All she could think about was going shopping.

"Don't give me that look, Luke. It just has been a while since we have done anything like this. It will be a break for all of us!" she said as she put her arms around him and squeezed.

"Maddie."

"What?"

"I can't breathe!" They both laughed out loud.

Luke called Levi, and he and Ellen were as excited as they to take a trip in an airplane. They had never done that before. They did not know anyone that had. It was exciting to think they could make a trip to Austin, Texas, by plane in less time than driving in an automobile from Paris to Little Rock!

Everyone was up early, ate, had their coffee, and still were at the airport before 9:00 am. They heard the planes before they saw them, and as they circled to land they could see Norman and Bonnie waving. The planes landed smoothly on the grass, stopped the engines, and only the pilots, Jimmy and Scottie got out. They refueled the planes while Luke got in with Norman and Bonnie with Maddie for the next leg of their journey.

"I hope it is okay for me to fly with you, Luke. I remember when Maddie was learning to drive. That is why I had to have a new car!"

Everyone laughed at his anxiety, but Luke took up for her.

"Maddie is an excellent pilot. Even I would not be afraid to go with her!"

Maddie shook her head up and down as if to say thank you.

"We will stop and refuel, and take a potty break in Dallas, and we should be in Austin by dinner time!"

"Yea!" the group said. Then Levi led the little group in prayer for safety and wisdom.

Once aloft the three planes formed a V with Maddie out front. She followed the railroad to Dallas and descended to a small air strip that was paved and had several planes parked around. After fueling and everyone using the restrooms, the little group was in the air again. Luke and Levi waved at one another and both could remember doing the same thing over France and Germany before going into battle. Maddie led the formation over Austin and The University of Texas. She pointed out the athletic field and the new Capitol building before she continued to the little airfield where Richard had arranged for the meeting.

As they landed and taxied up to the hangar, Richard got out of his Town Car with Lela Mae, and everyone was interested to see she was expecting. They all shook hands or hugged warmly. The chauffeur put their luggage into the back and held the door while the little group squeezed in. Richard took them to eat at a very classy place on the river where they had ribs and steaks, and Luke and Levi also had their first taste of Mexican fajitas. Both agreed it tasted great, but preferred the bland taste of grilled steak. They were amazed Richard could eat little green peppers that made Luke and Levi gasp for air and reach for water.

After the meal, the girls excused themselves and left to do some shopping. Richard had a conference room with a long table and office chairs reserved for the group. He offered drinks, but no one partook except for tea or water. He sat down, and looked at Norman as the senior person present as he said, "Okay, guys, what is it you want to do?"

Norman said, "I have the contract for an air mail route from Houston to California with stops in San Antonio, Austin, Dallas, Albuquerque, Phoenix, and into southern and northern California. I have 90 days to begin flying the route at least in Texas. I have most of the money for what we need to start, but we need money for at least 15 new DeHavilland DH4s, money for pilots, mechanics, and we need to arrange to at least rent facilities in those cities for landing and maintenance on the aircraft."

Richard hesitated but a moment and said, "Is that all?"

"Not unless you can think of anything else. I have a 12 page proposal with me that delineates everything, but what I just told you is the main part."

"What kind of payout do you foresee? How long before we make money?"

"The advance from the Postal Department covers a lot of the start up besides paying us in advance for 6 months mail delivery. I bid this to make money from the start or it wouldn't be worth it. In three months we will have it all paid back, and we are in the black. From then on, we just carry the money to the bank."

"How do you want to handle stock distribution?"

"Whatever is fair, Richard. The four men sitting in this room can trust our backs to the others. For you and me it is an investment. For Luke and Levi it is their livelihood. I was hoping to get a 4 way split, with each of us owning 25 per cent. I will listen if you think that is not fair because of the risk."

With a surprising amount of character unseen by the

men in the group before, Richard leaned forward with his elbows on the table and said, "I am born and raised in Texas. I am no stranger to risk. You see all those drilling rigs around? People don't know for sure what's under there. That's risk! To me, knowing some of the most trustworthy people I have ever met want to do business with me, and take as much risk as me, is enough. Count me in. Let's do it!"

There were warm handshakes all around and after reading Norman's proposal, Richard said, "I like to drive the best automobile, live well, and always go first class. I am doubling the amount you asked for to give us more clout with the bankers. Do you know a reliable banker in Arkansas?"

Norman smiled, "I think I do."

By the time the girls got back, it was a tight group. There was a lot of money to be made, and a lot of hard work to get it done. But worrying about not being able to trust one another was one problem they did not have.

Maddie and the others were excited to show off the clothes they had purchased. Maddie knew where the best stores for fashion and price were after living in Austin for

8 years. The girls were so excited one would have thought it was Christmas. Lela Mae told the girls there was absolutely nothing she could think of her mother-in-law had not bought for her coming child. They were just waiting to see what color to paint the nursery.

Luke was amused to see Maddie so happy, but he thought to himself, "It is a good thing we are going to have money at the rate she can spend it."

They spent the night at Richard's house which was larger than any hotel any of them had ever stayed. He even had an indoor pool to go with the outdoor pool. There were servants to bring anything from drinks to food. Norman and Bonnie both agreed they could get used to living like wealthy people instead of just merely "well to do."

The trip back to Little Rock by plane was a holiday with lots of laughter, waving, and blowing kisses back and forth between planes. Norman and Bonnie decided to spend another couple of days in Little Rock to organize the company and give everyone a little advance to buy for the office and some spending money for personal items. Luke designed floor plans for the offices in both Paris and Little

Rock. It was decided Maddie and Luke, Norman and Bonnie would fly out and look at properties in all the route cities within a few days, while Levi and Ellen would organize the company in Little Rock. Hopefully there would be some nice facilities that could be leased at the airports to save until nice facilities could be built.

Levi reported in the news about air mail service between Little Rock, California, and all the stops in between, beginning in just 60 to 90 days. The paper was deluged by people wanting to hear more. Even at an outrageous 20 cents per letter, people were putting down money to send mail. From three or four weeks to two days by air to California was unbelievable by most people.

The Howe-Johnson-Allen Air Services Company began operations in February 1920. The name was changed to HJA Air Services to be able to paint it all on the side of the plane. Jimmy flew to Houston and Scottie flew to a rented facility in Los Angeles for the first day of operations. The schedule was to start at 0800 hours from each direction. They each would fly, deliver, and pick up the mail at each stop, and after the route was done, the planes were checked over mechanically, refueled and were set to fly back to their original starting point the next day. Two flights a day from each stop, one from each direction, six days a week, was somewhat grueling for the pilots, but there were several pilots to trade off hours. They had to set up a schedule because the pilots were enjoying flying so much they were in danger of fatigue!

Within 3 months they were delivering the mail from Texas to California, and they also kept the short route between Fort Smith and Little Rock. Occasionally passengers rode along if the load permitted. They were using the new planes built by DeHavilland, the DH4 that had the 400 horsepower Liberty engines allowing them to zip along at 130 miles per hour carrying 500 pounds of mail or passengers. There were so many people wanting to ride, the company redesigned the planes to allow up to 4 passengers to ride. They made more profit on the passengers than the mail service.

In 1925 Henry Ford bought out the Stout Airplane Company and started building and selling the Ford Trimotor, a 3 engined plane that could carry up to 12 passengers. The company immediately purchased 5 planes to carry both mail and passengers. With several Ford

Trimotor planes flying passengers every day, the company changed the name of the passenger division to the Southern Air Transport Company. They were the largest air transportation company in the nation by 1928.

One of the biggest factors in the growth of the air transportation industry during this time was the development of a mail transport system by the U.S. Postal Service. The Kelly Airmail Act of 1925 had provided private airlines, like the Southern Air Transport Company, the opportunity to function as mail carriers through involvement in a competitive bidding system. These private carriers, through the airmail revenue, could then expand into carrying other forms of cargo, including passengers.

Passengers were targeted as a way to augment the income of the airmail systems. Slow starting, due to the perception of less than stellar safety performance and high fare costs, passenger volume grew tremendously and carriers multiplied. The Air Commerce Act, passed in 1926, allowed Federal regulation of air traffic rules. The aviation industry backed the passage of this act, believing that without the government's action to improve safety the commercial potential of the airplane would not be realized.

The postmaster general took control over the industry for a short time by limiting the number of carriers that were granted mail transport contracts. This practice was ruled anti-competitive and the industry was again opened up to competitive bidding for mail contracts. [1]

When the Postal Department took over completely all the mail routes to open them for bidding in 1926, the HJH Corporation formed another company just for air mail, and sold all the planes as well as the mail facilities to the new company to be able to concentrate more heavily on transporting passengers and freight. Although the government had a "turnkey" operation to continue mail delivery, they paid dearly for it. Norman and Richard spent lots of time in Washington until arriving home with a huge check.

The Southern Air Transport Company, the passenger division, bought several smaller airlines and the home offices were now in Little Rock instead of Paris, Arkansas. Richard and Lela Mae had stayed in Austin after the baby was born in 1920 to be near Richard's mother. She was a doting grandmother and the little, curly-haired girl looked like baby pictures of Lela Mae. She was beautiful like her mother.

By 1927, both Luke and Levi had children. Luke had a 5 year old boy named Austin and a 4 year old boy named James. Levi had a 4 and a half year old girl with blond hair and blue eyes named Anna Lee that had her daddy and uncle wrapped around her little finger. Both couples had new mansions built on the hill overlooking the Arkansas River in a new gated community that catered to rich wealthy whites. Luke and Levi tried to get August and Molly to move to Little Rock, but both were happy in Paris. Molly pointed out the kids and grandkids could spend the summers and holidays at "Grandma and Grandpa's house."

August's congregation had grown to the point that when he started planning a big revival he had to look for a larger church. The old Methodist Church was three times as large as his church, and when he asked, the elders of the church were glad to help. The people of August's church came and cleaned the inside of the church as well as the yard for the people to park.

August went downstairs into the basement just to see what was there. It was clear of debris, but it did show recent and continuous coming and going. There was one room under chain, lock and key at one end. August asked one of the men from the Methodist Church about it.

"We have a businessman that leases it to store old papers and some office furniture, like file cabinets and such is what we have been told. Is there any reason you will need that space too?"

"No, not at all. I was just curious, that's all."

After a few more questions August learned that John McGraw, the wealthy older brother of Jake McGraw, was the one using the cellar. John had a local grocery store which did very well. He had been raised in Paris and everyone knew him. He was there the first night of the revival.

August preached on virtue and living a true life based on truth and faith in God. Just before the closing of the sermon, John McGraw stood, and with tears streaming down his face, said, "Reverend August, I want to give my heart to Jesus now! I can't wait any longer!"

John's obvious sincerity touched several, and by the time he had come forward to the altar to be prayed for, there were several others on their knees praying and crying on either side of him. It was a good beginning to the revival.

After everyone left, John asked to speak privately to August. He took August and a flashlight and together they went down to the basement. John undid the lock and the chain and opened the door to the little storage area. Although the outside of the basement was dusty, the storage area was clean and orderly. There were shelves along three walls stacked with boxes plus stacks in the floor. John went to one of the stacks and opened one of the boxes marked "dry goods." In it was eight bottles of whiskey!

"I am tired of living a double life, Reverend. My own family, except for Jake, knows nothing about this. My still is why Jake became such a drunk. I made it and he had a ready source. After he gave his heart to the Lord, we argued about me keeping on doing this. So much so Jake does not come around much any more. However, he came by this past weekend and did not ask me to give this up at all. He hugged me and told me he just wanted me to know how much he loved me and looked up to me all our lives.

August, the guilt of all this was just too much. If you will help me, Jake will be here any moment with my flat bed truck. We are going to load every bit of this up, take it to my farm and destroy every bottle of this including the still! I promise, with the Lord's help, to never do anything like this again! I want you to never tell as my friend and I know Jake won't tell. He is about to bust his buttons he is so proud of me!"

August and John started carrying the boxes out to the center of the floor in the basement, and Jake, the former town drunk, came in with a two wheel dolly and the three men made quick work of loading the truck. No one saw or asked what was going on. They were all three well known in town, and they looked like they were just trucking in or out merchandise for the McGraw grocery store. They drove slowly through town and out to the McGraw farm, backed the truck up to the trash dump, and took sledge hammers and broke every bottle. They then heaped dirt and trash over the broken glass. They built a fire and burnt paper and rags from thrown away clothing over the big pile of dirt. No one would ever know except for the slight smell of liquor in the air for a few days.

After the success of The Southern Air Transport Company, a variety of air transport holding companies began, including Aviation Corporation. The air transport division of the company was called American Airways and later grew to become American Airlines, one of the largest commercial carriers in the United States. In 1928, what was to become another leading air transport company was created as a holding company by Boeing and its air transport division, United Aircraft and Transportation Corporation. In 1931 the four air transport divisions of United Aircraft became United Airlines. Charles Lindbergh, in the position of "technical adviser" to Pan Am World Airways, piloted that airline's first airmail service flight to South America in 1929.

Chapter Twenty

In December 1935, Luke, Maddie, Ellen, and Levi flew to Los Angeles for a short Christmas vacation. They had received a phone call from Richard Allen, who said he had invested in two motion pictures and he needed a stunt pilot or two for a few scenes. He called Luke and Levi to come and at least supervise the stunts. It did not take long for the group to decide to go. August and Molly kept the kids to have them for Christmas. Of course, they had to share them with the other sets of grandparents. Austin, James, and Anna Lee barely knew their parents were absent!

Hollywood in 1935 was in full swing. The end of the silent movies in the 1920's to the mid 1940's is considered the Golden Era of Hollywood. The 5 major studios were turning out over 750 motion pictures a year. The stars themselves off the screen were as celebrated as on the screen. They were paid enormous salaries for the time.

Gary Cooper, for example, was making over twenty five thousand dollars a week when over 25 per cent of the public was out of work and a good accountant might make 3000 dollars a year. Even during the Depression, most people could find a nickel to escape for a few minutes to the "silver screen." In an era that lacked special effects, and relied on story telling and acting to tell a story, the movies made in the Golden Era today are considered classics.

Richard had purchased several hundred acres and built a huge mansion close to Palm Springs, California. He had a place for planes to land, and several riding horses. Many show people came every time he had a party for he was a producer, or the man with the money. He knew all the big actors on a first name basis, and he had a big party planned for the first night the two couples arrived.

"Luke, we are living a fantasy! Movie stars are everywhere. I saw Clark Gable, James Stewart, even John Wayne!"

Luke responded with, "Okay, a few ground rules. What are you going to do if Clark Gable asked you to dance?"

"What do you think? I love you, but I am not going to miss a chance to dance with Clark Gable! Oh, by the way. No slow dancing with Mae West!"

"You either, with Clark Gable, wife of mine!"

Both laughed at the thought of dancing with movie stars. However, being good friends of Richard Allen's went a long way toward giving them instant credibility. When he explained the two couples were multi-millionaires themselves, people were pressing from all sides trying to gain their attention.

The movie they were shooting first was about barnstormers and starred Clark Gable. In the early 1920's up to 1935, barnstormers were traveling air shows. They were usually flying the slow flying planes, like the JN-4's or Jenny biplanes with 2 seats. These were the same planes The HJH Air Services Company had been flying for years. Luke had no problem doing the simple stunts, like upside down flyovers, loops, and "dead stick" acrobatics which caused the crowds to gasp in fright.

When the actress Richard had hired refused to walk the wing on a real plane, Maddie volunteered. Luke tried to rig a safety line just in case, but Maddie told Luke,

"Don't worry. That line is cumbersome and trips me anyway!"

"You don't have to do this," said Luke. "We will find another actress."

"It might take weeks, Luke. Just fly and I will hold on. Time is money for Richard with all these people on his payroll just sitting around."

Richard and Luke knew Maddie well enough to know she would not be talked out of the stunt. To her it was just another day at the office. She put on a bright pink jumpsuit and a blonde wig. She laughed and said, "The crowd knows only a blond would be dumb enough to do this!"

The plane took off with Maddie in the passenger's seat, climbed to about 300 feet, made a pass or two over the crowd with Maddie waving. She unbuckled her harness and stepped out on the wing. The crowd gasped and held their breath. Luke worried because he could not reach her in case she had trouble, and he flew just fast enough to maintain flight. She yelled at him to go a little faster because they looked like they were afraid to do the stunt. Luke went to about 45 miles per hour airspeed, and

Maddie walked out on the wing and waved to the crowd. They stood and pointed and applauded furiously. No one had ever seen such a dangerous event! The two "camera" planes, with Levi flying one, filmed the flight in just two takes because Maddie was such a "ham" and did it right.

Maddie complained jokingly to Luke it wasn't fair. She did all the work and the beautiful blonde co-star got the kiss from Clark Gable.

"I am the only one kissing on you, Maddie Johnson!" laughed Luke and held her tight.

The movie was "in the can" or finished, in a few short weeks, and Richard had a huge party for the cast and support people at his ranch. The party lasted for three days of swimming and eating and riding horses.

Maddie went for a ride with a small group that included Clark Gable. Somehow, everyone turned in their horses but Maddie and Clark. They had rode out and dismounted to look at the scenery on one end of Richard's property that looked up at the mountains. It had a series of springs where the horses could drink. Maddie grew quite as she thought about the propriety of being alone with one of the biggest stars in show business.

"Maybe we ought to go back, Clark."

"Are you afraid of me, Maddie?"

"I don't know, maybe I am afraid of me, but being alone with you makes me nervous."

"Look, I know you are married, and for all of my reputation to the contrary, I respect that. I wish I could find my own woman to love me as deeply as you do Luke."

"That country boy won my heart a long time ago, but tell you what. I do appreciate the fact you did not make a move on me, and you will know for always that you have made a friend."

She did hug him lightly and kissed him on the cheek.

"You know you just ruined my reputation as a big shot lover, don't you?"

"I will just smile when anyone asks, fair enough?"

They both laughed, mounted up, and raced back for the barn. Maddie beat him easily.

The movie in the theater was just as spectacular as it had looked during the filming. The night of the grand opening Maddie was an instant celebrity when someone shouted, "Look, it is the stunt woman from the film!"

She, Luke, Levi, Ellen, and Richard and Lela Mae had just arrived on the edge of the red carpet, and she was the last out of the car as Luke held the door and her hand to disembark from the limousine.

People were asking for her autograph and telling her how brave she was to the point Luke and she could not find a quiet place to be alone for the next few days. It was fun for a few times, but finally they started avoiding public places trying to get away from the pressing crowds. Maddie and Luke made the newspapers also in Little Rock. August and Molly and all their friends were astonished at what they had done.

The second film they were asked to help produce was about two men from the war that were after the same girl. Richard talked Levi and Luke into memorizing the few lines for two of the supporting cast members, and doing the flying. It made the film less costly in production to not have to stop action when the planes landed to change the pilots for the actors.

After a few days of filming, Levi was so quiet and reserved at a time when he should have been having fun that Luke asked, "What's up, brother?"

"You know, Luke, this is all great but it is bringing back so many memories. Some are disturbing to me."

"Levi, I faced the same thoughts, and here is what I concluded. Nothing will replace the lives of friends we lost, but I intend to live life to the fullest in their memory."

Levi shrugged and said, "You are right. And they call you the dumb one!"

At that, they both laughed.

Luke, Levi, and Maddie were paid very well by Richard, and he asked Maddie what kind of car did she want. Maddie was given a new 1936 Ford Roadster. It was red with tan leather seats and a black convertible top. Maddie and Luke drove along the Pacific Ocean and parked on the beach to go swimming and a picnic.

"What do you think about staying a while and becoming a star?" asked Maddie. They were laying on a blanket with Maddie's head on Luke's chest.

"I don't know, Maddie. These are not my people. I am not used to being hit on by women <u>and</u> men! Making movies is not real, most of the people are not real, and I am a small town person. I love taking a walk with you on our farm or our place in Little Rock, and eating some place quiet like Molly's. You are not letting this go to your head, are you?"

Maddie looked up at him with just a hint of tears and said solemnly, "I just wanted to hear you say it, Luke. I would not want to take you back to Arkansas with any regrets."

He held her close for a long moment and said, "I wanted to hear you say that too! I think I saw that Clark Gable guy, and some of those pretty boys, eyeing you up and down!"

"To tell you the truth, I was more worried about some of those starlets running off with you. I saw the way they were looking at you."

"Oh, really? You were? Maybe we could stay just a little longer! Did you get any names and phone numbers?"

"Luke Johnson, you won't ever change, will you? Come on, country boy. I better get you back to the real world."

She threw a big handful of sand on him, screamed, and took off running for the water when he came after her. He chased her out a few feet into the surf before he could grab her and pull her close.

"You are all the woman I could ever handle, Maddie Johnson."

He kissed her, and they walked arm in arm back to the blanket to gather their picnic basket and belongings. She rode with her head on Luke's shoulder as they drove back to town.

Richard promised to put Maddie's car on a train and ship it back to Little Rock to not have to put all the miles on it. Luke, Maddie, Levi, and Ellen boarded one of the new Douglas DC3's that belonged to the Southern Air Transport Company the next day. It had comfortable seats and carried 15 passengers and had a couple of sleeper bunks for the long flight of 7 hours back to Arkansas. As the plane began its descent into Little Rock, Maddie put her arm through his and squeezed.

"Welcome home, Luke."

"Welcome home, Maddie."

Chapter Twenty one

In January 1933, Adolf Hitler took the reins of a 14-year old German democratic republic which in the minds of many had long outlived its usefulness. By this time, the economic pressures of the Great Depression combined with the indecisive, self-serving nature of its elected politicians had brought government in Germany to a complete standstill. The people were without jobs, without food, afraid, and desperate for relief.

Hitler was sworn in as Chancellor on January 30th. His oath was: "I will employ my strength for the welfare of the German people, conscientiously discharge the duties imposed on me, and conduct my affairs of office impartially and with justice to everyone."

However, by this time, the oath had been repeatedly broken by previous chancellors out of desperation and personal ambition. Chancellors Schleicher and Papen had seriously suggested to Hindenburg the idea of replacing the republic itself with a military dictatorship to solve the crisis of political stagnation. He had turned them both down.

When a teary-eyed Adolf Hitler emerged from the presidential palace as the new chancellor, he was cheered by Nazis and their supporters who believed in him, not the constitution, or the republic.

"We've done it!" Hitler had jubilantly shouted to them. Papen and many non-Nazis thought having Hitler as chancellor was to their advantage. Conservative members of the former aristocratic ruling class desired an end to the republic and a return to an authoritarian government that would restore Germany to glory and bring back their old privileges. They knew it was likely he would wreck the republic. Then once the republic was abolished, they could put in someone of their own choosing.

Big bankers and industrialists, including Krupp and I. G. Farben had lobbied Hindenburg and schemed behind the scenes on behalf of Hitler because they believed he would be good for business. He promised to be for free enterprise, and keep down Communism and the trade union movements.

The military also placed its bet on Hitler, believing his repeated promise to tear up the Treaty of Versailles, expand the Army and bring back its former glory.

They all had one thing in common. They underestimated Hitler.

All over Germany people listened to this on the radio, waiting, and hearing the throngs calling for their Fuhrer. When he appeared in the beam of a spotlight, Hitler was greeted with an outpouring of worshipful adulation unlike anything ever seen before in Germany.

Meanwhile, an old comrade of Hitler's sent a telegram to President Hindenburg regarding his new chancellor. Former General Erich Ludendorff had once supported Hitler, and had even participated in the failed Beer Hall Putsch in 1923.

The telegram read, *"By appointing Hitler Chancellor of the Reich you have handed over our sacred German Fatherland to one of the greatest demagogues of all time. I prophesy to you this evil man will plunge our Reich into the abyss, and will inflict immeasurable woe on our nation. Future generations will curse you in your grave for this action."* [1]

Within weeks, Hitler would be absolute dictator of Germany and would set in motion a chain of events resulting in the Second World War and the eventual deaths of nearly 50 million humans through war and deliberate extermination.

Chapter Twenty Two

Little Rock, Arkansas 1940

Austin and James Johnson, and their first cousin, Anna Johnson, had just finished playing tennis at the Little Rock Country Club, and were sitting watching the others play from under an umbrella furnished with a table and chairs. There were several courts at play with mostly young adults.

"Wow, Anna, you were awesome today! Why you almost won several games from Jimmy and me!" When Austin laughed, Anna frowned, ran her hand through her short, blonde hair, and replied back.

"If I had had a woman for a partner instead of a clumsy man I would have beaten you bad!"

"Come on, Jerry Allen is a pretty good tennis player. You are just sore because we won."

"I don't suppose you want to take me on in singles, do you?"

"I don't think so. You think you could probably take me, and truthfully, you might!"

Anna smiled then at Austin's attempt to make peace. On her best day and Austin on his worst, she knew he would beat her. Austin was a great athlete just like his dad.

It was a hot June day in 1940. The heat rose off the painted asphalt tennis court in waves. Although all were already tan, the heat made the sweat soak their clothes and drip from foreheads and legs. They were discussing where to go and when to get out of the stifling heat.

Austin and Anna were close enough in age to have been in the same high school class. Both had just graduated with honors and Anna was the Valedictorian. Austin's grade point was a minuscule less which meant he was Salutatorian. Both were on their way to the University of Arkansas in the fall, and Austin was to leave in a few weeks to start football practices. He had been a state champion quarterback at Little Rock High School. Anna had already tried out and won a position as a cheerleader and would go to The University at the same time.

James, his younger brother, was the heir apparent to the quarterback position for the Little Rock High School, and had played backup to Austin for the last two years. All three were very close friends.

"Let's go get a Coke and a hamburger somewhere!" exclaimed Anna. "I want to drive your new car!"

"Now, wait a minute. My mother doesn't even drive my car."

"Well, I am not your mother!" She giggled a victorious laugh as Austin handed her the keys.

Austin and James looked at one another and just shook their heads as if there were no use in arguing. The truth is, Anna, Austin, and James, when he was old enough, all had a drivers license. In Arkansas the legal age to drive a car was 14. The legal age to fly an airplane was 16, and all three had their pilot's licenses also. Luke and Levi, their dads, had been pilots and instructors since World War I.

All had flown solo, and could fly well long before they were of legal age. Anna had met Amelia Earhart in 1936, and was devastated after her apparent death the next year. She had vowed to continue her legacy. Anna had her blonde hair cut short like Amelia. She still had a picture Amelia had signed of her and Anna at an air show in 1936. She wore riding pants more often than dresses unless she was going out. Kathryn Hepburn, the pants dressing movie star, was her new idol.

She was "worshiped from afar" by most of the young men at school and the country club for she could be merciless with her sharp wit and in her criticisms of the young men. Still, Anna had more friends that were male than female for she had no time for giggling, frilly dressed girls her own age.

The threesome inserted their wooden tennis racquets in their presses to keep them from warping, picked up their towels and balls, and started toward the shiny, new, black 1940 Ford Deluxe convertible which was Austin's graduation present from his parents for a job well done.

James had jumped up and down with excitement to inherit his mother's red 1936 Ford convertible, which Austin had been driving before. James was the one which had kept it washed and waxed, and while Austin drove their dad's Cadillac on his dates, James was perfectly satisfied to drive the little red Ford roadster.

Anna and Austin opened the doors and undid the convertible latches on the inside just above the windshield header, and all three helped fold and stow the top. Just as they finished, a duet of very pretty twin girls dressed in tennis outfits from James' high school class walked up to the car. They were twins although one was blonde and one was brunette. The brunette named Payton spoke up in a melodious voice, "Hi Jimmy. Can Mallory and I go with you?"

James looked at Austin and Anna, smiled, and said, "Sure, why not? I had rather drive my own car anyway."

Both girls squeezed into the seat with Payton next to James, who was grinning ear to ear. Austin and Anna laughed to see the threesome and knew he was in good hands.

James turned on the key, pushed the dash mounted starter button, and smiled as the engine started almost as quickly as an electric motor. The car barely had 10,000 miles and was in perfect shape.

The 1936 Ford had a three speed shifter in the floor, and as he put the transmission into first gear he touched

Payton's bare knee. His face reddened as he said quickly, "I am so sorry!"

Both girls laughed and Payton said, "Aw come on, Jimmy. Girls aren't stupid. You did that on purpose!"

As James' face got even more red, and he was getting tongue-tied trying to apologize, the girls were laughing hard at him. He finally laughed too when he realized the tease.

Once at the drive-in, both boys pulled their cars in under the shade of the overhang and at once were surrounded by laughing and loud youths. The Johnson boys and Anna were very popular.

"Nice car!" exclaimed the carhop as she skated up to the driver's side. Jill was a year out of high school and knew the threesome very well as she did all of the regulars. She had on a short red skating skirt and a white knit shirt with striping on the sleeves and collar. There was a patch which read, "Red's Drive-In."

Reluctant to have to admit it wasn't hers, Anna said, "It actually belongs to Austin and I had to beat him in tennis to get to drive it."

"Yeah, right. I don't believe that. Now, what can I get for you guys?"

"Two hamburgers and two orders of fries. I want a cherry coke and he will have a chocolate shake."

The girl looked at Austin, and in a very flirtatious voice said, "Don't you talk?"

"I only get to talk when she stops to take a breath."

Austin and the carhop laughed as Anna frowned and hit him on the arm. The girl smirked at Anna who frowned at her as she skated away laughing.

"You are so mean to me, Austin!"

"I am just trying to keep you humble."

A handsome young man in a white knit shirt and pressed Bermuda shorts separated himself from a group of guys and started walking toward the car.

"Here comes Mr. Cool," grinned Austin.

"Oh great," said Anna, but her smile gave her away. Of all the rich, handsome men in school, Ben Winston was one of the few she would talk to. He amused her because he was so full of himself, and she made fun of him just to belittle him. To Ben, he thought she might have special feelings for him.

"Hi, Benny. I didn't see you on the tennis court this morning."

"Nah, I got up late. I just came by to check out the action and pick up lunch."

Austin smiled to himself. Benjamin Winston the Third did not like to get sweaty or dirty. He looked like he had just stepped out of the bath and into freshly pressed shorts. No one wore pressed tennis shorts but Benny. His nose in the air posture and arched eyebrows irritated Austin. Just once he would like to throw him into a mud hole. The thought left a smile on his face as he nodded to him.

"Call me when the burgers come. I am going to go check on James."

Austin got out of the car, and before he could walk the few feet to James and the girls, he had a girl on either arm. He looked back at Anna and winked. She was smiling and just shaking her head. She was proud to know Austin and James were related to her.

Austin invited all the kids at the drive-in to his house to go swimming at 6 p.m. He called home and his mother gave her permission. She told him to stop by Tanner's

Market on the way home and she would call in and place an order for the items for the party.

Everyone was excited for the Johnsons lived on 20 acres of manicured landscaping with a swimming pool, tennis court, basketball court, and enough room with a backstop to play softball. They had a middle-aged Chinese man and wife, John and Lydia Wong, to cook and serve.

The big, walled estate was on Cantrell Road overlooking the Arkansas River. The house itself sat well back from the road with a circular drive up front and a six car garage behind the house. The front drive had a covering in case of inclement weather for visitors to get out of their vehicles.

The huge double doors opened into a tiled foyer with a staircase on either side to the second floor. The ceiling in the foyer was two stories tall. There was a large library on the ground floor as well as a smaller one on the second. The master bedroom was on the second floor as well as an office for Luke to do his architecture business. The small library was next to the bedroom. The house had six bedrooms, the pool house had a party room with separate showers and restrooms.

By 6:30 p.m. the place was full of loud, laughing young people. John Wong and his wife Lydia were hard pressed to keep up with hamburgers and hot dogs for everyone. John and Lydia had been part of the Johnson household for over 15 years. The Johnsons; Luke, Maddie, Austin, and James, treated them like family.

Austin saw what was happening, and put on a chef hat and apron over his swim trunks. He took the spatula out of the hand of a protesting John Wong's hand and said, "You serve this crowd, and I will cook!"

"Thank you, Master Austin. This very big group. Are you sure you know all these people?" His slight accent was showing.

Austin laughed, "Probably not, but it doesn't matter. Mom bought enough food for half of Little Rock!"

Luke and Maddie Johnson, Austin and James' parents, came out of the house with a large push cart full of ice and two wooden, hand cranked, ice cream mixers. A shout went up from the kids and a line formed to crank the handles. Salt was poured over the ice and the handles were being cranked so hard the kids had to be told to slow it down some to let the ice cream harden. Finally, the crank became harder and harder to turn and Luke stopped the young man on the first handle, opened up the container and announced, "It's ready!"

There were shouts and squeals of delight as the ice cream was put into bowls and Maddie and Lydia had cut up bananas and strawberries for toppings to go with the chocolate and caramel syrup flavorings. Lydia scraped out the containers, went inside and rinsed them out, and refilled them with more ice cream mix. This time she added a bottle of Orange Crush to give the ice cream an orange color and taste. Again, the kids were pressing forward with their bowls and, after two more creamers full, everyone decided they had had enough.

Even after being warned by Maddie to not go in swimming for at least 30 minutes after eating, there were several which jumped into the pool, splashing everyone.

Over half of the huge pool was only chest deep and people were enjoying standing and splashing one another. Maddie smiled and shook her head. She knew from her own experience it was hopeless to remind youngsters to wait. She didn't, and the kids didn't.

The younger kids started leaving by 9 p.m. and by 10 just the older kids were left sitting by the pool, or sitting on the edge and dangling their feet in the water. The conversations ranged from celebrities to sports, and there were lots of concerns about going off to college in the Fall when the world looked so unsettled. Germany had already invaded Poland and everyone questioned how long before they dragged the rest of the world into a war.

Austin and Mallory, and James and Payton, were on one side of the pool while Anna was on the other sitting between Jerry Allen and Benny Winston. Anna got up just as two muscular football player friends of Austin and James approached her.

"Anna!" said Fred, who was the biggest.

"Whut?" answered Anna in a voice full of sarcasm, making everyone laugh.

Somewhat embarrassed, Fred continued. "Mike and I think you need to take a swim."

"It took two of you to arrive at that decision? Does that mean you each have only half a brain? I am on my way to get a Coke. I don't want to get wet again, and, besides, I don't have time to play games with children!"

The group was suddenly quiet for the two boys were several inches taller and several pounds heavier than Anna's five foot five frame.

"Is it going to be a problem with you and James if we throw her in the pool?" asked Fred, looking directly at Austin. He did not want to have to confront Austin and James.

"Listen, Fred, you are the one with the problem if you try to throw her in the pool. She can more than take care of herself, but don't say I didn't warn you."

Fred and Mike smiled at one another as the two approached Anna. Fred put his hand out first as if to grab her, but Anna grabbed his wrist, twisted her body under him, and threw him over her shoulder into the pool.

Mike also made a grab but was grasping at air as she neatly sidestepped him, pulled his out stretched arm toward her, and with his own momentum yanked him sideways and let him go. He was flailing his arms as he yelled out, and he too went backwards into the pool.

"Now, leave me alone!"

Everyone stared in silent unbelief at the two hapless young men sputtering in the pool. Anna walked the few steps over to the edge of the patio, dipped her hand into the wash tub filled with ice and cold drinks, and picked out a bottle of Coca Cola. She pried open the bottle with the opener attached to the tub handle with a string, took a long drink, and looked back at the crowd of kids who were still staring silently with their mouths open.

"Now what? Haven't you ever seen anybody drink a Coke before?"

Austin and James laughed at what had happened, and went around to the edge of the pool to offer their friends assistance in getting out of the pool. Afterward, Fred and Mike were standing on the edge of the pool dripping.

"What happened?" asked Fred. "Where did she learn that stuff?"

"Our main man, John Wong, is a Chinese martial arts expert, and we have all been taking lessons since we could walk. I tried to warn you."

Fred knew he had been had and he smiled at Austin. "You could have tried a little bit harder to warn me. She's dangerous!"

Both laughed, and Fred put his head closer to Austin and said just above a whisper, "Do you think she would go out with me?"

Austin's surprise showed on his face as he said, "Now let me understand this. She just threw you in the pool, and you want to ask her out?"

"Yeah," Fred muttered sheepishly, as he shook his head up and down.

"Tell you what. You ask her out after you apologize, and if she doesn't throw you in the pool again, you have your answer!"

Austin patted him on the shoulder as he handed him a dry towel with a smile and said, "Good luck!"

As the group of kids from the party left, Fred hung around Austin and James and finally saw Anna alone. She was helping pick up towels and leftovers from the party. He walked over by her, picked up a pair of towels, handed them to her, and said, "I apologize."

"Why?" smiled Anna. "I am not the one that was in the pool."

He looked down for a moment, and said, "The truth is, I wanted you to notice me."

"Well, I think <u>everyone</u> noticed you," she laughed.

"Would you go out with me?" Fred blurted.

Anna studied him for a moment with her smile mostly vanished, as she questioned to herself if he was kidding or not. What Fred did not know is Anna had already decided back in grade school she liked him. She smiled a small, enigmatic smile, and said, "Yes, Fred Tanner, I would like that, but only if we don't go swimming."

"You don't have to worry about that!"

As she escorted him to his car, she put her arm through his. They made a date for the next night to go to the movies to see *Gone With The Wind*. He was to pick her up early enough to take her out to eat. At the car he put his arms around her and she smiled at him.

"I suppose I should apologize, Fred. I was a little hard on you."

"It's okay, really. Little things like I need to leave you alone and keep my hands to myself are things I need to know."

She giggled and kissed him quickly on the cheek and whispered, "See you tomorrow!"

Anna stood and waved as Fred drove away in his dad's red, 1940 Chevrolet convertible. His dad owned Tanner's Markets, which were several large grocery stores in Little Rock and North Little Rock. Although he said it was his car, Fred drove it so much no one believed him.

Austin and James walked up beside Anna, and Austin teased, "Now I know how to pick up girls! I let them throw me in the pool."

Anna smiled. "I thought I was going to have to grab him and throw him in myself. I am glad he thought of the idea. I wanted some way to break the ice with him."

All three laughed and James said, "I think you could safely say the ice is broken!"

The three best friends were laughing as they walked arm in arm into the house. Maddie watched through the kitchen window and smiled to herself. She remembered a time when she and Luke, and his twin brother, Levi, were just that close back home in Paris, Arkansas. It seemed so long ago at times, but reliving her childhood through the lives of her boys and Anna made it seem like just yesterday. She was still smiling as Luke put his arm around her to see what had made her smile.

"I remember those times too, Maddie. Anna is just as independent as if she were your own child. If I didn't know better, I would think you were training her!"

"Well, we do talk a lot about boys and stuff. She needs guidance as you might guess."

Luke shook his head and hugged Maddie to him and said, "I knew it! You have been responsible all along! You took that sweet little girl and turned her into another Maddie. Lord help us!"

They were both still smiling as the kids came into the kitchen through the patio doors. Seeing their parents smiling at them, both boys frowned as if they did not like to be the object of their affection. However, Anna smiled back.

"Is my room ready? I am tired," said Anna.

"You do know this is not where you live," smiled Maddie.

"Really? Then why do you have a bedroom just for me?"

"When you were little, you played so much and so long here at our house you would fall asleep, and it was easier to call your parents and put you to bed than to get in the car and take you the couple of miles to your house."

"Thank you, Aunt Maddie. I have already called home, and I needed to visit with you anyway. Fred Tanner asked me out after I threw him into the pool."

"Men are such weird, simple little creatures, aren't they? When we were kids I used to make Luke chase me, and I would only run just fast enough to let him catch me. He never caught on."

Luke put his arm around Maddie again and said, "That is why I was in such good shape for sports. It came from chasing her!"

They all had a good laugh, and Maddie and Anna walked arm in arm up the stairs to go to her bedroom. Lydia Wong came into the room to ask if there was anything else they wanted of her and John, and after being told she and John had done a good job at the party, they smiled, bowed, and went out the door to their quarters in the back.

Later, as Maddie sat at her dressing table and brushed her hair, Luke asked what she and Anna had talked about.

"Oh, it was just girl stuff. Our little Anna has her first crush and her first real date. I am feeling really old at how much she has matured."

"Yeah, I can see what you mean. Like throwing boys into the swimming pool!"

Both laughed for they could remember similar times from their own youth.

"Truth is," smiled Austin. "I bet he knows now to keep his hands to himself!"

Maddie smiled at him in the mirror and said, "Thankfully, they <u>never</u> learn that lesson."

"What else did you two talk about?"

"She told me she and Fred were going with Jimmy and Payton to see *Gone With The Wind* tomorrow night. She was so excited to finally get to go out with him. He had been the only boy she had had a crush on since they were in grade school."

"Well, he must have liked her also to ask her out after she threw him and Mike into the pool."

Maddie and Luke smiled as they both remembered a time when she had hit him in the stomach in Paris in the well house when he had teased her. She had tried to get away and go back to the dance, but he grabbed her and held her off the ground while he kissed her.

"I guess I did not move fast enough that night."

"Maddie, you moved just fast enough for me to catch you! You wanted me to kiss you!"

"I confess. Try it again and this time I won't run," she said smiling at him.

"It still seems as if Anna should be the little blonde 5 year old chasing the tennis balls on the court, or the 10 year old hitting the ball by the hour against the wall. She could beat anybody except Austin among her friends."

"Turn the light out, Uncle Luke, and come to bed."

Chapter Twenty Three

The next day was Friday, and Austin, up early as usual, was sitting by the pool with a cup of black coffee. James and Anna usually slept to mid morning until the smell of coffee and breakfast cooked by John and Lydia woke them.

"Mind if I join you?"

"No, of course not, Dad."

"I am sorry, son. I have taught you a bad habit of getting up early. Your mother would sleep until she starved to death if someone did not wake her!"

They both laughed and Luke admitted, "Okay, maybe it is not <u>that</u> bad. All the sleep she gets is why she is still so beautiful."

It was no secret to anyone who knew the Johnsons how beautiful Maddie Johnson was compared to any other middle-aged woman they knew, including celebrities. Although she secretly colored her hair a little, even the young guys looked as she walked by in town or at the pool. Luke also was still very fit as an ex-boxer and athlete. He worked out regularly at the fitness center in the country club with Austin and James, and he still could more than hold his own at tennis, handball, and golf. At 49 years of age, however, he was not looking with glee at turning 50 on August the 5th.

"Hey, I hear James and Anna both have dates tonight, what are you doing?"

"I guess I am taking Mallory Potter, Payton's twin sister, but she is such a kid."

"She is just a year younger than you, and she is gorgeous! I bet every guy in Little Rock would love to take her out."

Austin smiled and said, "Well, I am actually proud of taking her out and being seen with her. This will be our third date, and I think Mom is already planning a wedding!"

They both smiled and shook their heads for both Maddie and Luke thought Austin was old enough to have a girlfriend. The thought of a girlfriend to Austin was fine, but he wanted to still be able to see what the women were like at the University of Arkansas.

The movie, *Gone With The Wind*, was to begin at six o'clock, and Fred came for Anna at four o'clock, who was still at her aunt and uncle's house. Austin and James were to pick up their dates at the same time, and all three couples were to meet at the Italian restaurant across the street from the new Palace movie theater in downtown Little Rock. They wanted to get there early to sit in the balcony where the ushers with their flashlights did not patrol so much. Couples with children sat on the downstairs or main floor. It was no secret, but it was an unspoken custom of most classy theaters. The couples also knew a line would start to form about 5 p.m., and they did not want to stand in line very long.

The three couples were almost first in line. As they stepped up to pay, the teen age girl selling tickets smiled at Austin and said, "That will be one dollar apiece."

Austin, who was paying for everyone, asked, "Why so much? On most Saturdays we can see a double feature and a cartoon for only twenty-five cents!"

"It is a special movie, and it is real long. It even has an intermission. I don't set the prices anyway."

Austin laughed to let her know he was kidding, and she smiled back and said, "You sure are an onery cuss, aren't you?"

Austin handed her a ten dollar bill for everyone's tickets, and told her to keep the change. Anna, who knew the girl from school, said into the talk opening of the booth, "Yes, Janie, he is always like that. Don't pay any attention to him."

Janie put her head close to Anna and said in a low voice, "I wish he would pay attention to me!"

"I will put in a good word for you."

Both girls smiled at one another as the little group hurried up to the balcony. As soon as the lights went down for the movie to start, everyone took their dates' hands except Austin and Mallory. Anna squeezed Austin's arm, and when he turned to look at her, she looked down at her and Fred's hands and nodded toward Mallory. Austin rolled his eyes and put his hand over his date's hand. She turned and smiled at him, turned her hand over, and started holding his hand. Austin leaned over to Anna and whispered, "Would you quit trying to run my life?"

"You are so dense sometimes, Austin Johnson. Someone needs to teach you some etiquette and manners about going out on a date!" she whispered back.

She patted Austin's arm and smiled as she leaned over and put her head on Fred's shoulder who was smiling broadly and thinking to himself it was definitely worth a dip in the pool to be holding Anna Johnson's hand.

After the long movie, all three couples stopped for Cokes at the drive in, and as Austin and James took their dates home, Fred and Anna went to her house.

Levi and Ellen Johnson's home was similar in size and design to Luke and Maddie's, for Luke had drawn the designs and oversaw the construction for both.

Levi and Ellen, Anna's parents, were sitting and reading in the study as Anna opened the door. Fred held the door open as they entered the foyer. As they entered the room, Levi stood and smiled at the couple. He had known Fred and his dad for years. He extended his hand to

Fred and said, "Was it worth a dip in the pool to have a date with Anna?"

Fred, a little embarrassed, looked at Anna.

Anna shrugged her shoulders and said, "I did not tell them. Aunt Maddie told Mom."

Fred nodded and smiled at Anna, "Oh yeah. It was worth it."

Everyone laughed as Anna put her hand in his and rewarded him with a smile.

Ellen had cookies and drinks for the kids, and after serving, she and Levi were getting ready to go upstairs to bed. Anna began showing the house to Fred. As they walked around the study, Anna pointed out pictures and told him about Grandpa August and Molly, who were still pastoring a good sized church in Paris, Arkansas.

She showed pictures of her dad and Uncle Luke in World War One, and then of the early days in the air mail service. She showed him pictures of the air transport days and then of the pictures when the two couples went to Hollywood at the invitation of Robert Allen, the producer, to fly airplanes for stunts.

"Why, that is Clark Gable standing with your dad and mom, and your aunt and uncle! I recognize several other movie stars as well!"

"It was no big thing. Dad and Uncle Luke flew as stunt pilots in a couple of movies. Although, Aunt Maddie did do a little wing walking in one."

"Wow! I am impressed! You must get your crazy ways from your Aunt Maddie!"

"I am afraid she does, Fred. I am terribly afraid of heights," smiled Ellen, Anna's mom.

"We are going to be friends then, Mrs. Johnson. I am afraid of riding the Ferris Wheel at the fair!" Everyone laughed.

The Johnsons said good night, and Anna and Fred took their drinks out beside the pool and sat in the double swing on the patio. They had known one another for years, but both were a little shy toward one another as they talked and looked for parameters for their new relationship. Both were wondering where they were to go from there.

Anna put her head over on Fred's shoulder as he put his arm around her.

"You know, Fred, this just seems right somehow. I have known you since grade school, but I never dreamed you liked me too."

"Anna, you have thrown me into a swimming pool, and when we were younger you threw sand on me from the playground. You must have liked me a lot for a long time for you to be so mean to me! You must have known I liked you too."

"I guess I did, but I could just not get you to do anything about it. So, I am sorry, but when the opportunity came, I took matters into my own hands."

Fred kissed her quickly and said softly, "Well, I am glad you did."

"Listen, Anna, would you like to go to the Travelers game tomorrow afternoon? They are playing some team from Texas which is supposed to be pretty good."

"Sure! I have not been this summer. What time are you picking me up?"

"Game starts at one, but let's go early enough to watch batting practice. Say I pick you up at eleven thirty and we can eat something before we go."

"Great. I will be looking forward to it."

The Little Rock Travelers were a minor league baseball team which played in the old Texas League at Ray Winder Field which was built in 1931. It was a highlight of the Summer for nearly everyone both young and old to get to go and experience baseball at its best, complete with hotdogs and the sounds of the fans.

The couple talked and laughed about the pool incident, their friends, and discussed the movie which was already being banned for having a curse word at the very end. Both Fred and Anna were of the opinion this one word would lead to more and more cursing in movies.

"I better go, Anna."

Anna walked Fred to his car holding hands and kissed him as if her mother was watching, because she knew she was. It was still enough to make them feel warm, and Anna held him with her head on his chest for a moment before she let him go.

"Good night, Fred. I enjoyed it."

"Me too. Tomorrow can not get here fast enough!"

Anna's mother smiled at her as she came into the house. Anna hugged her mom and told her, "He is really nice, Mom. He treats me like a queen."

"He knows if he doesn't you will throw him back into the pool!"

They both giggled and then walked arm in arm into the house.

Chapter Twenty Four

The three couples started being seen together every day in some way. They went to see the Travs baseball team play and went swimming at Rockaway Beach. Some nights on the weekends they went to the Asher Drive In Movie, and at least one meal a day was usually spent at Pete's Drive In.

The group was sitting at the drive in under the canopy with Austin, Mallory, Anna, and Fred in Austin's car with the top down. James and Payton were in his car beside them also with the top down. Jill, the blonde, pretty carhop, who flirted with Austin just to irritate Anna, had already brought hamburgers and drinks.

"Austin, when are you heading for the University?" asked Fred. He and Austin were going to be roommates. It would give Anna a chance to be around both of her favorite men at the same time.

"We have to be there on Monday the 12th of August for the start of football two a days. So, I guess I will drive up on Saturday. How about you?"

"Yes, of course. If you want, we can travel together. Anna says she is riding up with me. She has to be there to practice cheerleading."

"Well, if the school would let Freshman women have cars on campus the way that guys get to, I could drive myself. I even <u>have</u> to live in the dorm. Not fun. I will probably get some loser for a roomie."

"I feel sorry for whoever gets you!" kidded Austin.

"Mallory, slap him for me. I can't reach him!" They all laughed.

"Besides, you don't even have a car."

"Well, I am looking, and taking my time. My family has several cars and if I need to borrow one they are available."

"What would you really like to have?"

Anna looked pensive for a moment as if she was wondering should she tell them the truth. She looked at Fred and then Austin.

"Believe it or not, I would like a new 1940 Ford Woody Station Wagon. When I went with my folks to New Hampshire last winter to go skiing, the hotel owner picked us up and all our luggage in one. There was room for people plus all their luggage. It was the neatest thing.

Then, when we all went to California last summer, some of the kids were driving older woody station wagons to carry their surfing paraphernalia. Okay, you asked, and I told you the truth."

"Anna, I think that would be a perfect car for you, especially as much as you like to camp and picnic with your friends. Don't look at me like that, for once I am being serious with you!"

Anna smiled at him in appreciation.

"Well, we better get home," she said, "We are eating at your house tonight and I want to clean up first. So, if you don't care, Austin, take Fred and me to my house. His car is over there for some reason. My dad is thinking about adding on to the garage to give him a stall of his own." Anna smiled at Fred and patted his knee, when everyone laughed at him.

"We are eating at six," said Austin, "and you know how John and Lydia like for everyone to be exactly on time. Sometimes I forget they are not really family, but they are so much a part of the Johnson household they may as well be."

"How did they come to be at your house?" asked Fred.

"It is a long, but great story. I will ask John to tell you sometime."

The meal of fried chicken, rice, egg rolls, and salads was served outside, and afterward everyone was sitting and visiting. John and Lydia joined them after making sure everyone was served. Fred told John he was interested in hearing his life story and how he came to be at the Johnson's. John and his wife looked at one another, and Lydia spoke quietly, "It is up to you, but everyone loves to hear it because it shows sometimes God blesses us in unexpected ways."

"Well," said John in a measured voice as if he were picking his words carefully. "You may or may not know China was ruled for centuries by dynasties of emperors and one of the final dynasties was the Xing Dynasty. China at that point was even ruled by two women, Empress

Dowager Ci'an and Empress Dowager Cixi. The most ambitious was Empress Dowager Cixi. She had been taken to the Emperor's court as a concubine at the age of 15. She passed her audition and was added to the Emperor's harem.

She began way down the "pecking order" on the princess line, but by having a son by the then emperor which she named Tongzhi she became an empress. Although he was only half legitimate, it was enough to ensure her presence in the palace. He became Emperor at the age of 18, but had been trained since he was 5 years old. However, Tongzhi died without a male heir which created a crisis in the succession of the dynastic line.

After great disagreement between the two dowagers, they finally agreed upon Zaitian who was the first born of First Prince Chun Yixuan and Cixi's sister.

He addressed Ci'an as "Huang O'niang" (Empress Mother) and Cixi as "Qin Baba" or (Biological Dad) to reinforce the image of her as the fatherly power figure. Empress Ci'an died, after a short illness, of smallpox in April 1881. Ci'an's death meant the balance of power was now in Empress Cixi's favor.

273

Prince Gong, a warrior prince and once a favorite of Cixi, was a strong leader and struggled to gain more power, but Cixi downgraded his position to "advisor" and promoted the more loyal Chun to President of the Navy and the Army. Prince Chun, in what looked like a move of great loyalty, took funds from the military and began to reconstruct the Imperial Summer Palace outside of Beijing. The invading Russians had burned the palace, and Chun pretended the move was for the retirement of Cixi. Prince Chun in reality did not want Cixi to interfere with the young Guangxu's rule once he became of age.

My father, Langxu, was Chun's second born, and was born just outside Beijing in 1875. As was the custom of the time, lesser born nobility were sent to America and other countries to study abroad. My father was trained in English and mathematics at Stanford University in California. He met a beautiful San Francisco socialite in college by the name of Louise Hearst who was a distant relative of Randolph Hearst. He wanted to marry her, but to do so meant he had to give up everything in Chinese nobility.

The Empress Dowager Cixi did not really care if he did because it meant her position and power was even more solid with him removed as a possible threat. In an unprecedented show of generosity, she gave him a wedding present of over a million dollars American in cash, plus quite a bit in stocks and bonds.

You can imagine what a 25 year old millionaire acquired in scurrilous friends from the Hearst family and other deceitful people. They lived very well for the time in San Francisco, and then moved to the Los Angeles and notably Monterey, California, area.

My father was very naïve, and lost most of his money by trusting this group of people which made a living, and their fortunes, from conning and cheating people.

I was born in 1898 and was already in college at UCLA when my mother went back to her people in San Francisco. My father went back to China and was heralded as a long lost son returning from a far country. He was loved and accepted all over again as the brother of the new Emperor. He died a few years later and was given a funeral ceremony as befitted a nobleman. He was buried by the time I found out, and I might not have gone back to China anyway.

I already had some money coming in from a trust fund to go to school, plus, I found I loved to cook, and took a part time job in a nice restaurant for extra money. I was only interested in martial arts, which is fairly nonexistent in America, and the job gave me something to do when not in school.

I met Miss Lydia in one of my philosophy classes. We were antagonists at first in most debates. I was from the Chinese culture and was very conservative. She was, and still is, a Progressive or a Socialist.

You know the scenario. What started as a war of words, grew into respect, then friendship, and finally I shocked all my friends by asking her to marry me!"

"Well how did you meet Mr. Johnson?"

"He and Miss Maddie loved to come to the upscale restaurant where I worked, whenever they were in Los Angeles. They kept sending very generous tips back to the Chef, which was me. So, after a few times, whenever they came to the restaurant, they would ask for me and I would come out personally and take their order. My manager did not mind at all. Luke Johnson tipped and paid <u>very</u> well!"

Everyone smiled and looked at Luke.

"What can I say? He was the best, and still is, chef I have ever met."

Everyone nodded their head and murmured agreement.

"Okay, but how did you become friends?" asked Fred.

"Let me answer this," smiled Luke.

"One night Maddie and I had stayed very late visiting with friends and business associates, and the restaurant was already closed by the time we left. John saw us and waved. We offered him a ride. He started walking and talking with us on our way to our car. He asked how we liked his signature dish, Beijing Chicken a'la John Wong. We were still talking when we were approached by four men in the empty parking lot.

'Give me all your money, pretty boy!' One of them said. When I said, 'no!', he looked at the others and laughed. 'Well I guess we will just have to <u>take</u> it!'

'You might want to pack a lunch, there are only 4 of you and there are two of us.'

'I think a pampered Pretty Boy and a little Chinaman we can handle. Besides, I have a knife!' he said, very cocky and self-assured.

'Let's see it,' spoke up John about that time. I am thinking, 'John stay out of this. I can handle it!'

The guy put out his hand and pushed the button on a switchblade knife. By the time the blade clicked fully open, John had grabbed the man's wrist, twisted it, took the knife away, and elbowed him in the face breaking his front teeth and causing blood to flow everywhere!

He was knocked backward from the blow and was about 3 paces away holding his bleeding mouth. John whirled around so fast he was a blur, and kicked the man in the chest. He went flying back and was caught in the arms of his three friends. He was out cold!

I don't know who was more surprised, the 4 guys or me! Here stood this little, five foot five Chinese Chef, no offense, John, still in his white uniform holding the man's switchblade and asking if they still wanted our money.

The men picked up their friend and went running off looking over their shoulders to make sure he did not follow them! Their eyes were wide open in fear and astonishment! John looked at me, I looked at Maddie, and I looked back at John, and said, 'So, <u>that</u> is what they mean by Kung Fu!' John quietly bowed a little bow."

John took over the narrative.

"Maddie and Luke gave me a ride back to the nice hotel where Lydia and I lived. I did not have a car or a license, and all the cabs had pretty much quit running by that time at night. Today, they run all the time. Anyway, we sat and visited in the lobby with Lydia, who had come down from our apartment, and we decided to go back to Little Rock together. Lydia could not have kids from a childhood illness, Austin and James were very young, and they needed someone to help take care of this huge house. So, here we are!"

"What a story!" exclaimed Fred. "So, that is where Anna and the guys picked up Kung Fu...from you!"

"Actually, as the son of nobility, I was taught Washu, which is lot more potent form of Kung Fu. I am also expert with sticks and double knives. In Chinese military, the nobility leads the men into battle. We have to know how to protect ourselves."

"I learned <u>my</u> lesson in Washu from Anna!"

279

Everyone laughed as Fred smiled at Anna.

As the party ended, the Potter sisters, Payton and Mallory, and Fred, now understood why even as "masters of the manor" the children joined in helping John and Lydia clean up and pick up. They had been doing it since childhood.

"I am impressed how your folks have taught you how to clean after a meal," said Fred to Anna and Austin. They both laughed out loud.

"<u>John</u> taught us, and mostly by example. We thought if a noble Chinese prince could clean, we could too. We have never questioned the practice. It makes his job easier."

"Your family is something special, Anna!" smiled Fred.

Anna walked Fred to his car. At his car Fred put his arms around her as she leaned against the driver's side door. The warm Arkansas night surrounded them with the sound of crickets and the flashing of fireflies. Anna put her head on Fred's chest after they kissed and held him tight.

"You smell better, Anna, than the honeysuckles and Magnolia blossoms!"

"Wow, look at you! My big football player is turning into a romantic! Next thing you will be spouting poetry!"

"I have never felt this way about anyone. For now, would you go steady with me?"

She raised her face up to him and said softly, "We <u>are</u> going steady, Fred. There's no one else for me either."

She kissed him again.

Austin and Mallory went for a drive along the Arkansas River, and parked overlooking the slow moving current.

"I thought you might want to watch the submarine races, Mallory."

Caught off guard for just a moment, she squinted her eyes and looked at the river. "What? I don't see anything."

Austin smiled but wanted to see just how far she would go before she caught on.

"Look, the red one is passing the yellow one!"

Mallory looked one more time before Austin burst out laughing.

"Mallory, they are <u>submarines.</u> They are under the water. You can't see them!"

"So, you were kidding me the whole time? I was wondering why I could not see them!"

Austin by then was nearly hysterical with laughter.

Mallory frowned and said, "Well, I don't think it is that funny!"

"Actually, I just wanted to bring you up here to go parking."

"Why didn't you just say so? It's okay by me!"

She put her arms around his neck. After a moment of very passionate kissing, he pushed her back and whispered, "Mallory, we can't. I do care for you, but I am going to be leaving in a few days. I am not going to be just a summer lover. Let's just enjoy the moments together, and see how we feel after you go to school for your Senior year."

She looked him in the eyes for a moment.

"Thank you, Austin. I am still a virgin and I confess my first time could have been with you tonight."

She kissed him sweetly on the lips and said, "I don't know where she is right now, but there is a woman somewhere that does not know she is going to meet a dreamboat named Austin Johnson!"

"You know, Mallory, the same goes for you. I am not what you need right now. You need consistency and a long term relationship, and I just cannot give it to you. Do you understand this is not rejection, but a declaration of how much I care and respect you?"

She shook her head up and down yes. As Austin drove her home with her head on his shoulder, he did not notice the tears.

Chapter Twenty Five

L uke and Levi Johnson's birthday was on Monday, August 5th, in 1940. Because they were to turn 50, Maddie and the family were planning to have their huge party at the Little Rock Country Club. What started as a party with just a few close friends, turned into a happening with several movie star friends wanting to attend. Robert Allen and his wife, Lela Mae, also sent word they were coming. With all the celebrities coming, the guest list had swelled to well over three hundred!

Luke took John Wong, Austin, and James with him to purchase each a new tuxedo. Levi was meeting them from his workplace, the *Arkansas Gazette Newspaper*, where he was the Senior Editor. They went to a small, family specialty clothing store called Lou Hoffman's. All three men were trying on formal wear when Luke stood looking at himself in the three way mirror. Levi walked up behind him and stood smiling.

"Do you remember when Pop was getting married to Molly, and we drove up to Fort Smith to buy all of us new suits? We never saw him laugh and smile as much as we all did on that trip."

"You know, Levi, I am really a private person. These sort of things make me nervous. I wish Maddie and my family would have just given us a private little party."

"Actually, that was the way we started out, but after we invited one friend we could not stop! Who do you not invite? Face it, Luke, you and I have a lot of friends from our glory days at the University of Arkansas, the fighter squadron in World War I, the mail and passenger air lines, the movies, the architect and building business, not to mention the people we have met here at the Country Club.

You are a good, honest family man and businessman, fun to be around, and every one that meets you goes away thinking they are your best friend. Face it, Luke, no one at this party will do anything but wish us the best."

"You're right, I guess. That is why they call you the smart one!"

They both laughed at the old, private joke, and Levi patted Luke on the back.

"There you go, my brother. I am proud to be your brother. Besides, YOUR birthday is MINE!"

They both laughed. Austin said, "See? You really are smarter than me! I forgot we are twins!"

The Country Club had two huge dance floors, and both were filled the night of Luke's party. The one ballroom inside was filled with more of the older guests there to hear the celebrities sing and dance to the orchestra. The dance floor outside by the huge pool was more youthful in decorations and guests. The loud music, instead of an orchestra, was a "swing band." Inside, while the older folks did the waltz, the guests outside were doing the hop and the jitterbug. The distinctive music and festivities between the two dance floors led Levi to make an observation.

"Every generation seems to be defined by their music. It is widening the generation gap even more by polarizing the youth and their music from the older folks and their music."

Maddie stood, and as the custom, all the men stood also. She grinned.

"Well, I don't want to be a fuddy duddy, and so, I think I will go out and dance to the band for a while instead of the orchestra. How about you, Mr. Fred Astaire? I am not Ginger Rogers, but I am not afraid to try!"

After only a moment or two on the dance floor, the two were alone as Maddie danced with arguably the most influential modern dancer that ever lived. Maddie did very well even though, in all fairness, the dance steps were kept simple for her. There were lots of whirling and Maddie holding Mr. Astaire's hand while he did the showy dance steps. Afterward, he escorted her back to the table, and bowed to her to a thunderous round of applause.

It was a loud, festive affair. With all the celebrities and distinguished guests attending, even the radio stations from around the country were present!

Sitting at the Guest of Honor table were several celebrities including Clark Gable, Carole Lombard, and others. Maddie got a nice smile and wink from Clark, and lots of eyebrows went up, and Maddie just laughed. She, Clark, and most importantly, Luke, knew they were just friends.

With Levi and several of his reporters present, the *Arkansas Gazette* carried the account of the party on the front page the next day. It even showed Maddie and Fred Astaire dancing.

Fred Tanner and Anna danced to Duke Ellington. Everyone wanted to see the new dances and new steps. Other "swing bands" included the bands of Glenn Miller, Tommy and Jimmy Dorsey, and even Louis Armstrong stood and played.

There was so much laughter coming from the main ballroom, when the band took a break, everyone went inside to listen. It was a small group of Jewish "Catskill comics" which included George Burns, Rodney Dangerfield, Jack Benny, Don Rickles, and more.

The jokes came one after another as the comedians stood in a line on the platform..

"I just got back from a pleasure trip," said one, "I took my mother-in-law to the airport!"

When the laughter died down enough to hear, another comedian said sadly, "I took my wife to the same hotel where we spent our wedding night. Only this time I stayed in the bathroom and cried!"

"We always hold hands when we go out. If I let go, she shops!"

"She was at the beauty shop for two hours. That was just for the estimate. She got a mudpack and looked great for two days. Then the mud fell off!"

A drunk was in front of the judge. The judge says, "You have been brought here for drinking. The drunk says, "Great, let's get started!"

Each comedian took his turn to amuse the crowd. Even though a lot of greats were present, Luke and Levi still received a tremendous round of applause when introduced as the "Birthday Boys." The cake was six feet tall and lit by 50 candles. Everyone received at least a small piece.

Later, at home with several friends sitting by the pool, Luke stood and clicked a spoon against his water glass.

"One is a very rich man to have this many friends. I thank you from the bottom of my heart for making this such a special day. Thanks to my wife and family, I will cherish this memory as long as I live."

Luke sat down quickly, but everyone saw him misting up from emotion. He could no longer speak. He pointed to

Levi and nodded for him to say something. There were several people dabbing at their eyes with handkerchiefs.

Levi stood and in almost a solemn voice looked at Luke and said, "I have always enjoyed being the "lesser" brother. No, I mean it! Luke is one of the finest people I have ever met. His integrity, courage, and intelligence are unlike anyone I know."

Robert Allen laughed, "We are not going to start singing and have a group hug are we?"

They all laughed and gathered around the two men to shake hands and pat them on the back.

Richard Allen and Lela Mae spent the night with Luke and Maddie, and Levi and Ellen joined them as they sat up and talked until the sun just started to lighten the Eastern sky.

"You know, thanks for everything, Richard. Our lives would have been totally different without you. I am proud you are my friend."

Richard stood and shook hands and then hugged him.

"Do you want to go steady?"

They all laughed out loud.

At the airport the next day, everyone shook hands with celebrities as well as family members which had traveled to the party. The newspaper again reported on the event as well as took dozens of pictures.

Chapter Twenty Six

The trip a week later to Fayetteville and the University of Arkansas was like a family outing. Mallory rode with Austin, and Luke, Maddie, Levi, and Ellen all went in Luke's big Cadillac. James and Payton went in his car, and Anna rode with Fred. Mallory's parents, had told their farewells back in Little Rock, and she and her twin sister, Payton, would ride back to Little Rock with James.

Once in the dorm, Anna and Austin waited an embarrassing few moments while their mothers made their beds. It was even worse when they got ready to leave when their parents gave them hugs and kisses.

"Aw, Mom," whined Austin. "It's not like we are leaving home. We will be home every long holiday and weekend. Besides, if we really had to see you, Dad can come up in our plane."

"Austin, it is not <u>you</u> I am worried about. It is <u>me</u> missing you!"

Austin put his arms around his mother and held her for a moment while she lay her head on his chest.

"Mom, this should be the best part of your life. It is like making a kite and then see if it is going to fly, and how well is it going to fly."

"You are right, Austin. You are going to do well in life. I am already proud of you, and when it comes James' turn to leave, he will do well too. But, I am a mom and I still hate letting go of my little boys!"

Austin hugged her tight and just shook his head, because he knew she was right, and this was hard on her. He could be embarrassed for her show of affection, but he loved his mother.

Austin, Anna, and Fred stood by the Spoofer's Stone on the quad and watched as everyone loaded and waved goodbye to their family. It was touching but they were ready to start their college careers.

"Well, needless to say, but you guys did okay on your roommates, but I wonder what I'll get. I saw her name on the door, and she is from Alabama. She must be a cheerleader too to be coming early, but she went to high school in Birmingham at a private school for girls. I am sure she is going to be a snob."

"You are prejudging someone you have never met. You can do better than that, Anna. You are almost a socialist in that you want to have everyone treated fairly and equally," said Fred.

"Fred's right, Anna. Give her the benefit of the doubt. At least wait and meet her."

"Her name is listed on the door as Elizabeth Ann Davis, and in parenthesis is (Beth Ann). Let's go over to the girl's dorm and see if she is here yet."

The threesome walked along the sidewalk and read the names on the bricks. Every year each Senior had his name put on the walk. It had been going on since 1876.

"Look!" exclaimed Anna, "There's dad and Uncle Luke's names! Class of 1911 for their undergraduate degrees, and Class of 1912 for their Master's! And there is Mom's name, Class of 1912!"

"Wait until you go to the gym and see my dad's name along with your dad's on the trophy for going undefeated in 1909 and winning the conference with a single defeat in

1910! Plus, dad was All-Conference in boxing! Seeing all this and knowing they walked this same campus makes me feel right at home! What about you, Fred?"

"My dad came for two years and then went back to Little Rock to help his dad open another grocery store. I am still very proud of him. He and his family own stores all over Little Rock, North Little Rock, and Hot Springs. My dad made it all happen. His dad died not long after he came home, but he had time to teach him the business and he has done well."

Anna put her hand in Fred's, smiled at him, and said, "He did well!" Then she kissed him quickly on the cheek.

"Public displays of affection are not allowed on campus, young lady!"

All three turned to see a woman dressed in gray and beige clothing. She could have been forty years old, or sixty, or even thirty, but she had a very commanding presence with a dour frown on her face. A middle-aged black man, with "salt and pepper" hair in a dark suit, was struggling under a huge armload of suitcases, hat boxes, and vanity cases. He was sweating while standing behind her. A smaller and younger version of the woman with similar hairdo and colored clothing was standing along side him while the mother had stepped forward to address Anna.

"Or what?" said Anna, and took a step toward her. Her eyes widened as Austin stepped between the two women. She was not used to people confronting her. He knew the woman at best was going to receive the first and worst tongue-lashing she had ever received, and at the worst....his mind reviewed and was alarmed at the possible havoc an out of control Anna might wreak on her. He tried to diffuse the situation.

"Look, Mam, we have only been here for a few hours. We should have read the part about kissing in public in our handbook. Although I have to admit I have seen others kissing and holding hands too. It obviously offends you and your husband, and we apologize."

The man with the luggage smiled behind her back and then quickly wiped it off.

"I am not married. This man is not my husband! Did you not notice he is black?"

"That is going on a lot these days. Most people <u>we</u> know are married though."

"You simpleton! This man is my chauffeur!"

"My mistake, mam. I apologize. Excuse us we are on our way to the new Freshman Girl's Dorm to visit my cousin's room." Austin smiled for he had been "putting her on" the entire time.

The woman sniffed, put her nose up in the air, turned around, and said sharply, "Samuel, get those bags up to Beth Ann's room and come back and get the others! Now!"

Anna looked at the girl and said, "I don't suppose your last name is anything but Davis, is it?"

The woman spoke again in a very impatient tone, "Yes, it is Davis! Why is that important to you?"

"Well, there is a Beth Ann Davis which was supposed to be coming today. She is a Freshman, and she is from Birmingham, Alabama. We were going to be roommates, but I am sure you can find another room."

"Why should we move?" the woman asked very haughtily.

Anna looked the lady in the eyes and said, "First, I am already moved in with the bed made and everything of mine on my half of that room. Second, my clothes are in the closet and put up. I am _not_ moving, and it is not open for discussion!"

Anna stepped around the woman and looking at the girl who had not said a word yet, smiled a little smile, and said, "She doesn't let you talk much, does she?"

The girl smiled timidly at Anna, glanced at her mother, and said, "I don't have to talk much. She speaks for all of us."

Her mother frowned and started walking toward the limousine. She looked over her shoulder at her daughter and Anna, stopped, and turned around to face them. She said with a little smile, "I know we do not agree on some things, Beth Ann, and coming all the way to Arkansas when we have great schools in Alabama is your way of getting away from me. However, I do want the best for you. I hope you are happy here."

She walked back toward the girls to within a couple of steps, smiled a surprisingly warm smile at Anna, and said, "You will take good care of my baby girl, will you not? She is all I have." Mrs. Davis stuck out her hand to Anna. She took her hand, and before the lady could do anything, Anna hugged her.

"We will be okay, Mrs. Davis. I promise. Stay in touch, and do not worry about her."

Tears began to well up in the lady's eyes.

"Thank you, Anna. I'm so glad she has found a friend like you, and I know I was somewhat harsh before. I am sorry."

Then, to everyone's amazement she hugged Beth Ann and pulled Anna to her too! She turned away quickly as if a "public display of affection" embarrassed her. Also, she did not want anyone to see her cry. She waved from the open window on the limousine as they pulled away from the curb leaving Beth Ann's luggage. The girls and the guys all waved as she drove off.

Fred, Austin, and Anna helped Beth Ann carry her luggage up to her room, and in just a few moments the bed was made and clothes put away.

"Go with us, Beth Ann. We were just going to eat. I'll even buy!" smiled Austin. Seeing the slight blush on Beth Ann's face, made Anna smile a little smile to herself.

"My Cuz!" she thought to herself.

By Monday morning Beth Ann was part of their group. Austin and Beth Ann even held hands coming home on

Sunday evening after church. The two couples sat in the lobby of the girl's dorm and visited until the lights were dimmed which signaled it was time for all male visitors to leave. This time the guys hugged the girls, and managed a quick peck on the cheek before they left for their own dorm.

The house mother was standing with crossed arms watching, and she cleared her throat. Austin winked at her. She actually flushed a little from not being used to having young men wink at her, especially with the audacity or good looks of Austin Johnson, but they left quickly. They did not want yet another confrontation over public displays of affection.

After the boys left, Anna and Beth Ann washed their faces and hands, removed what little makeup they wore, and put on their pajamas. They decided to sit up and visit. The girls were sitting on their beds with their legs folded under them. The first topic was about Austin, and was brought up by Beth Ann.

"Austin is quite a guy, isn't he? I have been around a lot of quality guys, but he is the finest I have ever met.

Don't look at me like that, because I know he is probably not ready for more than just friends."

"Hey, you are really wise. All the girls love Austin, but he is complicated. He really has never fallen for anyone. Not that you're not, but she will have to be something special. You give him space and time, and, who knows? We best be getting some sleep. Tomorrow is the first day of cheerleading!"

"Good night, Anna. I am glad I have you for a roomie. I was not sure what I might have. You will do til I find a better one!"

Beth Ann giggled, and Anna threw a small pillow at her and they both laughed.

"You are okay too. Good night."

Fred had been a favorite target as an offensive end for Austin in high school, and both were looking forward to playing together. They were part of the team and were dressed out and on the field by seven to take advantage of the cooler temperature for the first practice.

The Arkansas Razorbacks played their games in 1940 in Razorback Stadium which was constructed in 1938. It did not have lights at first, and all the games had to be day games.

At the first practice, Coach Fred Thomsen had everyone run for time in the 100 yard dash. Austin and a Senior named George Talbert tied for the fastest on the team. They lined up on the goal line and three of them threw the ball to see who could throw it the farthest. Austin threw the ball from the goal line to the 20 yard line. It was a throw of 80 yards in the air. George could only manage a 65 yard throw. The third could only manage 55 yards, and the coach and the team were starting to like what they saw.

Fred Tanner was just a couple of steps behind Austin and George in their race, and he was two inches taller and 20 pounds heavier than either. When the team moved to the hitting drills, it was apparent both Fred and Austin were used to going both ways, defense and offense, and knew what to do. After a few minutes of contact drills, they started lining up in positions, and because Austin and Fred were Freshmen, they were put on the second team.

The coach walked them through the few basic plays they ran, and was all smiles as he blew the whistle and sent them to the showers. He thought the team looked the best for the first practice of any team he had ever had. As Austin and Fred walked out of the gym locker room, the coach came up to Austin and shook his hand.

"So, you are Luke Johnson's son. I heard about him and his brother, Levi, on the undefeated season team in 1909, and the next year when they lost only one game. He was a great player!"

"Thank you, sir!"

"Don't thank me yet. You have some high expectations to fulfill!"

"I am sure I do, but I can handle it."

The coach gazed at him for a moment, smiled, and said, "Just like your old man. He backed up his big talk though with a big walk. I am glad to have you, Austin. I want to meet your dad if he comes up. Okay?"

Austin smiled and said, "I would not have ever been allowed to go anywhere else!" They both laughed. "You will like my dad."

After several days of "two a days" the coach wanted to have a little scrimmage with the first team against the second team. In 1940, before the modern "platoon" system, most players went both ways, and played offense and defense. Austin was the quarterback on offense and linebacker on defense for the second team.

The kickoff was first team to the second team to show them how to do it. The ball was placed on the 40 yard line, and when it was kicked, Austin handled the ball. He took the ball and made a couple of steps as if he were going to the left, but reversed his field, and, with a good block from Fred, he outran everyone to the end zone.

With all the interest in the new team, the stands had dozens of spectators. They went wild cheering on the Freshmen, who never had scored much in the past.

The kicker for extra points was Austin who drop-kicked the ball through the uprights which were placed on the goal line, and without running an offensive play, the second team was ahead 7-0.

"Your turn, Talbert. Let's see what you can do!" taunted Austin.

"You were just lucky, Johnson. We are going to run you off the field!"

"You gotta catch me first."

"We can do that!"

The coach smiled as they lined up for the kickoff. He thought to himself, "This should be interesting."

Fred punted the ball instead of using the tee. The ball went over 55 yards in the air, and when it finally came down, George had just put it under his arm when something which felt similar to a truck hit him so hard he almost lost consciousness, but, worst of all, the ball came loose and Fred covered it. George groaned as he tried to clear his head, and Austin patted him on the chest as he pushed up off him.

"Get used to it, Talbert. It's going to be that way all day!"

After only about 30 minutes of playing, and the coach stopping once in a while to point something out or make a comment, the score was 28-0 for the second team. He blew his whistle and said, "That's it for today! Hit the showers!" He was smiling a very broad smile.

Austin caught up with George Talbert who was limping back to the locker room with his leather helmet in his hand. He patted him on the back and said, "It was not personal at all, George. It was just football. Are we still friends?"

"Of course we are. Anyone that can beat me around on a football field like you just did is my best friend! I am glad you are on my side. Come on, I'll buy you a Coke."

Austin, George, and Fred Tanner showered, dressed and went to The Little Pig Drive In. Austin and Fred went in Austin's car and George went in his 1937 Ford Rumble Seat Coupe. It was a tossup which was more fun; the convertible or the rumble seat. Both were very popular with the dating crowd, especially if one was taking his date to the Drive-In Movie or to the "submarine races."

The young men went inside and sat at a table with six chairs. They were getting ready to place their orders when a new, turquoise colored 1940 Dodge convertible drove up with a load of five University of Arkansas cheerleaders. Anna and Beth Ann were among the laughing group of girls, and came in smiling. As usual, Anna was the first to speak.

"I knew we would find you guys here after practice! Don't you ever get enough to eat?"

The guys laughed, and Austin said, "You know we always have room for a hamburger. Besides, we had our first scrimmage today, and we used up a lot of energy!"

"Yes, we know. It is all over campus the second team beat the first team! Oops, sorry George. I forgot you are on the first team," said Anna.

"No problem. We are all on the same team and that is all that matters. Your cousin is a great football player!"

"Yes, he is, and at least he is humble!" everyone laughed.

After they ate and visited for a while, George and Belinda, his fiancee, were getting ready to leave on their own. They were to get married when the school year was over. George was finishing a degree in accounting, and, having been in the Army ROTC program at the University of Arkansas for the last four years, he was taking Belinda to Washington D.C. after they were married. His dad was a Colonel in the Army and wanted his son to be on his staff. Colonel Talbert was a very influential person to know.

George got up to leave, and shook Austin's hand.

"You know registration begins this week. So, the three of you meet me at the entrance to Old Main and I will help you get registered. I know all the teachers and can tell you the best ones to get."

"Why thank you, George," said Anna with a warm

smile. "I am lost already about where to go."

"It won't take long to find your way around. If football players can do it, you can do it, Anna."

He smiled back, and Belinda took his hand quickly and said, "Come on, we better go!"

Austin smiled at Anna as the couple left.

"Quite a little troublemaker, aren't we?"

"Okay, she may not ever be my best friend, but I am not interested at all in trading in my man Fred."

She put her arm around him and smiled.

Chapter Twenty Seven

Having a friend like the Senior, George Talbert, to help the group of Freshman find all their classes, and also help cut a few corners by knowing the enrolling process, was helpful. Everyone was ready for class to start the next day in only a few hours. Most everyone's classes were in the Old Main building, and it helped to find out where to go.

Anna was majoring in education to be a physical ed teacher back home in Little Rock. Austin and Fred both decided to major in Architecture like Austin's dad. He still owned a major firm in Little Rock, and he was excited his son would someday take it over.

Most of the young men had signed up for Army ROTC. They received uniforms and all immediately began marching all over campus to get used to the drills and cadence. Fred was shown by Austin how to keep their uniform creases razor sharp and his shoes were "spit shined" until they looked like patent leather. Both received outstanding in every personnel inspection.

The third week of school in ROTC was to be given to self defense training. They had all dressed in regulation workout sweatsuits, and Austin still managed to look neater than most of the other guys. A fatigue uniformed enlisted man from the Army by the name of Sergeant Zeke Warner was brought in to train them in hand to hand combat. Austin watched the man a few times as he threw the trainees around on the mat. After a while he had pretty well bruised most of the young men. He looked toward Austin and smiled a sinister grin.

"How about you, lady? You want to try me?"

"What are the rules? I am not going to let you work me over like you have these others. Am I allowed to defend myself?"

The Army non-com smiled and said, "You can do any thing you would like, but if I want to put you down, you will go down."

"Fair enough."

The two men circled one another warily. The sergeant was surprised at the grace and speed of this Freshman. He passed off every opening feint that he made with ease. All the college men were yelling for Austin to pin him, and it was starting to irritate the man. He finally tried a leg whip to bring him down, but Austin stepped inside of his leg and grabbed him by the front of his shirt with one hand and flipped the man quickly over on his belly on the mat with the other, and had him in a choke grip before he could defend himself. The grip around his throat by Austin's forearm and the pressure of his hand on the back of his head were causing him to start to lose consciousness.

"Okay! Okay! Release me! I must have slipped! Let's try it again and this time I won't be so nice!"

"Okay by me, sir. No broken bones or contusions will be the rules, but let's see something a little more special than what you have shown us so far."

The man flushed a dark red and said, "Why you insolent punk!"

He came at Austin in a run, but Austin sidestepped him and knelt on one knee for leverage and almost threw him off the mat on his back. Before he could do anything Austin had his leg held straight and was starting to bend it backwards. The pain from the stretching ligaments in his knee from just a little of Austin's pressure caused the man to yell.

"Don't break it! I give up!"

Austin rolled over like a cat and pushed himself off the mat in a flip to land on his feet. He smiled at the man who was holding his knee and whining. He extended his hand and offered to help him up, but the man slapped his hand away and yelled, "Class dismissed!"

Captain Barry Bucholz, the officer in charge of the ROTC program, smiled to himself. He had never liked Zeke, and had been watching the entire match from his office through a one way glass. Nearly every semester Zeke hurt someone by his bullying, but this time it was his turn. As the men filed by his office, he opened his door and said, "Johnson, may I speak with you?"

"Yes, Sir! Recruit Austin Johnson at your service, Sir!" He stood rigidly at attention looking straight ahead.

"At ease, recruit."

Austin immediately snapped to parade rest with his hands behind his back, and his head up looking the officer in the eyes.

There was a little twinkle in his eyes as he could see here was a class act. He had already bested his best man in hand to hand, and he had seen him run all over a football field as the team won 38-0 on the first weekend of the season.

"Where did you learn the Washu? I have only seen the nobles in China use that form of hand to hand."

"You are right, sir. We have a main man or butler, or whatever, from China which has been our caretaker for over 15 years. We have practiced every single day except Sunday since we were tots."

"I am impressed, Mr. Johnson. I will keep my eyes on you. You are an interesting young man."

"Thank you, sir. If I was out of line to Mr. Warner I will apologize to him."

"Between you and me it won't hurt him to be knocked down a notch. He can be heavy handed sometimes. I liked it!"

Officer Bucholz shook hands with him and dismissed him. Austin snapped to attention, saluted, and said, "Thank you, sir!"

As Austin left his office, Bucholz smiled at his gung ho attitude. He thought to himself how much he reminded him of his own youthful fervor. He would keep his eyes on him. Men like Austin Johnson did not come along very often.

Austin became somewhat famous on campus after the incident in the self-defense class. Yet, even Anna remarked how unchanged he seemed to be. She had come to expect the unexpected with him. He was mysterious and self-contained. He acted like nothing special had happened.

The Arkansas Razorbacks were a very small team in 1940 compared to the other teams in the Southwestern Conference. Even with Austin playing his best, the team only went 4-6 with only one win in the conference in the season. With the war going on in Europe, already young men from Arkansas were going off to the war in droves. They could not compete with the teams from Texas with much larger enrollments, and were hurt less from men enlisting. Austin and the rest of the team were glad when the season was over.

Fred and Anna continued to date and started being alone more and more. Beth Ann told Anna she knew Austin in his own way liked her, but there was a part of him he continued to shield from her and the world. He was complicated as Anna had commented. He was fun, good looking, talented, courteous, but she did not believe they were connecting.

Austin went out with Beth Ann every weekend, and sometimes they hung out with Fred and Anna at the University Center. He never said they were going steady or anything, but no one else ever asked her out. She was content to see Austin and be seen with him.

As the weather turned colder in the Fall, all of the couples sat around the big fireplace in the University Center, or one of the dormitories talking and laughing. Once in a while someone would play a guitar or even a ukelele. There were lots of singing some nights until the house mother turned the lights down. She gave them an extra hour on the weekends. She never smiled at any other young man except Austin as she stood by the door to lock it behind the men. He never failed to give her a quick hug and sometimes a peck on the cheek which invariably made her smile. Beth Ann and Anna kidded Austin about something going on between them, but he would only smile.

Chapter Twenty Eight

The University of Arkansas shut down the second week of December in 1940 for the Christmas, or midyear, break. Beth Ann and Austin went together to the train station for her to go home to Alabama for the holiday.

"Austin," began Beth Ann, "thank you for being my friend this semester. I enjoyed being thought of as your girl. It made me feel like I am somebody special."

"Beth Ann, you <u>are</u> somebody special. I am only 19, and I do not have a clue where I am going in life. I appreciate you not trying to put reins on me."

Beth Ann smiled and put her arms around him, and held him tight for a long moment. She looked up at him and quietly told him, "Austin, I am transferring to the

University of Alabama in January. I won't be coming back even though it has been a very hard decision. My mother and I are communicating for the first time in our lives. She is not in good health and I am going back to Birmingham to watch over her while I am going to school. I don't expect you to even remember my name a year from now, but if you think of me, write me once in a while, and let me know what you are doing and where you are. Would you?"

"Yes, I will. Honestly, I don't know how often, but I will write at least occasionally, I promise."

"My mother is going to have a cow when she sees my short hair and new wardrobe! I thought rather than have her worry I would not tell her. I will just surprise her."

"Well, you look great, Beth Ann. I enjoyed taking you places."

They kissed for a long time, and she smiled at him and said, "I would get in trouble with Mother over that kiss, but it would be worth it!"

He watched her smile at him as she boarded the train. She found a seat so she could see him through the window. She blew one kiss at him, and then held her palm out against the window in goodbye until the train took her out of sight. Austin stood for a moment gazing at the place where the train had been.

Austin drove home from school alone, and Fred and Anna traveled together in Fred's car. As he followed the couple down Highway 64 through Clarksville, Russellville, Morrilton, Conway, North Little Rock, and finally into Little Rock, Austin felt in a sober mood. He would miss Beth Ann for she understood he wanted his space and never seemed to question it. By the time they got to Little Rock and crossed the bridge over the Arkansas River, all of them were already looking forward to John's home cooking.

When Austin, Fred, and Anna left for school it was Summer, and now the lack of leaves on the gray trees coupled with the amber grass created a mood of melancholy which suddenly came over them as they turned off the highway and traveled up the drive.

They all smiled, however, at all the Christmas decorations. There were lights wrapped around the trees in the yard, and there was a huge tree shining through the windows as they approached the house. Suddenly the doors flew open and they heard James yell, "They're here!"

By the time the two cars stopped they were mobbed by family. James opened Anna's door and got a big hug for doing so. John and Lydia came, bowed, patted them, and told them how much they had been missed. Fred kissed Anna quickly on the lips and said his goodbye for he knew everyone was watching. Austin and Anna's parents all came out to greet them, and they waved at Fred as he left.

"Hey look! Even Grandpa August and Molly are here!" exclaimed Anna.

It was a joyous reunion. It had been several months since they had seen their grandparents, and all were excited.

August and Molly were driving a new Lincoln. August still had lots of hair, but it was no longer jet black. However, he was still fit and strong looking. Molly colored her hair, but she looked beautiful and robust for a woman of 70. After embraces all around, everyone went inside to sit by the fire. John and Lydia served hot chocolate and coffee for everyone. Plus, Lydia had already made the first fruitcake of the season in which she used rum for seasoning.

Luke kidded her by saying, "You know, Lydia, this is

wonderful, but you need to use more rum!"

Everyone laughed and Lydia replied, "You know one can not taste the rum after it is cooked. It only gives a pleasant aroma! I am not falling for that tease this year!"

After a huge meal and passing out gifts on Christmas Eve, everyone's conversations were on memories of Christmas past. The huge fireplace had stockings hung for every member of the families, including John and Lydia. Pine and cedar decorations were all over the room. The fresh scent reminded everyone it was Christmas.

On the mantle was a wooden antique nativity scene which had been lovingly hand carved by Norman Howe, and painted by Bonnie, Maddie's parents, which had died a few years before within just a few weeks of one another. Norman died first from a heart attack, and Bonnie could not live without him. She died from a flu attack brought on by not eating. Maddie could not get her mother to carry on her life without him.

On a lighter note, Luke kidded and reminded the blushing Maddie of the Christmas Levi proposed to Ellen, but she was not sure, and had even come home from college with another guy, Richard Allen, who now was an old family friend. Maddie told the astonished Luke, "You know, when I saw the ring you bought, if you had went ahead and asked, I would have said yes."

"Now you tell me! Maddie, look how many years we could have been together if we both had not been so stubborn! I was not going to go ahead and ask when you had just told me you were not sure. I did not want to be turned down in front of everybody."

Maddie put her arms around him and looked into his eyes as she said, "Luke, if it is any consolation, I never one time thought I did not love you. The money turned my head, for a while, but I did not want anyone, ever, except you."

"Good answer! Did you notice we are standing under the mistletoe? Come here, you!"

Luke held her off the ground for a moment as he kissed her. As he let her back down, he smiled with tears in his eyes, "Seems like old times, huh?"

Chapter Twenty Nine

By mid January, after the Christmas and New Year Holidays, the school work began to settle into a routine, and Austin began to study very intensely. He missed Beth Ann, but he had plenty of women to choose from if he needed to have an escort. His Architecture degree plan required several Math and Physics courses, as well as English. There was plenty to keep him busy and his mind from women.

"You know, Austin, I am worried you are not having any fun," said a serious Anna. They were sitting in a booth at the University Center with Fred.

"Would you quit trying to run my life?" he smiled.

"I am only trying to help. However, my dad is flying the plane up this afternoon to pick Fred and me up to fly to Birmingham to see Beth Ann. Why don't you come with us? Her mother's funeral was just two days ago, and I am sure she could use the distraction too. We can stay at their big mansion. She called last night and she asked about you. I think she still likes you, and she sorta needs you."

Austin heaved a big sigh and said, "Okay. I would like to see Beth Ann too. I really have not found anyone yet to take her place."

"I don't want to hear yet. I think you liked her more than you are letting on." When Anna smiled at him, he just shrugged his shoulders in answer and smiled.

"If I ever do have a wife I hope she does not nag like you!"

"If a woman doesn't nag, she doesn't love you. Don't you know that?"

Austin shook his head, looked at Fred, and said, "She's certifiable, you agree?"

"Don't get me in this. You are on your own. The last time I confronted her, I wound up in the pool! Actually, my friend, we just care about you."

"I know you do, but I am fine. I promise. I will go pack a suit, and an extra pair of socks for the trip."

Anna smiled and rolled her eyes at his remark. However, she was glad she had convinced Austin to go with them. She believed it was best for Austin and Beth Ann. She knew both cared more than they were showing to the world.

Levi and Ellen flew into the Fayetteville airport that afternoon around 2 p.m. They were in the Beechcraft twin engine plane belonging to the family. It was used for traveling back and forth to California for business mostly, but it had come in handy more than once to get people long distances in the shortest possible time. It had seats for eight not including the pilot and co-pilot.

All three were waiting at the airport with their bags. Ellen and Levi went to the restroom, the plane was refueled, and they flew from Fayetteville to Birmingham on a cloudless day.

There was a surprising amount of green mixed in with the tan and brown of pastures and fields which were being prepared for planting. Austin sat in the co-pilot's seat, and even took the controls until they were preparing to land when Levi took over.

"Thanks, Uncle Levi. I have not been up for a while and I really have missed flying. At school I have not had a chance to fly. It is a little hard without a plane, plus I am studying all the time."

"It has been great for me too. Your dad and I never got enough except when someone was shooting at us." Levi smiled.

As the plane landed, the black, Lincoln limousine belonging to the Davis family was there. As the plane rolled to a stop and the steps were put into position, the door was opened by Samuel, the black chauffeur, looking impeccable as always. Beth Ann got out quickly and started running across the tarmac. By the time she got to the foot of the steps, Anna was there to hug her tight as they both stood and cried.

"Look who else is on the plane!"

Austin was standing in the doorway smiling. He took the steps two at a time and swept Beth Ann into his arms and lifted her off the ground as he hugged her. He kissed her quickly on the lips, but both realized they were not alone. He put her back down, and kept his arm around her.

"Somebody had to come and keep Anna out of trouble!" All laughed as she made a face at him.

"It seems as if we have not seen one another for months, instead of a few weeks, so much has happened!" exclaimed a tearful Beth Ann. "I am so appreciative and glad you are here!"

Fred, Samuel, and Ellen's parents unloaded the luggage as Beth Ann walked between Anna and Austin arm in arm as they went on ahead to the limo. As the two girls got in, Austin helped load the final bags and sat beside Beth Ann. The big limousine held 6 comfortably, and though everyone was somewhat subdued because of the circumstances it was obvious the group was happy to be together again.

In the silence, Anna started talking first, "Beth Ann," as she leaned across and put her hand over hers, "I know this is the most trite question in the world, but are you okay?"

"Yes. Yes, I am. Mother and I sat and talked for hours. She had been so consumed with making a lady out of me she forgot to make a <u>daughter</u> out of me. Those were <u>her</u> words. We cried a lot because she knew she was very sick and was not going to see me finish growing up.

She told me you were such a fresh breath of air compared to all the little old biddies she knew, and she wanted me to be more like you. I needed to be able to stand on my own. She even confessed she loved my short hair and brighter clothes!"

"Good! I was so worried she would blame me for messing you up!" The two young women giggled at one another.

The Davis Estate was nearly as large as the Johnson's. The actual main house held the servants' quarters on one wing instead of behind the house as at Luke and Maddie's home. It did have a four car garage, and Beth Ann said all the servants had stayed. In fact, she thought they were probably glad to be treated with respect. The atmosphere itself was lighter and laughter was heard in the house for the first time in years.

"Mother was not as mean as everyone believed. She was afraid to let her guard down and thought she needed to be firm to run everything. Mother had been such a part of my father's publishing business for years, that when he died after a long illness, the leadership transfer was seamless."

The group was sitting in the library around a nice fire in big, overstuffed leather chairs. The two, pretty, light tan skinned servants, Mattie and Hattie, came and went quietly as they served coffee and tea. Mattie had baked a cake and sweet rolls and everyone smiled and thanked the two women. Later, Mattie would tell Hattie how nice the visitors were. Most visitors treated them very indifferently, as if they were still slaves.

Austin had his arm around Beth Ann, and the two were sitting in a two place love seat, and he looked at her and said quietly, "What now? Can you run the family business?"

"No, I won't have to. It is a corporation, and my dad's brother, Uncle Jim, has been the CEO of it for the last few years and will take over for Mother. Daddy and Mother left 40 percent of the business to him. I have 52 percent, and the rest is owned by shareholders. It is doing well. I trust him, and even though I have had offers to sell, I do want to someday run it. I am majoring in Business Management already. Speaking of which, I have a surprise for you.

Would you let me fly back with you? I have already re-enrolled at the University of Arkansas and they even allowed me to continue to be Anna's roomie!"

Everyone was happy, and Anna squealed and jumped up and down at the thought of having her roommate back. Austin was smiling as if he were glad too.

Levi and Ellen were invited to sleep in the Master Bedroom downstairs and there were shared rooms for Fred and Austin, and Anna and Beth Ann.

The next morning Beth Ann, as was her usual custom, got up early and almost tiptoed to the kitchen to not awaken anyone. She heard laughter coming from the kitchen. She pushed open the swinging kitchen door and Austin was visiting and kidding with Samuel, Hattie and Mattie.

"Oh, good morning! I hope we did not wake you. I was telling the girls how Anna threw Fred in the pool. We have a fresh pot of coffee going, want a cup?"

Hattie said, "I will get it for her. She likes a little cream in hers instead of black like you do, Mister Austin."

"I don't guess I ever thought you would be up early, Beth Ann. I was just making myself at home. I hope you don't mind. I used to get up early every morning and drink coffee with my dad before the day started."

"That's funny. I used to do the same thing when my dad was alive and I was young. It was our own private quiet time."

Austin smiled at her and was thinking Beth Ann was no diva expecting breakfast in bed. He liked her more and more. Most of the girls he knew, which came from homes with money, were so spoiled he very seldom dated.

"Do you like cars? Let's go for a ride before everyone gets up."

"It is my one vice!" He smiled and said.

She shook her head and said, "Oh, really. One vice."

He smiled again and said, "Okay I guess I do like chocolate milk shakes. I am not perfect, am I?"

Beth Ann laughed, and though she was <u>thinking</u> he was pretty close to perfect, she said, "If that is the worse vices you have, we can make this friendship work!"

She put her arm through his as they walked out through the kitchen into the garage. There were several cars, including the limo under covers, but Austin saw a pair of huge headlights under one of them.

When he pulled the cover back, he exclaimed, "Wow! That is a Duesenberg! I have wanted one since I was a kid! Can I drive? I promise to be careful."

Beth Ann smiled at his antics around the dark red convertible.

"Men!" she said out loud. The "dooozie" had been her dad's favorite car to take her for a ride. It brought back so many pleasant memories of happier times.

"Sure. Let me help take off the cover. "

Even before the cover was off, Samuel came in and helped get the car ready to drive. It was a little cool for the top down, but he started it and let it warm up for them. Austin and Beth Ann were all smiles as the heater warmed their toes as Austin slowly backed it out of the garage.

"You be careful with my baby! I mean BOTH of them!"

"Trust me, Mr. Samuel, no one could appreciate an automobile like this one more than me. By the way, I have a pilot's license."

Samuel laughed and said, "You may be glad you do when you open it up a little on the open road!"

The Duesenberg was capable of 140 mph. An unheard of number for its time. It was the first automobile in

America with hydraulic brakes, and a host of other ingenious ideas, such as dashboard mounted lights to tell when to change oil (750 miles), a light for when to check the battery (1500 miles), and other inventions that cars only in the last few years had begun to emulate. The supercharged SJ model would run an eight second 0 to 60 with a top speed of 140. With a price tag of around 25,000. dollars, it was a very pricey toy for only the super rich. Gary Cooper, Clark Gable, Greta Garbo, and James Cagney were examples of Duesenberg customers.

After about an hour, everyone was standing on the porch and waving as Austin and Beth Ann came driving slowly into the driveway. With the top down their hair was a little windblown, but they did not care. They had been for a drive in a Duesenberg!

Austin had several pictures taken of him and Beth Ann in and around the car. He knew no one back at school would believe he had driven such an icon of American conspicuous consumption.

Doctors and lawyers were making 3 to 5 thousand dollars a year. Austin told himself he could never justify owning a Duesenberg. He was indeed a multimillionaire, but public scorn and opinion would just be too much for him to deal with at his age. For the moment he had driven his dream car, which was enough. He did make a promise to himself to look at owning one later.

On the plane back to Fayetteville, Beth Ann took a nap with her head on Austin's shoulder. Every time he looked at Anna, she was smiling. He made a face at her, but he was smiling too.

After moving Beth Ann back into the room with Anna, things got back to normal chaos at school. Everyone studied hard, but there were numerous good times of dating, walking to class, attending basketball games, and as the weather warmed going into Spring, the foursome would go on long drives into the Ozark Mountains.

One weekend they surprised August and Molly by driving up unannounced. Austin was concerned he was falling in love for the first time in his life and he needed advice.

While Molly, Anna and Beth Ann were preparing a meal, Fred sat in a rocking chair on the porch. Austin and his grandfather went for a long walk out to the barn. Austin talked about his concerns while they re-stacked the hay and fed the livestock. After Austin opened up to him, his grandfather put his hand on his shoulder.

"Austin, you are my oldest grandchild. You have always been special to me for I can see a lot of your dad in you. You are mature well beyond your years, but let me say this. One of the reasons your dad was such a great wartime aviator is because he flew with such abandon. He was willing to take a risk for he knew the Germans were very meticulous about the way they flew. Your dad would sometimes fly upside down as he attacked! It got to where when they saw his bright red, white, and blue wings they would break off and run for home calling him the crazy American!"

Austin smiled at his grandfather for he had never heard that story. In fact his dad never bragged about anything from the war.

"Look, my son, I am very conservative myself, but I can say this about Beth Ann and the woman she is, enjoy yourself with her. I do think it may be a little early to start planning a wedding, especially with so much in front of you both, but graduate, make some plans for the future. Beth Ann loves you, and I promise you she is not going

337

anywhere. She will be welcome in the Johnson family. I promise."

The talk with his grandfather eased his mind. After the trip back to school, Austin took Beth Ann for a Sunday afternoon ride to a park around Huntsville and Rogers in northern Arkansas. On the way back to the school he stopped at a particularly spectacular view of the mountains and farms and houses far below. He put his arms around Beth Ann and said, "I love you. I have never told anyone else. Would you go steady with me?"

"You are something else, Austin. We are already going steady. I love you too, and I do not ever want anyone but you."

She rode back to the campus with her head on his shoulder and a smile on her face.

The rest of the semester included long talks between Austin and Beth Ann about goals and dreams, and what they wanted in a mate. It did not take too many times for both of them to realize they were experiencing something special.

Anna found Austin one day waiting for Beth Ann to come out of class, gave him a hug and said, "You are in trouble, Austin. I know the signs, and you are in love with my roomie. However, it is extremely mutual. I cannot get her to talk about anything or anyone but you."

"Now, that is funny. My roomie said the same thing about me!"

"Ain't love grand? Well, gotta go, here comes your main squeeze."

"Such language! She is my ONLY squeeze." They smiled at one another as Beth Ann walked up to Austin and took his hand. After a quick kiss they held hands as they walked across campus.

Chapter Thirty

School was over in mid May, and Austin drove Beth Ann to her home in Alabama. The servants were happy to be seeing "Mister Austin" again when she called to tell the staff to get the house ready.

When the few members of the Davis family came around to see what they could steal, they had had a confrontation with Samuel. For the family believed, since Mrs. Davis had passed, they were entitled to anything they wanted.

Beth Ann proved to have the mettle of her mother when it came to business. She made one phone call to the Chief of Police who was a personal friend of her and her dad. He had also seen Beth Ann on numerous occasions as she grew up, and treated her as a daughter.

He went to the man which claimed to be a distant cousin, and had collected a painting and some antiques, and explained in a very harsh tone, "Why didn't Samuel shoot you? I told him if anyone would not take no for an answer, to shoot 'em and I would rule it a justifiable homicide! Do I make myself clear?"

"Yes, sir." He hung his head in shame and he was very appreciative Beth Ann did not press charges.

"If money would do to me what I see you people do which have money, I would never want it! You never came around one time, when Mr. and Mrs. Davis were alive, to help Beth Ann care for them while they were sick. She had put her college education on hold to come home and nurse her mother. Her mother dying in just a few days was in a way a good thing for Beth Ann. If I catch anyone on the property, I will arrest them! It is off limits until Beth Ann gets here in a few days. That's her home now!"

Samuel and the two women, Hattie and Mattie, laughed at how quick everyone quit coming around when they related the story to Beth Ann and Austin. The visit by the Police Chief made them have a new understanding.

"How long are you staying, Mister Austin?"

"At least long enough to go for another drive in the Duesenberg!"

Later, after a huge meal of Southern cooking at its finest with fried chicken, new potatoes, turnip greens, and apple pie, all served by Hattie and Mattie. Austin and Beth Ann asked all three of the staff to sit down at the table and eat if they wished, or at least have dessert and coffee with them. The little threesome seemed nervous as if they were concerned they were being let go. Austin and Beth Ann addressed their employment concern first by smiling at them, and Beth Ann spoke first to the little group.

"I wanted to thank you personally for your years of service, and want to assure you that you have a job as long as you want to stay. Austin is officially my fiance, and we have talked at length about the things we would like to see changed. This is not the Old South.

Hopefully we are a long way from slavery. I know what each of you make in salary, and it is not enough to educate or raise a family. These three envelopes contain a check for each of you for one thousand dollars, and beginning this moment you will make a fair salary based on what you do. You are <u>employees</u> from now on, not servants."

The three black employees did not say anything for a long minute. They looked at Beth Ann and Austin as if they had not heard correctly. The girls began to cry softly.

"I just don't know what to say," began Samuel, the oldest at 45 years old. "We have not had families because we lived here. Although, I <u>do</u> have a couple of kids in town by a fine woman which I go see once or twice a week." He smiled, a little bashful at the disclosure.

"We knew, Samuel. We gave her a little money along on birthdays and holidays, and made her promise not to tell you! You have been here ten years and we wanted to keep you."

"And here I thought she was just good at managing her money!" laughed Samuel.

"What about you girls?" asked Austin.

"Hattie is 26 and I am 28, and we have had dates, but we could not quit working to get married. We give money to our mother who is working too. We have a little brother who is 20, and we are helping him get through his last year of college at Tuskegee. We want him to make a lawyer or a doctor. We believe he will not forget who helped get him there," confessed Mattie.

By then Austin also was tearing up a little. He thought about an entire family working for pocket change per day to make a difference in one family member's life.

"We would like to meet your family, including your mother and brother, girls, and <u>your</u> kids and wife to be, Samuel. Are you listening?" Austin was looking straight at him, and Samuel knew he planned for him to get married.

"Have the pastor of the little church you go to perform the ceremony in front of your friends and family. We want to be invited to the wedding, fair enough?"

"Yes sir, Mister Austin, and of course, you too, Miss Beth Ann!"

The staff was invited to continue living within the Davis house, but there was a new schedule and they were each only working 6 days a week, 8 hours a day. Hattie and Mattie alternated days off, and one worked early and one evenings to continue coverage for meals and cleaning. Samuel had Wednesdays off completely. He was asked to leave a phone number or call in once or twice, if he could. Austin had his car if he and Beth Ann ever needed to go out, and the only time Samuel would ever need to work on his day off was something special. Compared to the schedule which they had worked for years, the staff felt they were being treated more than fair. For the first time the staff was invited to use the swimming pool and outdoor grilling and party facilities if they were off duty and the facilities were not being used.

It did not take but a few days for the news to spread all over town concerning the changes at the Davis home. Jim Davis, Beth Ann's uncle, had been conspicuous because he had not already been by to see Beth Ann, and he called and wanted to see her at his office. She invited him to the house, because she did not want to go into town. He was there at two o'clock that afternoon.

Beth Ann went to the door when she heard the knock. She opened to her Uncle Jim, and he was not smiling at all.

"Are you having to answer the door yourself these days? I heard you no longer have servants, only employees."

"If you mean Hattie and Mattie, I told them I would answer the door because it was probably you. Come in. Would you like a cup of tea or coffee?"

"No, I can't stay long. I needed to ask you what you are going to do about Davis Publishing."

"Why? Is something wrong? I have never received a profit and loss statement, and I asked the accountant to give me one."

He was a little brusque as he tried to hide his surprise and said, "Why, what are you trying to find?"

"Is there something I will find?"

He flushed a little as he assured her, "No, nothing like that. I was afraid you were looking for something bad."

"Uncle Jim, I went to the bank and there is very little money in the accounts of the business or my personal account. Why is that? You told Mother we were doing well. You personally have several hundred thousand in your account."

"Oh, do you need some money, is that it?"

"The point is, I am supposed to already have money, and I don't. Against the advice of my lawyer, I am giving you 24 hours to do what you need to do to make everything right before the auditors come in. My dad and mother trusted you. Are we in agreement?"

"Yes, Beth Ann. Thank you." He treated her with respect for the first time in her life as he shook her hand and quickly left. Watching him drive away from the porch,

Beth Ann smiled to her self. She felt she was finally not intimidated by her uncle.

The audit had revealed suspected wrong doing, but several hundred thousand dollars appeared in Beth Ann's bank account and she declined to prosecute. She and Austin sat and talked about options.

"Some friends of my uncle have expressed an interest in buying the company. What do you think?"

"For you to run it, you would have to put your college on hold. Do you think you could trust your uncle now? If so, I think you should require consistency in profit and loss statements, and reports to find any irregularities before they happen. I know I am selfish, but I want you to come back to school with me. You can sell later once you decide what you want."

Beth Ann smiled at him, put her arms around his waist, and said, "What if I decide I want you?"

"That is a distinct possibility. I can not imagine my future without you in it, Beth Ann."

There was a meeting with Uncle Jim, Beth Ann's lawyer, and the accounting firm she had hired. Austin was present, and Jim quietly and privately asked Beth Ann, "You are a very rich young lady, Beth Ann. You could probably cash out for over a million dollars. Do you think there is a possibility this guy from Arkansas is after you for your money?"

Beth laughed at him. "You are a fool, Uncle Jim. Austin Johnson himself is a multi-millionaire, and his family is worth over a hundred million. No, his family might be asking am I after <u>his</u> money!"

Jim Davis was speechless. The thought of that much money made him start smiling at Austin, for surely, once Beth Ann and he were married, there would be a way for him to get some of it.

"Will you be okay for a few minutes? I need to take Samuel and go into town." asked Austin the next morning.

"Sure. Hattie and Mattie are helping me change the furniture around."

With a kiss and a, "See you later," Austin and Samuel drove into Birmingham and went to a jewelry store Austin saw while driving around in downtown. He went in and asked to see engagement and wedding rings. Samuel smiled and promised to not tell anyone.

After the evening meal, Austin and Beth Ann were sitting out by the pool under an umbrella. The scent of magnolias permeated the air so heavy it seemed to be the air itself.

"We really have not decided where we go from here, have we, Beth Ann?"

"I don't know. Do you have any thoughts?"

"Yeah, I do. Let me have your glass. I will go freshen our drinks. I don't know where everybody is."

Over her shoulder he could see three sets of eyes peering around the curtains. He went inside and put more ice in their glasses, and poured the tea. He pulled a little black box from his pocket, put it on the tray, and winked at the threesome who all were smiling at him.

"Here you go. Have I told you lately I love you? I probably haven't since this morning, but I do."

Beth Ann took her glass of tea from the tray and looked at the small black box.

"What is that?"

"Well, I'll be. Open it for I am curious too."

Beth figured Austin had purchased the new ear rings which they had seen at the jewelry store. She opened it to see a huge diamond engagement ring. She looked at Austin who was smiling but had tears in his eyes.

"Beth Ann Davis, will you marry me?"

Austin was still standing, but Beth Ann stood, grabbed him and hugged him and shouted, "Yes, yes, yes!" The motion almost put them backwards into the pool.

From the doorway came Samuel, Hattie, and Mattie. All were in tears but were clapping as they gathered around the couple. "Miss Beth Ann, we know you two are going to be happy together. I am so proud for you both!" exclaimed Samuel.

They gathered around Austin and Beth Ann. Hattie and Mattie had already baked a cake.

"How did you know I was going to say yes?"

"If you hadn't, I would have run off with him myself!" laughed Hattie.

Beth Ann hugged the girls and Samuel. "Thank you. You are all the family I have and I am glad you are here to share it with me."

Beth Ann pointed her finger at Austin and said, "You are a little scamp! I had no idea!"

"Well, Samuel and I went to town to buy some things for the lawn, and I thought to myself, I wonder if Beth Ann would like to get married?" Austin laughed, and Beth Ann just shook her head.

"I think we could get married right here, don't you? My dad and uncle can fly everyone into Birmingham. I just want my family around, not a bunch of strangers. Plus, if we have it here, our staff can attend. No one makes a better cake than Hattie and Mattie."

"What about your folks?"

"Pack a few clothes and we will drive over and spring the surprise on them. If we leave around 5 in the morning, we can eat supper in Little Rock. Yall start making plans for a wedding!" Austin told the jubilant threesome.

Around 5 o'clock in the afternoon the next day, James, Payton, Anna, and Fred were sitting by the pool and visiting about Beth Ann and Austin. Anna thought Austin would like to marry her roomie, but he was so secretive about everything to do with his life she told them they would have to read about it in the paper.

They were still laughing as a car drove into the driveway, came around the corner of the house to the garage which was close to the pool. They heard, "Beep, beep, beep!" It was Austin's signature "horn hello!"

Austin was just opening the door for Beth Ann when the group from the pool plus Austin and Anna's parents came running up to them.

With a big grin like he had been up to something mischievous, Austin stood with his arm around Beth Ann and said, "Folks, if you have not met her, I would like to introduce you to my fiancee, Beth Ann Davis!"

Anna started jumping up and down and hugging Beth Ann, while Fred and James were pumping August's hand as if they were trying to prime a well. Luke and Maddie hugged Beth Ann, and Maddie exclaimed, "Finally, I get a daughter-in-law! You are so welcome into this family!"

Levi and Ellen of course remembered meeting Beth Ann when they flew over to Birmingham for her mother's funeral. They still embraced, and told her how glad they were for both of them. As they walked into the house, Anna walked between Austin and Beth Ann with her arms around both of them.

"Who would ever have guessed this would happen the day we met, roomie? Certainly not your mother!"

They smiled at one another, and Beth Ann said, "Believe it or not, Mother picked Austin for the man she wanted me to marry, and she loved you as my friend. She told me she could pass and not worry about me, because you two would take care of me. Truthfully, it may be why she did not fight too hard to stay alive."

Anna hugged her hard and said, "We will."

After a meal of sandwiches and salads fixed by John and Lydia, who were also proud to see the way things turned out, the group sat and talked about which date to have the wedding. When told Austin and Beth Ann were considering having the wedding in Birmingham, Luke said, "Look, let us fly over and pick up the staff and whoever else wants to come, and have it here in Little Rock at The Country Club."

Austin and Beth Ann looked at one another and Beth Ann shrugged her shoulders and smiled, "Sure. Why not?"

It was already the first week of June and it was decided to have the wedding at 10 o'clock in the morning on June 29th, which was the last Saturday of the month, because Beth Ann wanted to be a June bride. Plus, having it early in the day would help get away from the heat.

Maddie, Ellen, and Anna took Beth Ann the next day and bought her a wedding dress after trying on most of the dresses in Little Rock. With her mother gone, the Johnson women decided they wanted to buy the bride a dress.

James was to be the Best Man, and Fred and Anna were in the wedding, of course, with Anna as Maid of Honor. The wedding was to be at the Country Club with August Johnson doing the honors.

Austin had several talks with his mother and dad and told them he was thinking about transferring to the University of Alabama in Tuscaloosa.

"Oh, my prodigal son! Don't break your daddy's heart!" Luke did smile, however, and ask why.

"Here is my logic. We already live on the southwestern side of Birmingham and we could commute from our home to school. We will hopefully be able to not have classes every day of the week, and not have to drive the 50 or 60 miles round trip to school but a maximum of three days a week. If not, another scenario is to rent an apartment closer to school and come home a couple times a week. Don't look so serious, you guys. Alabama even has a football team! I have already talked to the Alabama coaching legend, Frank Thomas, and he said he would be glad to have me. Last season they only lost to Tennessee and Mississippi State. This year they are hoping for a national ranking. With my help they might!" Luke grinned.

"You mean to tell me my son is going to play for another team? You would lift your hands against your brothers? What is this world coming to?"

Luke laughed, but he put his his hands on his shoulders and smiled at him. "Your plan to move and live in Alabama makes perfect sense to me, Austin. Beth Ann needs to keep her house and business going. She has a great staff to help her, and with you by her side I expect to hear great things from you two."

"You forgive your prodigal son then?"

"Yes, and so did the father in the Bible, but I know a little now how he felt." Everyone laughed at the remark.

A week before the wedding, Levi and Luke went over in their plane and picked up Mattie, Hattie and Samuel. The girls' mother and Samuel's new bride also came.

John and Lydia were disappointed at first to not be doing the cake, but after Austin put his arm around them and explained the staff from Birmingham wanted to have a part, they were appreciative of the extra help.

John told Austin how much he understood longtime loyalty. He shook Austin's hand because he had already heard of the emancipation of the staff and their promotion from servants to staff. He bowed to Austin and said, "I am proud of you. I taught you well." Austin hugged him and said, "Yes, you did, old friend. Yes, you did."

After a catered wedding at The Country Club with all the trimmings of expensive decorations, Austin borrowed his dad's plane and flew Beth Ann to Richard Allen's estate in Palm Springs, California. For over a week the newlyweds were taken to Hollywood and toured Los Angeles and the surrounding beaches. Through Richard's connections as a movie producer, they met several movie stars and celebrities. It was a "dream" honeymoon.

Austin and Beth Ann flew back to Little Rock for a few days, and then drove their car back to Birmingham. The staff was glad to see the new couple and clapped as Austin carried Beth Ann over the threshold into the house.

"I am so glad to be back home."

"Anywhere you are is home, Beth Ann."

Austin began a routine of getting up early and working out and running to get ready for football. Beth Ann played tennis and went swimming with him, and at times jogged along with him for shorter distances. By the middle of August and the start of "two a days'" Austin was a lean, tan, muscular, six foot two and 205 pounds.

The Alabama football team was coming off a good 1940 season with only two losses, Tennessee and Mississippi State. It was Alabama's third loss in a row to the University of Tennessee. The team went 7-2 overall and 4-2 in the Southeastern Conference. Acquiring Austin Johnson to be used on defense as well as wide receiver completed the team as far as Frank Thomas was concerned.

The 1941 season was an interesting one. Alabama beat Tulane 19-14 in spite of being outplayed in yardage. Special team play and Austin returning a punt for a touchdown was the key to victory. Their record was 9-2 overall and 5-2 in conference play. It was successful enough to be invited to play Texas A&M in the Cotton Bowl.

Texas A&M out gained the Tide 309 yards to 75. Alabama made one first down and A&M made 13. However, unbelievably, Texas A&M had 12 turnovers, including seven interceptions and five fumbles. Alabama scored on a punt return and an interception return. Texas A&M fumbled on their 21 and 24 yard line twice and Alabama scored on both possessions. The final score was an improbable Alabama 28 and A&M 21.

A few days later, on their way home from church on the first Sunday in December, people were running around in the street and yelling, "The war has started! The Japs bombed Pearl Harbor!"

All evening and into the night people were sitting by their radios listening to the results of the sneak attack. The next day President Roosevelt declared war on the Japanese. Austin called home to talk to his dad. He thought to himself he needed a point of reality .

"What should I do, Dad? With war declared, should I enlist?"

"James has already called too, but I think both of you need to stay in school for now. Like the First World War, good leaders which both of you will make with a college education, will be in demand. This will be another long and bloody war, my sons. Trust me, you will have a chance to fight."

Austin called James and invited him to Birmingham for a few days after school was out in May 1942. He drove over in his 1936 Ford Convertible. Although Beth Ann set him up with a date or two with pretty girls which she knew, he explained he and Payton were close to getting engaged. The only thing keeping it from happening was the war and school. He and Payton were just Sophomores at the University of Arkansas, and neither was ready for marriage, even though they were going steady and had been together for over two years.

In addition to home dates in Legion Field in Birmingham and Denny Stadium on campus in Tuscaloosa, the Tide played one game each at Cramton Bowl in Montgomery and Ladd Stadium in Mobile during the 1942 season.

A safety on a fumbled kickoff and a 38-yard touchdown run by running back Tom Jenkins were enough for an 8-0 win over Tennessee. However, in a game that decided the SEC championship for 1942, Alabama blew a 10-0 fourth quarter lead against Georgia. Frank Sinkwich, who went on to win the Heisman Trophy for 1942, threw two touchdown passes in the fourth, followed by a fumble return for a TD which iced Georgia's 21-10 victory.

With the United States mobilizing for World War II and millions of men joining the armed forces, Alabama's schedule for 1942 included two games against military all-star teams. 'Bama won 27-0 against Pensacola Naval Air Station, a team that included former Alabama end Ben McLeod as well as players formerly of Fordham, LSU and Nebraska, but lost to a Georgia Pre-Flight squad that boasted former All-Americans from Tennessee and Tulane as well as other players with college experience.

Alabama's first ever Orange Bowl was a wild affair against Boston College. Alabama trailed 14-0 at the end of the first quarter, scored 22 points in the second quarter to go into halftime up 22-21, then dominated the second half to win the game 37-21. [1]

Christmas of 1942 was spent in Little Rock. With nice-sized bonuses for the staff, Austin and Beth Ann closed up the house and traveled over from Birmingham. James and Anna came home from the university, and it was a joyous occasion. Two days before Christmas, after another huge John and Lydia meal, everyone was sitting around the fire in the family room. James put a log on the fire, turned and looked at the room and his father.

"Things are in chaos in the world, Dad. I have a friend on Guadalcanal. I haven't heard from him or about him. So, I guess he is okay."

"Are you feeling guilty about not already volunteering?"

"Maybe a little. I will at least finish the school year, but I may enlist in the Army Air Corps. I want to be a fighter pilot. I already have a pilot's license. I have been told I could go."

"What about you, Austin?" asked Luke.

"I hate to say it, but James is right. There is already talk Alabama is not going to field a football team for the 1943 season. I want to fly also. I have been watching the progress of the new P-51 Mustang and I want to fly it. That is one sweet airplane."

"Okay, what about you, Anna?" asked Levi.

I have been talking to the people about becoming a WASP and ferrying planes from the United States to Europe. They would not let me be a fighter pilot."

"I have to tell you, kids, it breaks my heart to think of you in harm's way, but Levi and I went too. So, I am not going to even try to talk you out of it. I just will be praying for you every moment of every day."

"What about me?" spoke up Beth Ann. "I may not be a combatant, but what I do is needed also. My publishing company received a contract from the War Department to print materials for everything from posters and propaganda to training manuals."

Austin put his arm around her and said softly, "Everyone is going to be just as proud of you as if you were a combatant. The war will have to be a team effort to win on so many fronts against so many countries. This is definitely a World War!" He kissed her on the cheek and held her tight for a moment.

The little group was quiet for a moment, and Luke said, "Let us pray."

Back home in Alabama, Austin and Beth Ann began to produce propaganda and training manuals while continuing to attend school. Beth Ann was impressed with how articulate Austin could be. He did most of the writing and she had to do very little editing to send it to the printers. The Navy Handbook required numerous pictures, and Austin took most of them using a press camera given to him by his Uncle Levi. It was left over from the days when he was a reporter for the Arkansas Gazette. After seeing some of his work, he told Austin he would give him a job, and Austin actually entertained the idea of being a War correspondent, but he wanted to fly.

In July 1943 Austin and James applied for Army flight school. After a 60 day officer candidate boot camp in Alabama they went home for 10 days. Austin went to Alabama and James stayed in Little Rock. Both were Lieutenant Junior Grade after having two to three years of college and graduating from OCS.

Austin and Beth Ann spent every moment together at their home in Alabama. James and Payton at home in Little Rock felt they wanted to wait about getting married. In late October both men received orders to Lubbock, Texas, for flight training at the Lubbock Army Airfield.

Lubbock, Texas, in 1943 had a population of approximately 30,000 which grew quickly during and after the war. The city had given 2,000 acres a few years before to build an Army Training facility, and in the years from 1938 to 1943 Lubbock had trained several thousand aviators. The training field was deemed safer than most by being surrounded with miles of flat farmland and blessed with a usually sunny, though sometimes cold in the winter, weather most of the year. It receives on the average of less than 19 inches of rain per year.

"Is this it?" grumbled James. "The only green I see around here is uniforms."

"Welcome to West Texas in the wintertime," smiled the non com there to pick them up who had heard the remark. "Don't worry, you will grow to love it."

"Yeah, I am sure I will," frowned James. He and Austin loaded their duffel bags into the Jeep and turned their collars up to the wind.

The ride in the jeep with no heater, and the top letting in the air with no windows, was bone chilling and numbing. Luckily the train ran close to the main gate. The driver stopped at the gate as Austin and James presented documents which allowed them on the base. The driver was friendly and even helped unload their bags in front of the barracks. He showed them where to find bunks and linens, and where the chow hall was.

"Thanks, man. I guess we are all set. We owe you one."

"Sounds good to me. You can buy a round at Pinky's. Oh, Pinky's is a local bar where mostly local veterans and soldiers hang out when we are not in class."

They both smiled and Austin said, "Will do! But it has to be warm. I am numb from the cold!"

The driver smiled back and said, "Know what you mean. I am from Arizona. You never really get used to this place!"

They found the man's name was Thomas Scott, and everyone called him Scottie. He was as laid back as James and he was well liked and a lot of fun. It was worth a drink just to get to hang out with him. He was only five foot five with black hair and blue eyes. The girls stood in line to dance with him.

Austin called home collect just to make sure Beth Ann was able to take care of business without him. They visited for only about 10 minutes, and Beth Ann said, "Austin, don't worry about me. You keep focused on what you are doing. I am fine. Samuel and the girls are taking good care of me and send their love."

"I know, but I miss you. I love you."

"I love you too. Say hello to James for me."

"I will. I will call at least once a week. Goodbye, my love."

The first Saturday night on the base Scottie came by the barracks and told Austin, "I see you and James checked out a Jeep. I am going on in to Pinky's with a couple of the guys, and do a little "trolling" before the crowd comes. I'll see you guys there." He smiled and winked and Austin just shook his head.

About an hour later, after standing in line to check out the Jeep, Austin and James took two more soldiers with them and drove into Lubbock, commented on the rough red brick streets of downtown, and out to "the Strip."

The Lubbock city fathers did not allow the purchase of liquor inside the city limits, and the bars and package stores were relegated to a stretch of the Andrews highway south of town nicknamed "the Strip." To Austin and James it was somewhat hypocritical in that the bars were usually full of locals.

As the Jeep with Austin and James pulled into the parking lot, they saw a crowd of people watching a fight with 3 locals and one hapless soldier in a bloody uniform. One burly cowboy was raising his arm back to hit the soldier held up by two more laughing, drunk cowboys when it was gripped in a painful vise that pushed him down to his knees.

"That's enough," said Austin through gritted teeth. "The fight is over. Unless you want to continue it with me!"

The cowboy rubbed on his forearm which bore the hand print of Austin's grip. He gazed up at Austin and said, "That's quite a grip you got there, soldier boy."

The obvious pain showed as he stood up. His friends let go of the soldier, and James caught the semi-conscious young man in his arms.

"Why, it is Scottie!" he exclaimed.

Austin turned and glared at the big cowboy.

"He was trying to pick up my girl. He was already dancing his second dance with her."

"Sounds like he had already picked her up. She probably was tired of an asinine buffoon like you pawing and slobbering at her. She wanted a gentleman."

There were several mutterings and laughs from the crowd who were afraid of Dixon and his rough friends.

"I have heard about men like you, Dixon. You are a coward. You are too afraid to go fight for your country, but to feel like a man you beat up young soldiers. Well, that stops tonight."

"You know, soldier boy. The numbers are not very good for you. There are three of us and only two of you," smirked Dixon.

"You know, you are right. We do need to even it up a little." Austin looked at a red-headed drunk cowboy who was urging on Dixon. Austin pointed a finger at him and said evenly, "What about you, carrot top? Why don't you help Dixon and these other low lifes out so the fight will be fair? After my brother and I kick your butts all over this parking lot, I don't want anyone to be able to say it wasn't a fair fight, okay?"

As the cowboy's face turned red from Austin's disrespect, he started to take a step toward the two brothers, Dixon put out a hand and stopped him.

"No, he's mine. I am gonna carve him like a turkey," he scowled. He pulled an 8 inch bladed hunting knife from a sheath on his belt. He held it out in front of him.

Austin smiled at him, and said, "Hey, Dixon, watch this!" In one quick move, Austin kicked the man's hand and caused the knife to fly into the air. As Dixon looked up in astonishment, he did not see Austin's kick coming hard enough to crush his chest and send him backwards into the arms of his companions. They held Dixon up as the knife came down into Austin's waiting hand. The two men's eyes opened wide as Austin jumped nimbly into the air and kicked both men in the face as they held on to Dixon. The Washu move caught both men by surprise as they fell back on the ground letting Dixon fall. Their noses were both broken and one had lost two front teeth as they lay on the ground groaning and looking at the blood dripping on the gravel parking lot.

"Okay, carrot top, your turn. It is just you and me!"

The man cursed and said, "No sir! I have seen enough. If you will let me go, I promise I will never pick a fight with a soldier again!"

The crowd roared at the remark and carrot top's hasty departure.

Dixon was having trouble breathing from his broken sternum, and he put his hand up and cringed as Austin stood over him and pulled him up by the front of his shirt with his left hand with the knife still in his right.

"Don't cut me! You win! I'm through!" He could barely talk, but his eyes were showing his fear.

"One last thing. I ever hear of you doing anything but buying a soldier a drink I will come for you and your friends. Next time I won't play. Do I make myself clear?"

Dixon was very polite as he wheezed , "Yes sir!"

"Now pick up your friends and go. I don't want to even see you for a long time.!"

Dixon grimaced at the pain in his chest as he and his friends limped to their pickup while the crowd jeered and laughed.

As Austin and James turned to look for Scottie, they discovered the pretty blonde cowgirl Dixon was trying to say was his girlfriend had Scottie's head cradled in her lap and was tenderly washing his mostly superficial wounds.

"Oh brother," laughed James as he rolled his eyes at the scene. Scottie opened his eyes, smiled, winked, and pulled the girl's hand back to his face and groaned a not very convincing sound. She went back to rubbing his forehead as he had his eyes closed and a smile on his face.

"Do you think he will survive the terrible beating he took from Dixon?" Austin asked with a big grin.

"He may not make it back to the base tonight, but, oh yeah, he is in fine hands!"

They both laughed and entered the bar which erupted in a standing ovation. Even the locals had been afraid of Dixon and his cronies, but now it would take some time for their wounds to heal before they confronted anyone else. Both brothers ordered their first beers and both agreed they could not understand why anyone would like that bitter taste. After forcing down two though, the room began to spin, and they knew it was time to go. They drove back to the base where the officer at the gate saluted and said, "Thanks for taking care of a problem for our men. He had beat up so many guys we were told to go to Pinky's at our own risk. Glad to have you aboard!"

Austin returned the man's salute and he and James went to the barracks. They undressed down to uniform pants and undershirts and socks. Both lay down to rest, and with everyone else in town on a Saturday night, they started talking to one another.

"Let's drive into town and go to church tomorrow," said Austin.

"I guess we probably need to after tonight," answered James. They both smiled.

The next day they went to the big First Baptist Church on Broadway close to Texas Tech. Both men enjoyed the service, and there were numerous service personnel and their families from the base. On the way back to the base, James told Austin, "You're fun, Austin, but I miss going to church with Payton and Mom and Dad."

"We are going to be okay, James. At least we have one another, and we know everyone at home are praying for us every day. Let's go find something to eat!"

Chapter Thirty One

After two weeks of hanging around the base and watching the bulletin boards of when they were going to start their training, finally Austin and James were called into the base commander's office.

Sitting at a long table with stacks of papers in front of them, were three officers. The only one the two recognized was the base commander.

"I see on your application to flight school you both already know how to fly a little," the base commander spoke first.

Standing at attention, Austin spoke first, "Sir, we both have had our pilots' licenses since we were 16 years old. We learned to fly single and multi-engine aircraft from being taught to fly the family's twin engine Beechcraft and the single engine Curtiss JN-4. We both have logged over 1400 hours in different aircraft including the JN-4 we were taught on, and I personally own a Piper Cub I am just finishing restoring."

Astonished, the base commander lay his papers aside.

"Well, well, well, Mr. Austin Johnson and Mr. James Johnson, that is interesting news indeed." The base commander looked at the other two officers and nodded as he smiled.

"Your country needs good pilots, but we also need men to train those good pilots. After your initial 7 month flight training, we will have two training billets here in Lubbock open if you would be interested. We don't need an answer this minute, but be thinking along those lines as you move through training.

Austin, I see here you are married. If you become a training officer, your wife could join you in on base housing. It might not be too bad in West Texas if you had your wife here. Besides, it might keep you out of trouble. I heard about the liaison work you two performed in neutralizing a local group of ruffians a couple of weeks ago. Unofficially, well done, but also let's remember why we are here, and keep the "making friends" to a minimum." He smiled, and when he did, the others followed suit. Austin and James snapped their heels together, saluted, and the base commander said, "Dismissed!"

The next morning was a clear, cold, West Texas day with little wind. In the cockpit of the AT-6 Texan used for training, Austin listened to the flight instructor run through the preflight check as did James in his airplane. Both were going on their first orientation flights. Both had already walked around the planes checking the tires, free movement of the control surfaces, such as the rudder and ailerons. When the instructors were satisfied with the physical condition of the exteriors, they started the engines and began to let them warm up to operating temperature.

After the little JN-4's which Austin and James had been flying, the AT-6 Texan aircraft seemed to be a very advanced airplane. As the instructor opened the throttle, the plane rose from the runway very easily into the air.

They only flew over and around the base at first, and then climbed to an altitude of approximately 3000 feet.

The instructors kept up a running conversation through the headsets as they pointed out local landmarks, neighboring towns, and navigation coordinates to familiarize the two with Lubbock and Lubbock County from the air.

After flying for about 30 minutes, Austin's flight instructor, Bill Burnett, asked Austin, "What do you think? Think you can learn to fly one of these?"

"Of course. Let me try it for a few minutes."

The instructor had seen several air cadets come through the training course which could fly a little, but he was not prepared for a student which could fly as well, or maybe even better, than he could!

"I am impressed. Who taught you to fly?"

"My dad and uncle, who are twin brothers, were fighter pilots and flight instructors during World War I, and they have had James and me and our first cousin, Anna Lee, as co-pilots ever since we could sit up or walk. I had a solo flight before I was 12 years old, and my dad let James and me fly on every flight to and from all sorts of destinations. They have business interests in California, and even delivered the mail at one point, although the company sold out later."

"What happened to your cousin?"

"She is training to become a WASP and ferry bombers across to Europe. She's a pistol! If any woman can take care of herself, she can!" Austin laughed. He then surprised Bill by doing a surprise barrel roll.

"This little trainer is really fun to fly, isn't it?"

Bill grinned into his face mask, "Yes, it is! But you don't want the Old Man to know I let a new cadet do a barrel roll on his first flight!"

"I sure won't tell him, but it felt so willing I was never uncomfortable at any time, were you?"

"Nope, not a bit. I knew I could trust your flying. Let's head for home. It's a tradition the cadet buys the trainer the first round after their orientation flight."

"I know you're lying. Though I will have to remember that line if I train my own cadets." Austin laughed out loud. "But I will be glad to buy!" He put his hand on his instructor's shoulder as they walked outside.

The North American T-6 Texan was known as the "pilot maker" because of its important role in preparing pilots for combat. Derived from the 1935 North American NA-16 prototype, a cantilever, low wing monoplane, the Texan filled the need for a basic combat trainer during World War II and beyond.

North American's rapid production of the T-6 Texan coincided with the wartime expansion of the United States air war commitment. As of 1940, the required flight hours for combat pilots to earn their wings had been cut to only 200 during a much shortened training period of seven months. Of those hours, 75 were logged in the AT-6.

It had a maximum speed of 205 mph and a ceiling of 21,500 feet making it a forgiving, durable trainer.

Austin was even allowed to land the plane. It was a very soft landing and afterward Bill was complimented by the tower captain how well he landed. He looked at Austin as they carried their flight gear into the locker room, smiled, and winked.

Later that evening the foursome of Austin, James, Bill Burnett, and Dennis Duryea, Austin's trainer, were sitting in a nearly empty Pinky's Bar and Grill. They all got a laugh when Bill told the story how surprised the tower captain would have been to know it was Austin which had landed the plane, not him. Austin and James purchased a pitcher of draft beer apiece and the conversation finally took a more serious note.

Bill asked, "Have you and James thought any more about becoming flight instructors?"

"We have talked a little. How long have you been here?" asked Austin.

"I have been here 18 months. I love having my family here, but I am itching to leave and feeling a little guilty about not fighting alongside my students. I am one of the billets which, if you take the instructor position, will be replaced."

"How does your wife feel?" James asked.

"She's a good Army wife, and she knows how I feel. She and my son will move back to Russellville, Arkansas, to live in our home we left. You probably don't even know where that is."

"Sure we do. My dad and uncle grew up in Paris right up the road from Russellville. My grandfather is a Pentecostal preacher in Paris still today!"

"I thought you were from Alabama."

"I am from Little Rock, and met and married a pretty young thing named Beth Ann Davis from Birmingham, Alabama, which I met at the University of Arkansas. She has a business there and we moved to Birmingham to let her run it after her folks passed away. I transferred to the University of Alabama for two years before I joined the Army."

"Are you the same notorious Austin Johnson which played football for the University of Alabama just a couple of years ago?"

"Yep," smiled Austin.

"I happened to read about you returning that punt which won the game when you guys beat Tulane. Also, the bowl game against Texas A&M was on the radio. You were a standout there too! You had three interceptions!"

The only patrons in the bar were a couple of middle-aged people and a large table of Texas Tech students who had heard the conversation about Austin. One of the students came over and spoke to Austin.

"I am not trying to intrude at all, Mister Johnson, but I don't guess you would want to play for Tech, would you?"

said a smiling, slender, dark haired young man wearing glasses and a sport coat and tie. He had two giggling blonde girlfriends standing with him which kept batting their eyes at the four young soldiers.

"Thank you for the compliment, but no, my football is put on hold until after my enlistment."

"Fair enough. We are glad to have you in Lubbock, and if you have a chance, the basketball team is starting to play conference games soon if you wanted to come and watch them play."

"You know what? I would like that. Thank you for the invitation." He held out his hand and the young man shook his hand. The two girls and the rest of the table gathered around and shook hands, and one or two of the girls even hugged the soldiers. The men ate, finished their drinks, and left for the base smiling and waving at the students.

As Austin and James walked into the barracks, there was a note laying on Austin's bunk to call Anna at a phone number he did not recognize. He called the number and a female voice answered, "Women Airforce Service Pilots, to whom did you wish to speak?"

"This is Austin Johnson, and I am a family member of Anna Johnson. I missed her call and I am returning it. Is she around there close?"

"Yes she is. Hold on I can see her!" The girl held the phone and yelled, "Anna some guy is calling and says he is a family member!"

A breathless Anna picked up the phone and said excitedly into the phone as to who it could be, "Hello?"

"Hey troublemaker, are you still raising a ruckus? Where are you?"

"Austin! You won't believe this! I am in Sweetwater for WASP training just an hour away by air! How's James?"

"He's fine and here with me. We took our first orientation flights today. We are training in the AT-6 and it is a neat little plane. I even did a barrel roll and secretly landed it on my first flight!"

"You didn't! They are so protective with us women it is boring. I have been meaning to call but I have only been here a couple of weeks and this is my first chance."

She got to visit for a few minutes with James and they all agreed the first time possible they were going to get together.

Both air training facilities were shutting down for Thanksgiving weekend in two weeks and Anna had talked her dad into flying the family to Lubbock after picking her up. They would spend the weekend together in Lubbock.

Austin and James hung up the phone after visiting with Anna and both agreed it was going to be a long two weeks while they waited.

It snowed several inches in Lubbock the first of November, and for the first time, the Commander stopped all flying. The men played cards, drove a Jeep into town and smuggled a little booze back to the base.

After receiving a visit from the base commander, they gave away a bottle of whiskey and a case of beer. The chow hall was opened up for snacks, and that evening was spent listening to sad songs on the radio and news reports. The Allies were starting to win the war.

Chapter Thirty Two

On August 5, 1943, the Women's Flying Training Detachment (WFTD) and the Women's Auxiliary Ferrying Squadron (WAFS) were combined to form the paramilitary WASP (Women Airforce Service Pilots) organization.

Twenty-five thousand women applied to join the Wasp, but only 1,830 were accepted and took the oath, and out of those only 1,074 women passed the training and joined, becoming the first women to fly American military aircraft.

After Austin and James left for Lubbock at the end of October 1943, Anna Lee joined the WASP. One of the requirement's for all WASP was to have a pilot's license, and she had hers from the time she was 16 years old. Fred and she were engaged unofficially but he hurt his knee in training after joining the Army, and was transferring to Washington to accept an attache position with Colonel Talbert, the father of George Talbert, his friend and teammate at the University of Arkansas.

The thought of being alone in Little Rock was a big reason she was ready to leave. Anna and Fred had talked before he left for the Army and he was encouraging her to join to get her to be able to possibly fly into Washington. She had arrived in Sweetwater, Texas, in late October, and was already flying training flights before she had the chance to call Austin and James.

Austin and James drove over to the Lubbock Municipal Airport on Wednesday afternoon before Thanksgiving Day to wait for the plane.

"Hey, there it is!" exclaimed James.

The stainless hulled Beechcraft gleamed in the late sunlight as it circled once and then settled onto the runway nice and easy.

"Must have been Dad flying," said Austin.

"Well, it probably wasn't Anna!" smiled James. They were still smiling as the plane taxied to a stop and both looked at one another as Anna waved from the cockpit.

"I can't believe it!" laughed Luke.

The door opened and the steps extended and Austin was the first to the bottom of the steps. To his surprise Beth Ann was the first one out the door and down the steps. She leaped the final two and Austin caught her in his arms and held her off the ground as he kissed her.

"What are you doing here? You did not say a word about coming!"

"The whole family cooked this up. We thought you guys might need a lift! We even have a surprise for James. Look!"

Payton was at the top of the steps, but James did not wait. He bounded up the steps and kissed her, and walked with his arm around her as they came down.

There were tears and hugs and kisses everywhere as Luke, Maddie, Levi, and Ellen came down the steps. Finally, Anna came down after shutting down the cockpit.

"You know, Anna, you are getting better at landing. James and I were worried the Army would make you pay for all the crashed aircraft!" He hugged her close with tears in his eyes. Without saying so, she knew how much the three of them cared for one another.

"We had to have three Jeeps to get everyone picked up, and I got a guy to help us by driving one of the Jeeps. There he is now."

Everyone turned to see a uniformed soldier coming out of the terminal. No one said anything for a moment, and them Anna almost screamed.

"Fred!"

She ran across the pavement and into his arms as he whirled her around and kissed her. She furrowed her brow as she asked, "But how?"

"Ask Austin. He made a call to George Talbert, who asked his dad, the colonel, and officially there happened to be a meeting come up in Lubbock. So, here I am!"

Anna turned to Austin, grabbed him and kissed him on the cheek. "I love you!" Everyone laughed.

"I will have to go by and give the base commander some papers from my dad for this to be a legitimate meeting." He smiled.

Later that evening, the little group sat in the lobby of the Lubbock Hotel and talked about the future. Fred had asked Anna to marry him and come back to Washington D.C. with him.

"Fred, you know the answer is yes, but I am still in training in Sweetwater, and I feel very strongly about serving in the WASP. I know your mother and dad are not here, but what if we got married this weekend, went back to work, and I will see if I can get stationed in D.C. after training. We will be deployed in over 120 different airfields, and several are around Washington. I am sure with your dad's help, okay, maybe Austin too, I can be stationed with you." She smiled: for once a little bashful at the thought of spending the night with Fred.

Anna turned to her mother and Aunt Maddie and said, "Before you get too sad. Let me say this is not a spur of the moment thing. I promise as soon as the war is over, Fred and I will renew our vows and give you the pleasure of a church wedding. Fair enough?"

Anna's mother, Ellen, said with tears in her eyes, "The ceremony is not what marriage is all about. I would not mind at all for you two to have this weekend together. I know firsthand the uncertainty of war."

The day after Thanksgiving Day, Fred and Anna were married in front of Reverend Rogers of a little Pentecostal church in Lubbock. Both were in uniform as were Austin, his best man, and James as a male attendant. Beth Ann was Maid of Honor and carried the flowers for her while Payton was bridesmaid.

Back at the hotel, Anna and Fred received an upgrade to the bridal suite complete with a bottle of champagne which never was opened. It was cold outside on Saturday and it was about noon before the newlyweds made their appearance in the dining room. Both were embarrassed from the applause of everyone, even the patrons at the hotel when Austin stood and applauded.

Austin and James shook hands with Fred and hugged Anna.

"To think it all started with a dip in the pool!" smiled Austin at Anna.

Fred's return plane did not leave until Monday morning, but Anna had to be back before 10 p.m. Sunday night.

"It is just like being in college all over again," grumbled Anna. "Except here the house mother is a gripy old man." Then she giggled as she told the story of Austin flirting with the house mother at the University of Arkansas.

Anna and Fred were both trying to be brave for the other, but as soon as Anna was on the plane and airborne, she cried.

James and Payton decided to get married over the Christmas break and she would move to Lubbock to be near Austin and Beth Ann. The base commander was excited to have Austin and James commit to a year as training instructors after they received their wings the next June.

Austin and James both got a ten day leave for Christmas, and Luke flew the plane up to take everyone back to Little Rock for the wedding of Payton and James. Grandpa August agreed to perform the ceremony, and Austin was best man. Mallory, Payton's twin sister, was the Maid of Honor which meant Austin was to be her escort.

"Well hello, Austin." Mallory came up alongside and casually put her hand on Austin's back. Austin turned and one of the first things he noticed was the big diamond engagement ring on her left hand. He was relieved a little because he believed things would not get out of hand if she were already engaged. He wanted nothing to come between him and Beth Ann.

"Well hello yourself, Miss Mallory." He smiled at her and said, "Who is the lucky guy?"

"Benny Winston has had a crush on me since we were in grade school. He begged me until I gave in!" She giggled, and just for a moment he remembered just how beautiful she was. Then he felt Beth Ann's arm snake through his and Beth Ann's silky voice.

"Why, this must be Mallory, Payton's little sister. My name is Beth Ann, Austin's wife, and I am glad to meet any of Austin's friends."

To the casual <u>male</u> observer, it was just a conversation between two women who had just met. The tone of voice, the direct eye contact, her arm through Austin's, and her controlled smile, let Mallory know with whom she was dealing. Beth Ann Johnson was a woman with a lifetime of dealing with little girls like Mallory, and she could more than hold her own as the wife of the best looking guy at the wedding. As a woman, the fact was not lost on Mallory, and she cleared her throat and said, "I better go find Benny. He's probably nursing a drink somewhere."

She kept looking at Beth Ann but was pointing over her shoulder and waving at something vague. She backed into a chair but recovered her balance. Her eyes did not leave Beth Ann's.

"It was really nice to meet you, Mallory," purred Beth Ann as Mallory backed away. She squeezed Austin's arm to reassure him she had the situation well under control.

"Oooo. I could see the claws come out. You were something else! I imagine she will barely walk down the aisle beside me now. I have to admit, I have never been as intimidated by any man as Mallory was by you just now!"

Austin saw Mallory later at the rehearsal but she would not make eye contact. When it came time to link arms to walk the aisle she kept her body well away from his. Beth Ann's point was made with Mallory. The savagery of women was not lost on Austin, and he just smiled to himself for he was very proud of Beth Ann.

After Austin, Beth Ann, James, and Payton returned to Lubbock after Christmas, the girls worked on decorating their little homes. Base housing was basic with gas stove, refrigerator, furniture including bed, chest of drawers, and living room furniture which included chair, couch and coffee table. The girls went shopping nearly every day to find prints for the walls, rugs, nicer dishes, and curtains for the windows. They repainted with different colors inside and out, and within a few days they were settled into their own first homes.

"Every day I come home it is to a different home!" exclaimed Austin.

"Are you saying you don't like it?"

"No, darling, I was just making a comment. I actually enjoy it because I know you and Payton have to be bored."

"I have been thinking I might ride the bus to Birmingham for a few days to check on things, if you will be alright."

Austin frowned and said, "I guess I have been expecting it. We don't have kids for you to look after like some of the other wives, and you have a lot of responsibility as the owner of a business which they don't even comprehend. I will miss nights and morning coffee with you, but I do understand. When are you planning to leave?"

"No big rush I suppose. This is Friday. What if I leave Monday morning? The bus leaves at 0600. See, I am already learning military time."

"I will get permission to go in at 7:30. I can not stand the thought of not seeing you off!"

"You big softie," Beth Ann smiled at him. She put her arms around him and squeezed. "We do have three days. We better make the best of it!"

The windup alarm clock went off at 4:30 a.m. on Monday morning. After turning off the alarm, Austin put his arm over on Beth Ann's side of the bed, but it was empty. He noticed the light under the bathroom door, and when he opened the door, Beth Ann was fully dressed brushing her hair.

"Goodness. You must be in a hurry to leave."

"Knowing I am going left me a little restless, and I could not sleep. You have a few minutes if you want to take a nap."

"I can sleep while you are gone."

Beth Ann left Lubbock around the first of February, but came back in Austin's car just in time for her birthday on March 17th. The party was held on the base, and friends and other instructors and their wives attended. The base commander even put in an appearance and got to dance with the "Birthday Girl."

"Are we going to be able to keep Austin here, Commander, after he earns his wings? He wants to be fighting so bad."

"Beth Ann, I know how he feels, but he settled down a little after I had a talk with him. If Austin went to Europe right now, he would do well, no doubt in my mind, but what if he could train numerous pilots to be as good as he is? He and James can make a very significant contribution to the war effort doing just what they are doing. He takes his training of cadets very seriously, and he will be producing some of the best pilots around."

"Are we both being selfish wanting to not see him go?" she asked seriously.

"Probably some," he smiled, "but what he is doing is vital to our winning the war." He smiled at her as the song ended, and then he bowed a little bow and escorted her back to their table.

As Austin and Beth Ann got up to dance Austin smiled and asked, "Was he trying to get you to run away with him?"

"He asked, but I said no!" She laughed a small squeal as Austin squeezed her to him, and both laughed as people looked at them.

Chapter Thirty Three

June 1, 1944, Austin and James graduated from the flight training program at the Lubbock Army Air Base, and received their wings. The family had flown up from Little Rock and the base commander enjoyed showing Luke and Levi around the base while the officer's wives took off with the wives to eat some place fancy and encourage the wives with woman talk.

The next day they began their first training classes. The base commander spoke to the instructors old and new before he called a meeting of cadets and introduced each instructor.

"Men, within a week, the Allied Forces led by General Eisenhower will invade Europe in the largest assault in the history of warfare. There are several million troops involved. The cadets you will be responsible for training will be going up against veteran German pilots with excellent planes and nothing to lose. We are told to give them only 200 hours of combat training and send them. I understand the burden that will put on you and them, but we will do our best to see we send capable pilots to the front. God bless America!"

Each instructor was responsible for two trainees at first, but pilots were needed so badly the number jumped to four cadets each. Flying time was one and half hours a day for each of the cadets, which made for a long day sometimes for the instructors. Morale was not a problem, but fatigue sometimes could be.

The instructors stayed in shape as well as keeping their minds relaxed by grilling out steaks, hamburgers, chicken, and getting together as much as possible. However, sometimes on the weekends, Austin and Beth Ann, Payton and James would put the top down, and go for a drive through the surrounding countryside.

Lubbock, Texas, is built on a plateau and sits roughly at an altitude of 3202 feet above sea level. There are numerous small towns, lakes, and parks including Ransom Canyon, Roaring Springs, and Lake Sweetwater, which is only a three hour drive. It has been a spot for tourists and locals to swim and picnic since before 1900.

The foursome enjoyed their time off but Austin and James were wanting to be in Europe to help fight the war from the cockpit of a real fighter. It was the main topic of conversation.

It became apparent by October 1944 when the Allies captured the German town of Aachen the war was being lost in Europe. There was a seemingly endless stream of German troops from the front which had been surrounded and then surrendered. Hitler's general, Rommel, committed suicide after the fall of Greece. No one but Hitler believed the war could be won, and the Germans fell back to behind the Seigfrid line and began the Battle of The Bulge.

The Battle of the Bulge (also known as the Ardennes Offensive and the Von Runstedt Offensive) was the last major German offensive launched at the end of the war through the densely forested Ardennes Mountains region of Wallonia in Belgium, hence its French name (Bataille des Ardennes), and France and Luxembourg on the Western Front.

The Wehrnacht's code name for the offensive was Unternehmen Wacht am Rhine ("Operation Watch on the Rhine"), after the German Patriotic hymn Die Wacht am Rhein. This German offensive was officially named the Ardennes-Alsace campaign by the U.S. Army, but it is known to the English-speaking general public simply as the Battle of the Bulge. The "bulge" being the initial incursion of the Germans put into the Allies line of advance, as seen in maps presented in contemporary newspapers.

The German offensive was supported by several subordinate operations known as Unternehem Bodenplatte, Greif, and Wahrung. Germany's goal was to split the British and American Allied line in half, capturing Antwerp, Belgium, and then proceed to encircle and destroy four Allied armies forcing the Western Allies to negotiate a peace treaty in the Axis' Powers' favor. Once accomplished, Hitler could return his attention and the bulk of his forces to the Soviet Armies in the East.

The offensive was planned with the utmost secrecy, minimizing radio traffic and moving troops and equipment under cover of darkness. Although ULTRA suggested a possible attack, and the Third U.S. Army's intelligence predicted a major German offensive, the Allies were still caught by surprise, due to a combination of Allied overconfidence, preoccupation with their own offensive plans and poor aerial reconnaissance.

Near-complete surprise against a weakly defended section of the Allied line was achieved during heavy overcast weather, which grounded the Allies' overwhelmingly superior Air Forces. Fierce resistance, particularly around the key town of Bastogne, and terrain favoring the defenders threw the German timetable behind schedule. Allied reinforcements, including General George Patton's Third Army, and improving weather conditions which permitted air attacks on German forces and supply lines, sealed the failure of the offensive.

In the wake of the defeat, many experienced German units were left severely depleted of men and equipment as survivors retreated to the defenses of the Siegfried Line.

For the Americans, with about 500,000 to 840,000 men committed, and some 70,000 to 89,000 casualties, including 19,000 killed, the Battle of the Bulge was the largest and bloodiest battle Americans fought in World

War II.

The best part of hearing about the offensive battle to Austin and James was a significant number of the pilots trained by them were instrumental in destroying or neutralizing the Luftwaffe for the rest of the war.

Austin, however, had become even more reserved and unto himself. Beth Ann knew it was because he felt his time was being wasted. His one year commitment was up and he was to go before his base commander the next day.

"You want to go for a ride? I need to get out of Lubbock for a while. Pack a lunch and we will go to Ransom Canyon and eat."

Beth Ann put her arms around him and said quietly, "Austin, thank you for sticking this instructor thing out so that we could be together just you and me." She sighed a deep sigh and continued, "Have you thought about where you want to go? I want you to be fulfilled. I will go home to Alabama and keep myself busy until you come home."

"You are something else, Beth Ann. Your mother would be proud of you."

They spread a blanket on the rim of the canyon and she lay in his arms as they watched the last rays of the

West Texas sunset turn the skies from blue to scarlet to indigo to darkness.

The next morning he knocked on the base commander's door after the attache had let him know he was there.

"Come in, Austin."

Austin stood at attention and the commander's face softened, for he had grown to have a lot of affection for this young man, but he also knew that it was time to let him go. The war was over and he had done a job like no one else he ever had.

He said, "At ease. Have a seat," and he waved to a stuffed chair to one side of the room. The base commander sat down in an adjacent chair, and they both listened to an AT-6 leaving the runway and clawing for altitude. He turned to him after a moment and quietly asked, "Where do you want to go?"

The Supreme Headquarters Allied Expeditionary Force (SHAEF) under General Eisenhower issued a directive to create T-Force soon after the Normandy Landings. T-Forces were ordered to "identify, secure, guard, and exploit valuable and special information, including documents, equipment and persons of value to the Allied armies." T-Force units were attached to the three army groups on the western front; the 6th United States Army Group, 21st Army Group, and 12th Army Group. The targets of the T-Force were selected and recommended by the Combined Intelligence Objectives Subcommittee (CIOS). T-Force units were lightly armed but highly mobile.[1]

In post war Germany, T-Force was tasked with carrying out abductions of German scientists and businessmen. One of the objectives of these abductions was to recover Nazi military secrets. In addition to this, the abductions of the scientists enabled Britain and the United States to use their knowledge to build back up the British and American economy after the war, and also prevented the Soviet Union from obtaining their knowledge.

For example, Courtauld's received the latest information on manmade fibers, Dorman Long benefited from information and equipment originating from the Hermann Goering Steel Works, and even the British coal industry had pit props sent to them from the Harz Mountains. On the military side much information was gathered, which could have been vital had the war in the Far East not ended so soon.

Apart from this, there were wider political and economic implications, including the significance of the early liberation of Kiel, which prevented the Russians from adding Schleswig-Holstein and the Jutland Peninsula to their area of influence.

Chapter Thirty Four

Berlin, Germany 1945

Hans Gruber, former Nazi SS assassin, and now working for the Soviets, had been following the young American Army officer for over two hours. Hans had been alerted by a double agent on the inside of the occupying allied military about a secret document transfer, and was sitting in his car waiting for a courier to come out of the Army headquarters building. After a while, a tall, fit looking, American Army officer emerged with a briefcase handcuffed to his left wrist. He looked side to side and got in a jeep parked at the curb.

Although he made sure he tailed him at a distance in his black 1934 Mercedes sedan, Hans followed him all over the city as the American ran a circuitous course to "shake" or lose someone if he was being followed. Finally, the man seemed to have convinced himself he was alone.

Hans sat in his car and watched the American park his jeep in front of the White Lily Pub and Bar. It was in a partially bombed out building, one of only a few with very little damage, not far from downtown Berlin. The young officer looked at his watch, got out of the Jeep, and started walking slowly among the burnt out buildings as if he were sightseeing. He looked up and down shaking his head at the destruction, obviously in no hurry for his appointment.

"How trusting these young Americans are!" Hans thought to himself. He was confident this was going to be easy. He did not follow the young man, but was content to wait and let him come to him. He sat down outside the pub on the patio at a small table for two, and ordered a dark German beer as he watched him out of the corner of his eye.

The American, after a few minutes, took another look at his watch and turned around to head back to the pub. Hans knew he needed to make his move before the officer met his appointment and gave away the briefcase.

Hans watched the entrance to the restroom. He knew most Americans wash their hands before they eat. The

American looked around to satisfy himself his party had not arrived, and walked directly to the restroom which was off the floor of the restaurant. It was down a small hall lit with only one bare electric light. The door opened outward, and once inside, the room had seen better days. It smelled of urine and filth from not having a regular cleaning. It was dim lit and Hans waited a moment to allow his eyes to adjust. At the other end of a row of urinals the young American was standing looking down. Hans looked and made sure the hallway was empty before entering. He shut the door behind him and started to reach for his Luger in a hidden shoulder holster under his suit coat.

"I've been waiting for you to make your move, Gerry. I have known since headquarters you were following me."

The slight drawl, thought Hans to himself, placed the American as being from somewhere in the South in the United States. His hand froze on his pistol as he looked and realized the man had turned toward him. Hans was facing an Army issue Colt 45 in the hand of a young Army officer that showed no sign of fear or wavering.

"The war is over, you know. You lost."

413

"Not for me it isn't!" Hans' hand jerked on the butt of the Luger, and as it cleared the holster the American shot him twice, once in the chest. He staggered back against the stucco wall as his pistol fell clattering on the tile floor. His hand went to his chest and came away dripping blood, and he slid down the wall to a sitting position leaving a trail of crimson. As his eyes began to dim in death, Hans could only cringe slightly as the man leaned over him and spoke to him quietly.

"That's where you're wrong, Gerry. It's over <u>especially</u> for you!"

Captain Austin Johnson of the 6th United States Army T-Force hurriedly searched the man: found several passports, sets of papers, and a fat wallet with three thousand American dollars in hundred dollar bills. He took one passport for Switzerland and one for England. He also took out all but three one hundred dollar bills.

The door burst open and two Army MP's were pointing their own 45's at him as they stood in the doorway.

"Man, I am so glad you are here! He drew a gun and made a grab for my briefcase. I had noticed him following me and so I came in here. I already had my pistol in my hand pretending to be going to the toilet when he came through the door. As he reached in his shoulder holster, I shot him."

The two men looked at one another and lowered their pistols. One of the men happened to recognize Austin as being from headquarters.

"Good job, Captain!"

"Listen, men, he obviously is a spy or assassin of some sort. I searched him and in his wallet he had a snapshot of him and a girl in front of a Nazi flag. One of the passports he was carrying is German and has his name as Hans Gruber. I am here to meet up with a British diplomat and deliver some important documents. Can you men take over from here?"

The men nodded.

Austin smiled, "I will be glad to say in my report the wallet was empty."

The two men looked at one another. They were used to finding people shot and having few facts to back up what happened. After the three hundred dollar gift, they were willing to swear they found Gruber already dead when they burst into the restroom, and they were not going to even mention the Army officer.

"Thanks men, I will see you on the base. I'll buy the first round!"

"Sure! Sure! You got a deal, captain! Get outta here!"

They both patted him on the back as he went by them out the door, down the hallway and out the back. By that time people were coming into the pub to see what had happened. He jogged around to his jeep to find a pretty blonde woman in a British officer's uniform sitting in the front passenger's seat holding a large manila envelope and a small clutch purse. She smiled at him and said, "Captain Johnson, my name is Hannah Olsen, and I believe we need to have a sense of urgency about leaving this area!"

Austin grinned at the woman's use of the King's English as he vaulted over the door opening, turned on the ignition switch, hit the floor starter in the Jeep, and without spinning the tires, accelerated hard enough to push them both into their seats as they fled down the street and turned the first corner which came up after a few blocks.

Once they were a few more blocks away from the pub, Austin slowed the Jeep to just fast enough to have a conversation and still not draw any undue attention.

The woman said. "You can give me the briefcase now and I will take over from here."

Austin looked quickly at her and said, "I had instructions to meet a Dr. Barnhardt here and escort him to the British sector."

She smiled at him and said, "Don't you trust me?"

He had slowed the jeep to just more than a crawl to go around piles of bricks and lumber lying in the street. It was the shattered carcass of the once proud Third Reich.

He looked into her green eyes and said flatly, "No."

Flustered momentarily, she asked, "Why not? Don't I look trustworthy?"

"No offense, but actually I have not seen anything to make me trust you. A man I never saw before somehow knew I was coming, and tried to kill me in the restroom. I get to my Jeep and the most beautiful woman I have ever seen is sitting there. How did you know that was my jeep?"

"By the time I arrived, the jeep was the only military vehicle I saw."

"Where is your vehicle?"

"I was dropped off because I was told you would take me to where I wanted to go."

"Then how were you going to *take over from here*, to use your choice of words?"

Although her left hand still held the envelope, her right hand was in her lap as if to inch inside her small purse.

"Furthermore, Hannah Olsen, or whatever your name is, if you start to pull anything except a compact out of that purse, I am going to punch your lights out!"

She was startled for a moment by his sharp tone and quick transformation from a hillbilly soldier to a deadly foe. She looked at him for a moment, and quietly said, "I think you would, Captain Johnson. I think you would."

"And another thing, how do you know my name?"

"Find a lit place where we can have some privacy, and I will show you my identification as a British officer. I am Royal Secret Service similar to you and my code name is Dr. Barnhardt. I was sent to meet you."

For the first time, Austin relaxed a little and even smiled, "Fair enough."

He thought to himself, "Killing Gruber was one thing, but I would hate to have to hurt a woman as beautiful as this one!"

Austin stopped the jeep under one of the very few working street lamps and checked her identification. He still held on to the briefcase, however. He would wait until they got to the British sector checkpoint and he could give the briefcase over to her with witnesses. Whatever was in the briefcase was important enough to have already cost one life, and he did not want the next one to be his.

Thirty Five

The rough-riding Jeep with Austin and Hannah Olsen slowed to a crawl as they headed for the British sector of Berlin. Austin could feel the hair on the back of his neck tingle as if there were a cross hair zeroed in on it. He looked right and left and watched the mirrors for any sign of movement as they crept along.

Suddenly, a black Mercedes Sedan similar to what Hans Grubel had been driving pulled across the street in an area of close quarters where the rubble only allowed one car at a time, blocking it completely.

Austin stopped the Jeep and as the window in the back of the car began to lower, he hit the bright lights, temporarily blinding the occupants of the car. He grabbed Hannah by the hand and half dragged her out as they jumped from the Jeep.

"PLINK, PLINK, PLINK!" the sound of bullets from a gun with a silencer were hitting the Jeep as they ran for cover to the first darkened building. Austin did not know how many there were; so he just kept low and kept pulling Hannah till for a brief moment they stopped in an adjacent building after entering on the ground floor and racing up several flights of stairs. They waited and listened. He could hear German and Russian being spoken and after some curses in German the men returned to the car and sped away as another military Jeep turned the corner.

Barely allowing themselves to breathe even though they were gasping for air, they listened to two men going over the jeep, and talking in English among themselves quietly. In a few minutes, they could hear footsteps, and a voice said loudly but not yelling, "Captain Austin, is that you? Are you here?" It was the two MP's he had left at the pub.

As the men got closer, Austin said, "Don't shine your flashlights for they will know you found us. Is my Jeep okay?"

"Well, you got a few scars, but it is still drivable."

"Okay, go by it, turn off the lights and drive off. We will let you get about a block away, and then you turn at the first corner to the right and drive like Hades around the block and take up our rear! Got it? We will make a run for the checkpoint which is only a few more blocks, but I am depending on you two to keep them off us to let us get there!"

The two men were talking as if they had not found anything, stopped at the Jeep, turned off the lights and got in theirs and took off at a good clip but nothing to cause anyone to notice.

Austin and Hannah made it to the Jeep, vaulted over the door entrance into their seats, and Austin started the engine but did not turn on the lights till they were moving. Just as soon as he turned on the lights, he heard squealing tires behind him pulling from an alley. He floored the Jeep, and turned to the left, ran between two still standing concrete columns, killed the lights and pulled his 45.

"May I pull my pistol, Captain?" Hannah whispered.

"Yes, but aim it somewhere out there!" He smiled.

The black sedan flew by in a cloud of dust, and Austin grinned to see the MP's Jeep not far behind with the passenger pointing a pistol and shouting for them to stop. He even fired a warning shot but the car did not slow down.

With the sedan not worrying about Austin for the moment, they drove quickly until the lights of the British checkpoint appeared out of the fog which was beginning to come down.

Seeing the British officer Hannah, the guard held up his hand in the curious, to an American, open handed British salute as he passed her and Austin into the compound.

They pulled up in front of a well lit office building with several people coming and going, turned off the Jeep, and both took a deep breath. They got out of the Jeep, went up the few steps and into the outer office.

"Hey, Hannah!" cried one of the young enlisted men. "We heard some shots fired, did you happen to notice anything?"

Hannah smiled a little smile with a quick glance at Austin and said, "You know how it is. Could have been anything."

The briefcase was uncuffed from Austin's wrist by a British Colonel, who smiled at the two of them but did not open the briefcase. He took it toward an inner office and over his shoulder said, "You are free to go!"

Hannah walked out the door with Austin as he went back to his Jeep.

"I sleep here in the compound, and I suppose you are going back to the base."

"Actually, I have a room at a little hotel. As a member of T-Force, I get a few perks. In fact, I have a few days off. I will write a letter or two and see if I have any mail. I may even drive around in the daylight a little."

"Wow, you are living the high life!" she smiled.

"Meet me at the Berlin Cafe tomorrow around 1100 hours, anywhere but the White Lily Pub! I will buy us lunch. The Berlin Cafe is where most of the officers from T-Force hang out. No pressure, but I would like to get to know more about you."

"If you do, you might be disappointed. I am pretty much just a small city girl. But, I will be there."

The next day Austin was in uniform sitting with a group of other officers at the Cafe. He heard one of them comment on what had just walked through the door. He turned and looked too, and just for a moment, he did not recognize Hannah. She was in street clothes, and she was even more stunning than before.

Austin shrugged, "Oh, that's just my lunch date."

All the men were silent as he stood to meet her and walked over to another table. The conversation waned as people stared, but started again as Austin frowned at them.

"Behave!" he mouthed behind her back as he escorted Hannah to their table.

Austin was enjoying the smiles and knowing winks and just shook his head.

"All men are dogs," he thought to himself.

Even he conceded she looked hot. She was dressed in a form fitting black and white patterned dress with black high heels. She had on a white hat that was broad brimmed and turned down on one side to not only make her look gorgeous, but it lent an air of mystery to her. Every male in the place was staring.

Austin helped her with her fur wrap, and she smiled and purred, "Thank you, Captain Johnson."

Austin could have sworn he heard one of the men groan under his breath. The air was charged with excitement. Austin realized Hannah was used to just such reactions, but he still asked, "Had you rather go somewhere else?"

"Look, there is not a nicer place to eat in Berlin, and these guys are going to cry if we leave right now!" she giggled.

They both laughed as if it were an inside joke. She even went so far as to put her hand on his arm and lean over and whisper into his ear, "I know you are married, Austin, but we will give them something to talk about!" She laughed again, showing her pretty teeth and smile.

"You know, you are quite a wench! These guys are drooling. I hate to say this, I would not be surprised I could make a lot of money by auctioning off your phone number! Do women like this sort of attention?"

"What do you think? I rarely ever get to "walk the dog" as you Americans call it."

Austin laughed out loud at her remark, causing all the men to turn and look at him, and he could see them mouthing obscenities in fun as he leaned over and whispered into Hannah's ear. "The phrase, Hannah, is 'putting <u>on</u> the dog'!"

Hannah blushed slightly, but laughed as if at a very funny private joke. She put her hand over on Austin's forearm and put her head against his shoulder as she laughed at her obvious *faux pas.*

Several of the men looked at one another knowingly and winked, and one leaned back and put out his hands in a gesture as if to say, "Are you kidding me?"

No one but Austin and Hannah knew what really had happened. After the meal the two rode around Berlin for a short time before the took her back to her base. He helped her from the jeep, and as he put out his hand, she kissed him quickly on the cheek. She smiled as he blushed.

With a few days of "down time" Austin drove around on the air base to the flight line to look at the row of P-51 Mustangs. He got out and climbed up on one and looked into the open cockpit. He was dressed in uniform with his pilot's wings glistening.

"Hey, Captain Johnson, have you ever flown one of these?" It was Colonel "Big Red" Carmody from the base command.

He ran his hand over the cowl and said, "No, but I have always wanted to."

"Well, this is your lucky day. I can make it happen," said the man with enough gold braid on his hat to cause a solar flare. He was a full bird Colonel, and had been a squadron leader during the war. He confessed to Austin he was taking one up to just stay in practice, and he could fly wing man to help in case there were questions.

In a very few minutes, Austin had put on a helmet, jacket, and parachute and was climbing into the cockpit and getting a feel for what it must have been like.

He nearly shouted as the two planes lifted off the runway. He managed to maintain enough of a straight face to fly alongside Colonel Carmody who was enjoying the flight almost as much.

"I flew high cover for bombers during the war as we bombed Berlin night and day. I never got tired of the feeling of diving through the clouds to engage the Germans in a dog fight. I have 12 confirmed kills of my own, plus a few more probables."

Austin smiled as he imagined what could have been. The two men chased one another through the clouds pretending to shoot at one another like kids with play guns tied to the handlebars of their bicycles.

"Hey, Johnson, you are a heck of a pilot! I would have loved to have had you as a real wing man!"

"Thanks, Colonel. It means a lot coming from you."

All too soon for Austin it was over. The men landed, put away the planes, and went to the ready room.

As they opened the door to the ready room, the base commander motioned for Austin to come to his office.

"We are not in trouble for joyriding in the Mustang, are we?" Austin whispered aside to Colonel Carmody.

"No way, look at the brass in that room. It is something much bigger than that!"

Even the Colonel snapped to attention and saluted.

"At ease, men. I want to introduce you, Austin, to your next assignment. This is Doctor Richard Weiss. He and Doctor Einstein and Werner Von Braun collaborated on several projects for Hitler, and he would like to go to America and work for our side. It may sound simple but we need you and Doctor Barnhardt to accompany him. His English is not as good as his German. Hannah can speak fluent German, and she will be helpful on your journey.

"Okay, how do we get him out of Berlin? I am sure the Russians and the rogue SS troops are looking for him too."

"You are so right, Austin. The three of you will be shot on sight if you are caught. We are smuggling him out tonight along with both of you. There is a C-47 loaded with farm tools ready to go from an old airfield beside the Rhine River. Can you fly it?"

"Sure."

"It will be dark in another hour. We can get you off the base, but after that you are on your own to get to that airfield. The plane will be ready to go."

Austin took Hannah and the doctor to another room to change clothes. One of Hannah's scarves over the Doctor's long hair and one of her work dresses started the transformation. She put heavy wool white socks and farm shoes on him, and with an old tattered work jacket from a janitor they had found--he was ready.

Hannah told Austin to wait for a moment and then when she came out he could not believe it. She had on a male officer's uniform, and even a slight shadow mascara mustache.

"Maybe I am going crazy, Hannah, but you still look sexy!"

"You're weird, Austin. We have papers, if we can wing it a little, as two soldiers escorting a widow back to Britain. Pray we don't have to use them. I doubt if we will fool many people."

"I agree, most male soldiers are not as pretty as you."

She slapped his hand away and said seriously, "This won't be a picnic if we are discovered."

"I am not taking it lightly. How am I going to explain to my wife if I get shot alongside you?"

"Maybe you better hope if you get shot they kill you, or your wife might!"

"That ain't funny!"

"It wasn't really meant to be. Okay, we gotta go."

The guard at the gate had been alerted to let the threesome pass without stopping because the little old lady was very sick and the two soldiers were taking her home off the base."

The guard at the gate was one of the MP's which Austin knew, and he just saluted as the threesome eased through the gate. They were driving one of the base command cars which was a Mercedes Sedan. The windows were darkened and Austin was pleased with the power.

The war was over, and there were command cars coming and going all the time. Going down the city streets the car just looked like it was looking for a place to eat or a place to have a drink. No one seemed interested in the car at all.

Downtown Berlin had been bombed without mercy, but as soon as they cleared the city there were a surprising number of homes back in use. Austin drove fairly fast but did not want to draw any attention.

Soon, they saw the little industrial airport. The fuel trucks were pulling away from the plane as Austin came to a halt beside the runway.

"Hannah, I am going to walk across the runway and show the papers from the Colonel which state we are making a routine flight to southwestern Germany and Holland to deliver new farm equipment, and the little lady is very sick and needs to get to her home, which is just outside Amsterdam, our destination. As soon as you hear the engines start up, bring Dr. Weiss carefully and load him. As soon as we get him on the plane, no matter what happens, we don't stop. Okay? Make sure the Doctor knows what the plan is. He seems to be pretty spry and he may can pull this off."

Austin drove the car to the bottom of the on ramp steps and went up to the cockpit while Hannah, dressed as a soldier, helped the doctor carefully up the steps. They had just shut the door and an orderly was driving the car away when a black Mercedes car came careening around the guard shack.

Austin had already started to roll and he had the engines revved to the max. It did not take long for the plane to be moving fast enough the car could not keep up. A head and a luger appeared in one window.

"Get down and get behind something heavy duty. We are going to take some lead!" Austin shouted.

Just as the plane's wheels left the ground, the sound of gunfire erupted and there were bullets bouncing around inside the plane. Hannah had her body over the doctor and they were behind a stack of plow points on a pallet.

"Go! Go! Go, baby, go!" She could hear Austin yelling. The load had been packed light on purpose, and, as Austin pulled back on the wheel, they made it airborne!

As they circled for altitude, Austin was in constant communication with the base tower and received clearance to head southwestern for the English Channel. His code name was "Plow Point."

He was flying without lights trying to make it to the empty countryside before anyone knew. He had been alerted previously the Russians had two planes up looking for him. So, he could not fly at a high altitude and be seen on radar. He was flying very low and more afraid of hitting something than anything else.

All of sudden there were tracer bullets flying by the cockpit as a Russian Airacobra fired a warning salvo from behind him to try to force him to land. If they had indeed found him, Austin reasoned, he might as well climb enough to be able to maneuver. The idea of being a ground level, slow moving, unarmed target did not sound like fun.

The C-47 with a light load climbed quickly to about 10,000 feet. He looked out the windscreen and could pick out the silhouette of the fighter coming almost head on from a cloud bank. However, the plane abruptly broke off and started a banking climb several hundred yards away. The Airacobra was almost perpendicular when an

American Air Force P-51 Mustang came roaring overhead with a burst from all 6 cannons. With a second burst, the plane exploded.

Austin's headset crackled, "Hey there, Plow Point! This is your flying buddy, Ol' Big Red, and I will be an overhead escort to the coast. Have a nice day!"

"Thank you, sir! You're the best!" Austin exclaimed as he saw the fireball from the damaged plane drifting to earth and then explode. The plane with the trio aboard climbed even higher for the rest of the journey.

The plane landed in Amsterdam, and British T-Force authorities came aboard and welcomed the group. They patted Doctor Weiss on the back and shook hands as Hannah translated to him he was safe. The look of relief and joy in the little old man's face brought tears to her eyes.

"I didn't know Brits ever cried," teased Austin.

"I think I have something in my eye," she returned, a little embarrassed that he had caught her.

"Come on. I will buy you a drink."

"Yes, please! I think I just now let out the breath I have been holding!"

All they could find was a small, crowded bar not far from the base. No one was going to pay any attention to Hannah who was still dressed as a male soldier. They left the borrowed Jeep out front and went inside to order.

The Dutch had very good beer according to Hannah, and Austin agreed after he tasted the light colored brew. He wiped his mouth with a napkin and looked across the table at Hannah.

"Are you going to be okay?"

"Of course. I am flying home to Britain tomorrow. I will be fine. I am taking an agent's position at British Intelligence. They will soon be shutting down the T-Force."

"Sounds great. I'll know where to find you if I ever come to England."

"I am sure you will, Austin. You are going home and you will not even remember my name a month from now."

"You and I both know that will not be the case."

Hannah reached across the table and squeezed his hand in affection. She smiled slightly, and whispered with tears in her eyes, "I know."

"Hannah, you know there is a connection between us. I am sure it could be more, but I have a wife and I am leaving in a few days. I don't want to sacrifice my integrity for just a few nights. Do you understand?"

"Austin, I would never believe you would do anything different. Your wife is a lucky woman."

Hannah went to the airport to say goodbye to Austin and Doctor Weiss. They were flying back to Washington D.C. and Austin would ensure the doctor's safety as he traveled. From there he had a flight arranged to take him to Birmingham. It was the second week of December in 1945, and he wanted to be home before Christmas.

"Do you know which type of plane you are taking home?"

"The base commander told me we were returning a B-24 back to the States. They are not taking any chances with us."

"Austin, I gotta go, but you take care of yourself, okay? You are one of the good ones. As far as you and me; another place, another time." She smiled. She did not kiss him on the lips, but she held him several long seconds before she kissed him on the cheek and walked away.

Austin picked up his duffel bag and took the good doctor by the arm. As they walked toward the plane, he saw Hannah watching from a window. He smiled at her and she blew him a kiss.

Once on the plane they had to wait a few minutes for the pilot and co-pilot. One of the men flying with them leaned over and in a joking tone said, "Believe it or not the pilot is a female! She probably wants to take one last look at the map." He laughed, but it died on his lips as he looked over Austin's shoulder to see the female pilot glaring at him. She had a short, blonde, stylish haircut, piercing blue eyes, and a frown.

"I suppose one of you guys think you could do a better job?"

Austin turned around when he heard her voice and stood up. "Dang right I can!"

The pilot's mouth opened in surprise before she started laughing.

"Of all the men in the world I know, you are the only one I would agree with! How are you doing, Cuz?" It was Anna Lee! She grabbed him and hugged him tight. "Austin, no one from home has heard from you in months. James will be home soon. He was a fighter pilot in the Pacific flying the Hellcat. We didn't know if you were alive or dead."

"I am truly sorry for that, but T-Force is such a secret, security phobic place I was told to not contact even my wife until I got back to America. How is Beth Ann doing?"

"She has more faith than any of us. She has never even considered the possibility you were not coming back.

I have a surprise waiting for you, Austin, when you get back to Washington. We land at 0600 their time, and I have been told a P-51 Mustang is waiting for you to continue on to Birmingham. You should be home about dark. It is a perk for being a hero. Some Colonel Carmody put it together with a little help from General Talbert. I will visit with you later!"

She hugged him, kissed him on the cheek as she teared up, and said tenderly, "Let's go home!"

The cab slowed to turn in to the Davis Estate drive, but Austin stopped him and said, "I want to surprise them." The driver smiled as Austin handed him a twenty dollar bill as he got out and retrieved his suitcase from the seat beside him. "Merry Christmas," Austin said.

"Merry Christmas to you and yours, Sir!"

Austin picked up the suitcase, patted the man on the back, and said, "Thank you."

Beth Ann and the staff were finishing the evening meal in the dining room in the inner part of the house when the door bell rang.

"Who in the world?" said Beth Ann. "I am finished eating. I will get it."

The big, double glassed doors were cut to see someone was there but it was so distorted all Beth Ann could see was a uniform. Curious and concerned, she opened the door quickly.

Samuel and the girls heard her scream. By the time they ran to the foyer, Austin and Beth Ann were both kissing and crying. Austin broke the kiss, and with Beth Ann's arms still around him, he reached and shook hands with Samuel and hugged the girls. They were all nearly hysterical with joy. The Prodigal was home!

THE END

Bibliography

1. Wikipedia Online

2. "A history of the world's airlines", R.E.G. Davies, Oxford U.P, 1964

3. Mintz, S. (2007). *Digital History*. Retrieved 11/2010 from

   http://www.digitalhistory.uh

Other books by
Don Horne:

Red Jacket and Yellow Squash

This is a faith-building, awe inspiring, book compiled from true, first person testimonies of what God can do.

From Ann Margret
To Battle Stations

A coming of age/love story set in the 1960's and 1970's based on time spent aboard the carrier Kitty Hawk in Viet Nam.

www.ingramcontent.com/pod-product-compliance
Lightning Source LLC
Chambersburg PA
CBHW070346260626
47161CB00001B/30